PRAIS\

M000306337

The Alone Time

"Absolutely chilling, *The Alone Time* delves into the lives of sisters Fiona and Violet as they navigate life after surviving the plane crash that killed their parents. Each layer of the story is expertly revealed, leaving you in shock as you wonder what is the truth and what is only imagined."

—Lyn Liao Butler, Amazon bestselling author of *Someone Else's Life*

"Marr's *The Alone Time* is a captivating, thrilling, deeply haunting tale about familial bonds, family secrets, memory, and trauma. This book is so twisty that it will give you whiplash! Absorbing, beautifully written, and fraught with tension, *The Alone Time* will keep you in its grip until the very last page. Fantastic. It will leave you reeling!"

—Lisa Regan, *USA Today* and *Wall Street Journal* bestselling author

"In this story nothing is as it seems. Part mystery, part survival tale, and part family drama, this intricately woven tale had me flipping through the pages quickly. Told alternately between the present and the past, the pieces clicked into place one by one, each chapter adding another layer of mystery and suspense. There were several twists at the end, one that had me reeling. A beautifully written story with high-stakes suspense! You don't want to miss this one."

—Amber Garza, author of *In a Quiet Town*

The Family Bones

"Marr expertly builds tension by alternating between the two narratives, which eventually merge and build to an explosive conclusion. Readers will be captivated from the very first page."

—*Publishers Weekly* (starred review)

"With a fresh take on the locked-room mystery, Elle Marr weaves a perilous and pulse-pounding tale of nature versus nurture. *The Family Bones* is a clever, wild, riveting ride that amps up the tension until I couldn't flip the page fast enough. The interconnected threads, subtle clues, and jaw-dropping twists lead to a whopper of an ending."

—Samantha M. Bailey, *USA Today* and #1 national bestselling author of *Woman on the Edge* and *Watch Out for Her*

"'Dysfunctional' doesn't even begin to describe the Eriksen clan during this family reunion from hell. Elle Marr's twisty plot and even more twisted characters make *The Family Bones* a dark, delectable, and fascinating thriller that questions how well we know not only our relatives but also our own minds."

—Megan Collins, author of *The Family Plot*

"Smart, razor sharp, and shocking, *The Family Bones* will keep you up late with all the lights on. A family of psychopaths trapped by bad weather at an isolated retreat—what could possibly go wrong? With dual storylines racing toward a chilling climax, *The Family Bones* is a tense, must-read thriller."

—Kaira Rouda, *USA Today* and Amazon Charts bestselling author

Strangers We Know

"The increasingly tense plot takes turns the reader won't see coming. Marr is a writer to watch."

—*Publishers Weekly*

"Elle Marr is an author to know. Just when you think you understand the motives behind her characters and the way their storylines are being presented—bam!—Elle will hit you with twists you won't see coming. Told from multiple points of view, *Strangers We Know* is about more than Ivy learning of her past and, shockingly, the serial killer within her family; it's also about knowing who to trust and how to discern who's telling the complete story. Because if everyone has secrets, are they truly family or only strangers? Read *Strangers We Know* to find out."

—Georgina Cross, bestselling author of *The Stepdaughter*

"Elle Marr burst onto the suspense scene in 2020 with her bestselling debut, *The Missing Sister*, and followed up a year later with *Lies We Bury*, another trust-no-one murder mystery. With her third novel, *Strangers We Know*, Marr firmly establishes herself as a master of 'did that really just happen?' thrillers. *Strangers We Know* has plot twists so unexpected and characters so creepy you won't want to turn out the lights, and the ending is surprising in multiple ways. Who knew a deranged-serial-killer whodunit could leave you with all the feels?"

—A.H. Kim, author of *A Good Family*

"Dark family secrets, serial murder, and a cult? Yes, please. Twisty and a little twisted, the highly addictive and surprise-packed *Strangers We Know* will have you pulling an all-nighter."

—Heather Chavez, author of *No Bad Deed*

"From the first page I was gripped by *Strangers We Know* and read through the night till the end. The novel is thrilling beyond belief, with suspense and twists ratcheting up on each page. Elle Marr is brilliant at delving into the darkness of a seemingly normal family, and by the time she pulls back the curtains on each character, the terror has built so excruciatingly, you just have to keep going till you find out every single thing—you're afraid to know, but you have to know. This is the year's must read."

—Luanne Rice, bestselling author of *The Shadow Box*

Lies We Bury

"A deep, deep dive into unspeakable memories and their unimaginably shocking legacy."

—*Kirkus Reviews* (starred review)

"The suspenseful plot is matched by the convincing portrayal of the vulnerable Claire, who just wants to lead a normal life. Marr is a writer to watch."

—*Publishers Weekly*

"Marr's #OwnVoices, trust-no-one thriller unravels with horrifying 'THEN' interruptions, producing a jolting creepfest of twisted revenge."

—*Booklist*

"In *Lies We Bury*, Elle Marr (bestselling author of *The Missing Sister*) has brought a cleverly plotted and compelling new mystery with unique characters and truly surprising twists."

—The Nerd Daily

"A deep, thrilling dive into the painful memories that haunt us and the fight between moving on or digging in and seeking revenge."

—Medium

"Elle Marr's second novel tucks a mystery inside a mystery . . . The big twist near the end is a doozy."

—*The Oregonian*

"A twisted mash-up of *Room* and a murder mystery, Marr's *Lies We Bury* is a story that creeps into your bones, a sneaky tale about the danger of secrets and the power the past holds to lead us into a deliciously devious present. Say goodbye to sleep and read it like I did, in one breathless sitting."

—Kimberly Belle, international bestselling author of *Dear Wife* and *Stranger in the Lake*

"Dark and compelling, Elle Marr has written another atmospheric and twisted thriller that you don't want to miss. *Lies We Bury* delves into the darkest of pasts and explores the fascinating tension between moving on and revenge. This is a fly-through-the-pages thriller."

—Vanessa Lillie, Amazon bestselling author of *Little Voices* and *For the Best*

"This haunting and emotional thriller will keep you up at night looking for answers."

—Dea Poirier, international bestselling author of *Next Girl to Die*

"A clever, twisty murder mystery packed full of secrets and lies that will keep you turning the pages way past bedtime. *Lies We Bury* hooked me from page one and kept me guessing until its dramatic conclusion."

—Lisa Gray, bestselling author of *Thin Air*

The Missing Sister

"Marr's debut novel follows a San Diego medical student to, around, and ultimately beneath Paris in search of the twin sister she'd been drifting away from. Notable for its exploration of the uncanny bonds twins share and the killer's memorably macabre motive."

—*Kirkus Reviews*

"[A] gritty debut . . . The intriguing premise, along with a few twists, lend this psychological thriller some weight."

—*Publishers Weekly*

"Elle Marr's first novel has an intriguing premise . . . The characters are well drawn and complex, and Marr's prose offers some surprising twists."

—New York Journal of Books

"A promising plotline."

—*Library Journal*

"*The Missing Sister* is a very promising debut—atmospheric, gripping, and set in Paris. In other words, the perfect ingredients for a satisfying result."

—Criminal Element

"Brimming with eerie mystery and hair-raising details . . . A chilling read that shows the unique bond of twins."

—*Woman's World*

"This thrilling debut novel from Elle Marr is a look into the importance of identity and the strength of sisterhood."

—*Brooklyn Digest*

"An electrifying thriller. A must read—Karin Slaughter with a touch of international flair. Just when you think you have it all figured out, Marr throws you for another loop and the roller-coaster ride continues!"

—Matt Farrell, *Washington Post* bestselling author of
What Have You Done

"A riveting, fast-paced thriller. Elle Marr hooks you from the start, taking you on a dark and twisted journey. Layered beneath the mystery of a twin's disappearance is a nuanced, and at times disturbing, exploration of the ties that bind sisters together. With crisp prose, a gripping investigation, and a compelling protagonist, *The Missing Sister* is not to be missed."

—Brianna Labuskes, *Washington Post* bestselling author of
Girls of Glass

"A gripping thriller. *The Missing Sister* delivers twists and turns in an exciting, page-turning read that delves into the unique bond that makes—and breaks—siblings."

—Mike Chen, author of *Here and Now and Then*

THE
ALONE
TIME

OTHER TITLES BY ELLE MARR

The Family Bones
Strangers We Know
Lies We Bury
The Missing Sister

THE
ALONE
TIME

ELLE
MARR

THOMAS & MERCER

This is a work of fiction. Names, characters, organizations, places, events, and incidents are either products of the author's imagination or are used fictitiously. Otherwise, any resemblance to actual persons, living or dead, is purely coincidental.

Text copyright © 2024 by Elle Marr
All rights reserved.

No part of this book may be reproduced, or stored in a retrieval system, or transmitted in any form or by any means, electronic, mechanical, photocopying, recording, or otherwise, without express written permission of the publisher.

Published by Thomas & Mercer, Seattle

www.apub.com

Amazon, the Amazon logo, and Thomas & Mercer are trademarks of Amazon.com, Inc., or its affiliates.

ISBN-13: 9781662513817 (paperback)
ISBN-13: 9781662513824 (digital)

Cover design by Shasti O'Leary Soudant
Cover image: © Rialto Images / Stocksy

Printed in the United States of America

For the lemonade makers

The creative adult is the child who survived.
—Unknown

1

FIONA

Art is never more than a reflection of an artist's twisted mind. The twigs that I harvested from the forested park that sits at the edge of my property seem to prove that idea, refusing to behave in my latest sculpture. Instead of a three-dimensional re-creation of a mountaintop, the one I can't seem to shake from my dreams, the piece resembles more of a pincushion. Leaves, tiny branches, feathers, and an errant pine cone I stepped on during a walk last week each seem in opposition to my increasingly knobby fingers.

Something falls in my kitchen, scattering to the hardwood. "Marshall, stop going through the trash, buddy. Darleen is going to be here any minute."

I stomp into the kitchen, all bark and no bite, then wag a finger at my Great Dane. "Jeez, look at this. You don't even like tomato."

Sweeping the remnants from yesterday's BLT back into the plastic bag, I right the bin against the wall. With Marshall's big brown eyes trained on me in fleeting remorse, I stack a cookbook on the lid. "No more of that."

Normally, I hate wasting food. But when the BLT I ordered to go from San Diego's hottest rooftop bar and restaurant contained a long human hair, I spit it out and then threw the whole thing away. Some people would do the same, but no one shares the same reasons as me. Except for Violet.

"Knock knock," a voice calls through my screen door.

"In the kitchen."

Shuffling footsteps pass the dining table, and then my art dealer, Darleen Hallow, appears in the doorway. Marshall follows close behind, reaching her elbow. "Is that a new piece you're working on back there? Love the pine cone."

Fading red hair is cut in an artful lob that lands on Darleen's rounded shoulders. She could be a relative for the sharp hazel eyes we share, but that's where any resemblance stops. Her creamy skin that seems impossible under San Diego's consistent sunshine glows in the dim lighting of my home. A light bulb flickers above my sink—one of the endless household tasks I can't seem to focus on when manifesting a new idea. Nothing else can grasp my attention while I'm in the thick of creativity—not for long, at least. Laundry piles up, dishes multiply on counters, and take-out boxes dwarf my recycling bin. Considering I still need to create another half dozen pieces for the art gallery exhibition slated for next month, I might need help hurdling over pizza boxes to exit my house by then.

Since the Alone Time, I've had trouble multitasking. A therapist might say it's a residual effect of my trauma—of being stranded in the wilderness with my family. In reality, it's emerging from the wild without all of them that continues to haunt me.

"It's getting there," I reply. "My last visit to Balboa Park was productive. Found the blue-and-gold feather in a fountain. Drink?"

"No, I'm good. Thanks."

Darleen, Marshall, and I head to the front of my house, to the sitting room, beside the front door I never use. It reminds me too much of my parents' door—just down in El Cajon.

Darleen settles onto the couch that doubles as Marshall's bed. "Okay, Fiona. Thanks again for this quick visit. I know you're super busy."

I smile, sliding into an armchair. "Yeah, it's been a little stressful. Thanks again for coordinating everything with the gallery."

"My friend, it's an honor. I don't know if you're aware, but everyone in the art world is talking about you right now."

I stiffen. "Really?"

"Well, no—sorry. Not—not like that. Everyone is excited to see your new creations."

She sputters just like everyone else does when they recall the real reason people are intrigued by my artwork, and how it took years before they talked about anything other than me. I survived a plane crash that took my parents' lives, that left me and my younger sister, Violet, to fend for ourselves for months. When a rogue hiker finally spotted us and came to our rescue twelve weeks after the crash, we had become so accustomed to the world as we knew it, we didn't want to leave. Well, I did. I wanted shelter and a hot shower as a thirteen-year-old girl. Violet, as a seven-year-old, had accepted the woods were her home now. She was harder to coax onto a small airplane that resembled the one that killed our mom and dad.

"Darleen, I get it. But this is my first major show all by myself and . . . I'm kind of terrified."

She softens, leaning toward me. "Sure, sweetie. That makes sense."

"Like . . . what if no one comes? What if I don't sell one piece?"

Darleen shakes her head. "Not possible. Not after the way you were featured at the Coachella Biennial last year. Most artists wait decades for the kind of appreciation you're getting now."

I purse my lips. "Appreciation or criticism?"

"Well . . . ," Darleen draws out.

She doesn't have to finish her sentence; we've been over this. Some people think I'm exploiting my parents' deaths since my pieces are inspired by our time in the wild. But lots of others, many more, just want to support me. One of the girl-survivors.

"Regardless of the naysayers," Darleen continues, "if this show goes well, it could catapult your work up to San Francisco and New York. Maybe even Europe."

"That would be amazing," I reply, wistful. "Violet would love all of that."

"Right. I'm sure." Darleen gives my hand a squeeze. It's one of my favorite refrains at this point—me wishing my baby sister would find a way to move forward from the trauma, to lead a fulfilling life and stop wallowing in the past. Better to completely turn the page and channel the experience into something good. Like art. Like I'm doing. So far the only productive thing Violet has accomplished is dropping out of college. Twice.

"Do you think Violet would join you for the art show next month? You said it yourself: it's kind of a big deal."

I smile. Darleen has my best interests at heart, I know it. "I haven't spoken to my sister in over a year. Now—when there's so much riding on this gallery show—isn't great timing."

"Well, I had to ask. You know, there have been a few inquiries. Requests for interviews and features. There's a documentary that was announced a few weeks ag—"

"It's a no for me," I cut in. "Definitely."

"Got it." She holds up both hands, palms out. "Understood."

The conversation turns toward the dozen pieces that I promised the Hughes Gallery. Darleen asks well-meaning questions, tilting her head to the side just like my mom used to do. When she rises to leave, she pulls me in for a tight hug.

As Darleen's blue Civic backs out, Marshall sits at the screen door facing the curved driveway of my home. As if yearning for a friend who doesn't care if he paws at cold sandwich bits.

Birdsong twirls through the air at dusk. The noise of traffic and cars honking grows faint against the rural whisperings on the edge of town.

Once, Darleen asked me why I keep my door open during the day, only locking it at night. I nodded to Marshall and said, "My bodyguard scares anyone off. And I like a breeze."

She said, "Aren't you afraid he might overpower you, living just the two of you? He's such a big guy."

I touched my dog's head. Patted the skull I know exactly how to crush, whose bony plates would collapse together like Styrofoam under the right weight and angle.

"No," I replied. "I'm not afraid of my dog at all."

Certain that she's long gone, Marshall trots through my one-story house. He returns to the front room's couch, then curls up on the blanket that's wedged against the corner cushions for him.

I approach my dilapidated sculpture. Since I don't have roommates and don't entertain guests outside of my art dealer and the wayward boyfriend, my dining room is the most versatile workshop I could ask for. Tweezers, meat tongs, and latex gloves are scattered along the table's border.

The pine cone tilts away from the summit like a hitchhiker's thumb, whereas before it seemed the perfect addition to the sticks and twigs that formed a mountaintop twelve inches in height. The cardboard box I use as a base, and which I specially order in bulk from a warehouse in Los Angeles, seems too narrow now, given the shift.

I heave a sigh. "Why did I think this was a good idea, again?"

Over the years, interviewers at galleries—the only interviews I'll give—have asked me when I began creating art from organic materials. Whether the idea was born from the Alone Time, as my sister and I called the twelve weeks that we were stranded in the wild, or afterward, during my wandering adolescence at my aunt's house in La Jolla.

Every single time, I reply, "Oh, afterward." I always wonder then if I've managed the right balance of spontaneity and genuine reflection to appear truthful.

My phone rings, jarring me from my process. Marshall whines from the front room, lifting his head and jingling his collar to further alert me. He doesn't like it when I receive calls either.

As I reach my cell where I left it beside the trash bin, an unknown number buzzes across the screen. An automatic no for me.

I silence the call, returning to my dining table.

Then my phone buzzes again. The same unknown number calling. When a voice mail hits my inbox, I play the recording, already anticipating the bomb.

A silken voice begins, "Hi, this message is for Fiona Seng. I'm Nathan Wallace from the *Boston Times*. In light of your upcoming gallery show, I was hoping to—"

I snatch my phone from my table, then jam my finger against the delete button.

A deep breath rattles in my throat. I pause to recenter myself, to refocus. Try to block out the nasty energy of rubberneckers seeking more page views at my emotional expense.

Cool air passes through the screen door, circling my mountain sculpture and tipping a gray-and-white feather from the middle. The short tuft of plumage slides out of position, resembling a cloud that drops in elevation. Falling out of line. Refusing orders.

I set my shoulders. Draw strength from the soothing coo of a turtledove that twirls somewhere outside. Although my sister has shunned most forms of nature since our return to civilization, I've never lost my appreciation for the outdoors. Our experience in the wild took so much from us, but I have clung to my love of sunsets, landscapes, and animals in their natural habitats. Against all odds.

I reach for the tweezers with a shaking hand.

As my mother used to say to us girls, before she tramped past the damaged wing of the airplane into the darkness of a mountain ridge: if you get knocked down, make sure you get back up.

Fueled by the memory of her voice—the way it echoed against the cliff's edge—I reposition the feather at the mountain's peak. Higher than it was before.

2

JANET

The Crash

At fourteen thousand feet, air glides along the body of our passenger plane like a car wash throttling a Mini Cooper. The insulation from sound—and heat—I've come to expect from flying on major airlines is nonexistent in the little Cessna that my husband, Henry, borrowed from a friend. I wrap the blanket I brought with us closer across my body in the copilot seat. Henry beams at the open skyline and blanket of fluffy white clouds underneath, the most excited I've seen him in years. Considering I called a divorce attorney just last week to explore my options, this is a huge change for us: we seem happy.

Turning over my shoulder, I peek into the back seat, where my girls slump. Fiona, my thirteen-year-old, plays some video game on her Game Boy, whose sound I'm always telling her to turn down. I can hear its percussive melody in my head even now, despite the plane's engine roaring through my chest. The headphones she wears—that we all wear—have fallen lopsided, probably while she napped earlier. I tap her knee, then motion for her to fix them. The last thing we need is for Fiona to sustain some kind of hearing loss up here.

My youngest, Violet, is my natural wallflower. She'll find a way to blend into any background and will only join a fray of kids if she is prompted, or encouraged with a treat. Petite for her age, my girl already prefers reading and has just begun writing. Though she holds the new baby-blue journal she asked for in her lap, Violet bites the end of a pen between her teeth as she stares out the scratched safety glass of the window. She's seven years old, going on seventy, my girl.

When my own mother immigrated to California from China, she envisioned a life where we would want for nothing: a wealthy childhood for her kids, then theirs. Little did she know, before she passed away from cardiac arrest last year, her youngest granddaughter would prefer the least expensive pursuits: hand-me-down books, and brand-new notebooks where she jots down events from her day.

Recently Violet shared with me one such entry, wherein she called me her best friend. My heart swelled like a balloon then, and I had to bite back tears as I told her that was very nice, that she was my best friend too. Fiona, who was sitting at the table in the next room and overheard our exchange, only scoffed. I hoped I hadn't hurt her feelings. Fiona is of hardy stuff, though. She never seems like she needs anyone as a thirteen-year-old, certainly not her mother. Not like Violet and me.

"See that?" Henry asks, pointing to a break in the never-ending blanket of fluff. "That's Yosemite. That's Half Dome down there."

I try to make out the landmark, one that I visited twice as a kid growing up in Oakland, but can't decipher the green-and-brown expanse below. Instead I nod. "It's so beautiful."

My voice comes in clear through all four of our headsets, but I still have to shout above the noise of the wind coursing around us. The engine makes a *put-put* sound every so often, like an old jalopy, as it defies gravity.

I've never been a big flier. Maybe it's because I didn't take my first plane ride until I was twenty, but I've always preferred to drive, even across long distances. More control that way. More say in how and if I go from this world. Or the semblance of it anyway.

Last week, when Henry and I were fighting so loud our neighbors turned on their lights, he spun to me in the middle of it and said, "Let's do it. Let's do the trip to Canada, just like we planned. I'll fly us and we can borrow Ned's Cessna. Let's choose us for once."

Hope painted his big brown eyes like a puppy's. I wanted to strangle him then and there. To suggest that we resume our picturesque family vacation—place our lives in his hands and his newly acquired private pilot's license—felt like such a dismissal of the hurt he had caused us. Well, the girls weren't up to speed about his transgressions, I don't think. But I knew. So I hated myself when I took his hand and said, "Okay."

"One more shot?" he asked with a sheepish grin—the one he always used when I caught him doing something illicit: that time he ate the last piece of Fiona's birthday cake; when he was suspended from work for harassment of his colleagues and I found him lounging at home on a Tuesday afternoon; the anniversary he revealed he had three speeding tickets from the prior six months.

But it was also the endearing, charming smile that I first fell in love with when we were just two servers in a beachfront café in San Diego. The lopsided expression that reassured me, despite his wild pie-in-the-sky dreams that sucked up our family savings, everything would be okay.

"One more shot," I replied.

Several hours pass, with Henry occasionally pointing at another landmark below that I pretend to recognize. Fluffy white clouds resemble a down comforter well underneath the four-seater Cessna. It's magical, viewing the miles of marshmallow bedding up close that Henry says is only possible due to this altitude's low atmospheric pressure. During this stretch of serene sky, I understand exactly why Henry was so eager to share it with us, with his family. He once told me that, while flying, he felt like the most powerful man in the world.

As a first-generation American and an Asian man, Henry was always going on about respect when we first met fifteen years ago. He wanted to prove to everyone that he deserved recognition and respect from all fifty states, not just the coasts. I used to think that focus was rooted in our shared cultural scope—of being American yet Chinese, and hugging that duality like a hand-me-down jacket on little kid shoulders.

Then I realized, after he got fired from our beachside café job, after he was discharged from the marines, and after he failed his pilot's license test twice, that Henry was an idealist. He rarely liked to grapple with reality head-on. He preferred the context that he concocted in his head. Case in point, when he was caught flirting with another server at the restaurant, a girl from Santee, who I never liked. He told me at the time that they were just friends and that I was acting jealous. Later, when he was sleeping over at my apartment, I found a note in his pocket—bleeding ink scribbles on a napkin. It was a reminder to call her later, with her phone number written underneath.

"Did you see that?" Fiona asks Violet. Giggles erupt in the back seat of the plane. Violet leans close to Fiona's shoulder, where her older sister battles some Super Mario foe, teasing big smiles from them both. The baby-blue journal remains clutched in Violet's lap.

Henry and I broke up after the next suspicious note that I found in his pocket. Though I wasn't snooping, I swear. Each time, he suggested I grab some gum for him from the front chest pocket of his cargo jacket. I wondered then if he was trying to get out of a relationship with me—away from my hopes and dreams of ultimately becoming a mother and happily married. I wondered if he didn't want the same things as me at all.

"Girls, how's the temp back there? You okay?" Henry asks through the headset.

"Yup," Fiona replies, not looking up.

I touch Violet's leg underneath the other blanket we brought. "Violet, honey?"

She nods, meeting my gaze. "Cozy. But I'm hungry. When is snack?"

"Both of your lunches are in the paper bags by your feet. Ham and cheese for Fiona. Char siu and tomato sandwich for you."

Without glancing down, my girls reach for the food. Their eyes remain transfixed on the Game Boy's tiny screen. I hope the zombie glaze on their faces doesn't become a trend.

Violet chews a bite while she rummages in her bag. "Any Dijon mustard?"

"For your char siu?" Chinese barbecue pork is delicious without any other sauce or condiment. "Is it dry? I turned off the grill five minutes earlier this time."

"No, it's yummy, Mommy. I just had a thought. It might be good together." Violet takes another bite of her sandwich, red-hued pork visible along the crust.

I smile. "No, my little foodie. No mustard on this trip."

Violet shrugs. Something catches her eye on the Game Boy, and she continues watching over Fiona's shoulder.

Henry initiated autopilot over an hour ago. His hands rest on the bottom rung of the steering wheel, I'd guess out of habit. Humming travels through the headset, the song during which he first told me he loved me—way back in 1984.

Being up here and flying higher than even the birds, in such a small aircraft, makes it feel like the usual rules don't apply. What happens in the clouds stays in the clouds. Although I'm still angry with Henry, the rage and pain I felt on the ground lessen with each mile that we cross.

I sneak my hand from underneath the wool blanket I brought on a whim. Calgary will be cold in November, but snowfall shouldn't be more than an inch. The hotel we booked last minute for a four-day, three-night getaway will be plenty warm.

The impulse to touch Henry—the sleeve of his shirt or his pant leg—twitches my fingers. I hesitate for several reasons—so much has transpired between us over the last month. And yet my muscle memory yearns for him, even at ten thousand feet.

Suddenly, Henry grabs me with such force that I gasp, jerking away. The plane jostles from our shift in balance. Reminding me just how precarious flight really is, of the delicate physics that allow us to remain suspended along hundreds of miles.

He laughs. "Scared you, Janet? Don't get complacent over there. We've got two more hours to go."

"Is that all?" I return, my heart still in my throat. The girls both keep their heads down, unbothered.

His touch softens along the ridges of my fingers. When Henry faces me, the setting sun gleams bright in his eyes, causing him to squint. The result is unnerving, like a bad mood has fallen over him or I've wounded him somehow.

"Don't worry, darling. We'll be on the ground again before you know it."

"I can't wait—"

High-pitched beeping interrupts my playful reply. It's coming from the dashboard. A small blinking red light accompanies the noise.

"Henry?"

But my husband adjusts knobs on his dashboard. Pushes and pulls the instruments, while the beeping seems to climb in pitch.

As his movements become more frantic, the clouds rise to our height, as if emphasizing just how powerless Henry is to stop them.

"Henry, how can I—" But the view change cuts my words short. Puffy cotton balls envelop us as we drop below cloud level, thick white cushions swallowing us whole.

3

Violet

Words fly on wind
Like wings on air
Perfunctory in their void of care
Sweet whispered lies
Embracing tight
To offer warmth
And pass the night

Voices rise in the lecture hall as my humanities professor dismisses the class. I scan the curved chalkboard a dozen rows of seats below for the assignment. Another reading from Dante's *Inferno*.

"Don't forget to do the exploration exercise afterward," Professor Tran says above the din. "Creative writing in particular is so helpful to reveal details in our subconscious that we may have forgotten. Kind of like therapy in that way."

Keeping my head low, I dog-ear the page with the poem I was writing. I'll want to finesse it later. I stuff my notebook into my backpack. Hunch down into the baggy sweatshirt I wear, knowing better than to attract attention in tight clothing. Laughter erupts from a group of guys in matching Greek letters, but I keep my eyes forward.

This is my only class of the day, and all I want is to make it home in time for *General Hospital*. No chitchat. No fake smiles. No tenuous friendships that won't make it past the ten-week quarters of the California college system. I need my bag of Hot Tamales and Fritos, stat.

A lot of people my age—not my classmates, as they're all younger than me by years—would turn up their noses at my happy hour plans, but a little junk food makes me happy. Doesn't everyone deserve a little happiness? Don't I?

My fingers twitch at my sides. I usually know better than to ask myself that question.

One more day, one step forward. That's my mantra. Just make it to one more day and the morning might look different. If cellophane wrappers from fried corn dogs made in 7-Eleven serve as my stepping stones, so be it.

Santee smells like rain when I reach my car, an unusual scent in this part of town. Normally, I'd lament any sign of cold—at any point. The kind of trauma I experienced as a child will have that triggering effect. However, San Diego could use a quenching. Thunder claps overhead like cymbals in an orchestra, and I slide into my driver's seat before the clouds break.

I navigate the parking lot filled with students all attempting to leave at once. It's Friday, and I can't imagine anyone else working on school assignments tonight—but I'm "dedicated, hardworking, and determined to get my bachelor's degree," I told the admissions board. Despite dropping out twice over the last seven years, now as a thirty-two-year-old, I'm ready. I'm mature. And I feel massive survivor's guilt because I walked out of the Washington wilderness without my parents. An English degree will make me feel like I finally did something with this life, an accomplishment, I told the board—and if all goes well after that: a writing career. Maybe as an author or a journalist. I don't know. The only thing certain is that before the plane ride that cost us our lives—all of them, not just my parents'—my seven-year-old heart loved documenting the mundane details of a child's day in a journal that I carried with me everywhere. After the Alone Time and outside of a school setting, I didn't pick up a pen for years.

If I could move on from everything that happened out there, I would. But I can't.

My apartment lies squarely centered in a block of similar cookie-cutter buildings. On a clear day, I can see all the way to the ocean, but I didn't choose it for the sliver of a view. Despite considering apartments in every neighborhood in San Diego County, this one—with its crowded neighbors, poor sound insulation, and cramped parking lot—was perfect. I knew it when I first walked through the layout and heard a child crying in the apartment beneath. The urban hum of conversations and car doors slamming is a soothing reminder that I am two miles away from a grocery store, the police, and a fire station just in case they're needed—my lullaby.

After stepping into my second-story apartment in the three-floor building, I remember I don't have anything to eat in my fridge. Only a package of deli meat past its expiration date. I shuffle down the concrete steps and head toward the convenience store at the end of the block where I get all my major food groups. Cars stream past, music pouring from their windows. A big rig roars through the intersection ahead, flipping on its headlights just in time for dusk. I shiver as a gust of air from the big rig's path whips along my body, the only thing that seems to acknowledge me as I tread the dirty sidewalk.

Fluorescent lamps come alive in the near darkness, a beacon for drivers prepping for a long route, and lazy college students, like I guess I am. When we were kids, my mother was insistent that my older sister should learn to cook at least three good meals before she went off to college. Both to avoid starving—or submitting to a fate of prepackaged food—and to ensure she was a good wife to whomever she chose. Last I heard from Fiona, she was married to her art, or whatever. So enthralled with her creations that she couldn't bother to celebrate my birthday then, or the five that followed.

The door chimes when I enter my local Quick Shop. Nobody looks up. Not the cashier, who rings up an older woman with tattoos across her forearm, or the guy wearing a Padres baseball cap standing in front of the jerky aisle. And why would they? I'm frequently ignored because I like it that way. Because, after years of trying to make friends and failing to keep them once they know what happened, I find it's better to go about my business. Save everyone the trouble. Inevitably, either in the first ten minutes of knowing who I am or after a drunken night out, the questions come.

Keeping my head low, I make toward the instant noodles aisle and past the display of eight-ounce Diet Cokes stacked in a tower. Straight to the prepackaged pasta dinners that I visit at least once a week. Although I do know how to make spaghetti on my own, the comfort food on a Friday night will hit the spot in front of the reality show I've been bingeing.

"Is that any good?" The Padres lover nods his chin to the fettuccine I'm eyeing.

"It's not bad. If you're desperate and don't really love food to begin with."

He laughs. Up close, he's got dark-brown eyes that are almost black—bottomless inkwells. Sharp features end in full lips and a pointed chin. "Have I seen you here before?"

I look around us—at the scuffed white tile, the automotive section to my left, and the tampons on the end-of-aisle shelf. "Not exactly the spot to pick up women."

He smirks. He's young. My age or a little younger. "I don't really love food either. It's more of a way to—"

"Get your nutrition in," I finish. "Yeah."

A moment passes between us while I try to gauge what's happening. Does he recognize me? He wouldn't, as I've never given interviews, but there are pages of reports on us online. My sister, Fiona, and I deliberately stayed away from the media once we were rescued. We swore to never engage with the public about our ordeal—or rather, Fiona made me swear never to talk. And I agreed.

"Well, I'm going to be sitting outside if you want to get your"— he shoots my cellophane-wrapped dish a skeptical look—"nutrients in together."

Holding aloft a stick of beef jerky, he walks backward down the aisle. Mischief dances across his face, self-deprecating and charming.

I smile. I can't help it. Confusion and pleasure mix in my chest, then leave me feeling anxious. Chimes ring as his thick black hair seems to float past a shelf of Chef Boyardee cans out onto the sidewalk.

I pay for my meal, unsure of my next move. It's not a good idea— it's a waste of energy to sit and get to know someone who will only freak when they learn the truth about me. But I'm also planning to eat my quick meal alone in front of the TV, in the apartment I rent thanks to generous GoFundMe donations and damages checks from the airplane manufacturer whose model killed half my family. What's the harm in eating beside someone whose void of culinary taste matches—or even surpasses—my own?

Plenty.

After paying for my pasta and a package of peanut butter cups, I take the entrance at a nice clip. Loose the chimes. Then speed walk past the first guy who's shown an interest in me in ages.

"*Buon appetito,*" he says. A yellow moving van slams on its brakes at the stoplight. Metal on metal screeches, drowning out the rest of his words.

When I reach my apartment complex, I turn over my shoulder, certain he or someone else has followed me home. A plastic bag greets me, swirling in the wind. My only stalker.

The switchblade I carry with me presses warm and comforting against my closed palm.

In the days and weeks that followed our rescue, the police questioned us over and over again: What happened to your parents?

We never wavered, never faltered in our answer: the crash. The impact of us colliding with the earth was the death of them both.

But if any police bothered to follow up with me now as an adult, to observe the compulsion I have of carrying a blade on me when walking alone, they would know. The stink of my lie would perfume any interrogation room. Thicker than the smell of hot dogs on a rotating convenience store spit.

Upstairs in my apartment, I rip open the plastic of my meal, then pop the pasta in the microwave. Turn on the TV as background noise, since I missed *General Hospital* due to mass traffic as I left campus. Someone talks about an exciting new guest on a morning talk show, making waves with her revelations from the past.

Class today focused on Dante and his first canticle. The professor emphasized how Dante relied on imagery to scare the daylights out of his readers in the fourteenth century, though I found myself caught up in his choice of words. *They yearn for what they fear for.*

Is that true for me? I yearn for my family, though that's an irreparable idea long since trashed. I yearn for wholeness and balance—nothing too extravagant for Violet Seng. Do I also fear those things?

Pressure between my index finger and thumb alerts me that I should stay busy. Not think too deeply about the past or who I wish I had become. Although a benign gesture on its surface, the incessant rotation of my pointer finger against my thumb pad has led to problems. Tearing of my skin. Infections. Scarring. Increased anxiety levels when I don't perform the act, which compound during the next period while I'm able to abstain. Until the next time I cave, that is.

The microwave dings, announcing my meal is ready.

I move into my cramped kitchen and retrieve a squeeze bottle of bright-yellow mustard from my fridge. It takes a few shakes, but I get the condiment to loosen from the base. It's the kind seen at ballparks and kiddie birthdays: cheap and without any fancy ingredients.

Using a coffee mug, I mix together two tablespoons of mustard, then a tablespoon of the white wine I keep in my fridge door, and top off the mixture with brown mustard seeds that I got from Whole Foods.

Sure, buying premade luxury stuff would save me some time and increase the quality of my meal. But the public donations Fiona and I received after the fifteenth anniversary of the plane crash—through the GoFundMe set up by our lawyers, who were seeking a boost to their profiles—must be stretched out. If I can save a few bucks yet still enjoy nice flavors, I'll make the effort.

Then again, every time I do, the taste is only an echo of what it should be. It's never quite what I aim for, reminding me that my attempt has fallen short yet again. I'm consistent in that sense.

As I twist the chicken fettuccine together in my homemade Dijon mustard, the answer to Dante's question comes to me. I yearn for a better quality of life—I fear the cost of it in the same breath.

4

Henry

The Crash

Shrill beeping matches the steady cadence of a blinking light on the dashboard. The fuel reservoir is empty. *Beep beep beep beep.* I can't focus—can't think—with it screaming in the cockpit. I switch it off.

Silence replaces it. A bellowing, reverberating void of noise, painful in its god-awful echo. Seconds ago, funnels of wind racked the metal body of the passenger plane I borrowed from a friend, like a carnival ride I loved as a kid that batters you left and right. All you can do is clutch the ripped upholstery that covers the ride's handles and hold on for dear life and squeal for joy. But there is none of that in this vehicle. I clutch the steering wheel as the plane's complex fuel system shuts down, starting with the autopilot function.

Battering rams of air that I'd almost grown used to during the hours before were deafening through the thick headset I'm wearing. Now, they've become a diminishing whistle. A cartoon noise that might signal an Acme anvil is about to drop out of the sky, instead of our suddenly engine-less death bird.

"Henry," Janet whispers. "What happened?"

Her voice is another shock. I can hear it clearly with no roaring anything to devour her words.

The blanket of white clouds is getting closer. We're dropping. Losing altitude.

"Henry?" Louder this time. "Why did the engine cut out?"

"I don't know," I answer. "I don't know. I don't know, I don't know." I pump the primer lever three times—*one, two, three*—push the throttle in a half inch, then turn the ignition. No dice. I try again, to no result. I twist various knobs, adjusting instruments across the dashboard, but nothing seems to work—to lift us higher and farther from the fat cumulus cotton balls that are about to dissolve to nothing. I note our coordinates. We're still hundreds of miles away from Calgary, not even close to the airport I chose as our destination.

When I was a kid, I used to run along beneath the puffs of cold air, the contrails that an airplane leaves behind in its path along the sky. I would run, mesmerized by these metal feats of human innovation and the disappearing evidence that we once joined birds on the currents above. I would sprint, gaping mouth and wide eyes, until the sidewalk ended and I would have had to run into traffic to continue. At an early age, I knew I wanted to be a pilot. It took me a few different careers and sources of income to finally obtain a license, but I didn't care. I did it.

I also knew at an early age that I wanted a family. Now I've got everything I ever wanted, and I seem to be losing it all in the same harrowing moment. The clouds are coming faster now. The wind that the Cessna's wings exploit is inconsistent, dropping us lower with each break in buoyancy. Another roller-coaster memory flashes to mind where a kid from my neighborhood fell to his death from the topmost seat of the Ferris wheel.

"Girls. Girls!" Janet snaps to the back seat. "Seat belts. Put them on now."

Two clicks confirm our daughters are listening. They're silent, no doubt rippling with fear just as I am. I can't look at them. I won't. I'll remember them by their innocent faces that I used to gaze at for hours in their cribs. The sweet giggles, the demands for horsey rides on my back. The more recent eye rolls, then intervals on the couch watching *Jeopardy!* together. All of it was such a gift. And a long drop to the earth and death is how I repay the kindness.

"Henry!" Janet shouts in my ear. God, she's loud without the engine. "Henry, what the fuck is going on? The plane!"

Five feet—ten feet—are snatched from us as the Cessna drops in a sharp dip. We're through the clouds now. Green and white are visible below, though still specks of color.

Again, I attack the engine. Pump the primer lever—*one, two, three*—push the throttle in a half inch, and turn the ignition. The engine breaks the silence with a roar, and I let out a joyful whoop.

"She's back!"

The body of the plane trembles—*put-puts*—like just before the engine died last time. Sweat drips down my chin as I check the fuel valves on both tanks. Port side, the tank is empty and resting on the fat, angry red line. Starboard, the arrow hovers just above empty.

I pull the throttle out to decrease the engine speed. Lower our altitude to conserve energy, then start scanning the approaching horizon for a flat place to land.

Pause. Drop. Pause. Drop. As gusts of wind that are stronger than the output from the engine collide with the Cessna, the plane floats for a few moments each time, catching the air. Like a kite. A hang glider.

I've been on a hang glider only once before, and with a certified instructor on my back, but the memory rushes forward. *Wait for the right time,* he said. *Wait for it. Wait for it.*

The plane jolts as a gust of wind slaps the wings, and I press the steering wheel down. We lean forward into the wind, picking up speed, the only creature this high off the ground.

Janet and both girls scream. Then the plane jumps like it smashed into a solid wall. The plunge stops. For a moment of piss-poor bliss, we remain airborne. Level. We coast aloft while I adjust the steering a centimeter this way or that. Ridges along my knuckles are bone white.

With a shaking hand, I reach for the radio already tuned to the frequency assigned to me by air traffic control. I compress the button and pull from my throat the words no pilot ever wants to speak: "Mayday, Mayday. This is Cessna two-four-seven-bravo. Mayday, we are going down. Coordinates are . . ."

I list off our latitude and longitude automatically, without thought, as was drilled into me by my flight instructor and the dozens of hours in a cockpit that prepared me in the tiniest way. My flight instructor said, *Leave a record. Help us to find you if you get lost.* I repeat our coordinates into the void—hope that somewhere nearby, a person is listening.

White static shoots through the radio. Garbled words.

"Hello? Hello?" Panic douses my calm at the possibility of contact. "Is this ATC? Can you hear me?"

"Cessna two-four-seven-bravo, we read you. Tell us—"

The transmission cuts out. "What? Repeat, over? What did you say, over? Hello?"

"—your—"

"What?" I scream into the radio. Fiona and Violet are both crying in the back seat, and Janet has taken out prayer beads I didn't know she owned. She's rubbing them together in her hand while mumbling something.

"Repeat. What are your—" The voice cuts off again.

"Goddammit!" I hit the steering wheel with the two-bit, janky radio. We slide right, then drop another ten feet—fifteen feet, this time. More screams from the girls. Janet rubs her beads like she's trying to spark a flame.

I grasp the wheel, then plunge it forward into a low-hanging stratus cloud. The green and white have taken shape at this altitude. Mountains. A snow-capped peak surrounded by green trees on the slopes below. Not nearly enough snow to be Canada and no sign of city lights for miles. Where are we?

We catch another air drift, then glide lower at an angle. "Mayday, Mayday," I start again. Pain radiates from my joints as I continue wrestling the steering wheel for a straight trajectory. "Hello? Is anyone out there?"

Static. A voice. Multiple voices. "Repeat. Your lo—"

"What?"

The plane falls. We lose our wind, dropping faster, even faster now toward the hard, unforgiving earth. "What?" I shout again.

"Your co—what is your loc—reading as—"

"We're at forty-seven degrees north, 123 degrees west."

"Negative. Negative, we do not confirm. What is your loc—"

"Forty-seven degrees north, 123 degrees—"

"Negative, pilot. Repeat—"

I switch off the radio, not desiring to die while screaming to an unknown person with bad hearing.

As the tops of fir trees take on crisp form, I realize no one—not the person on the radio, or anyone else—has a clue where we are. A search party, if it's sent at all, will be wildly off course.

"Daddy! Daddy!" Violet cries.

"Do something, Dad!" Fiona yells. Janet continues to rub her beads.

Branches extend toward us as if welcoming us into their lush grave, then ground, rocks, and boulders peek from between trees and impact is imminent.

"Our Father—"

"Janet, do you have your—Janet, put on your seat belt!"

"—who art in heaven, hallowed be thy—"

"Your seat belt, goddammit! What are you—"

Dust, dirt, and glass explode into my lungs. Then the light Janet is always preaching to me becomes blinding, searing my corneas.

Hours go by.

Days, weeks seem to go by.

A bird whistles. And confirms what I fear most: I'm still alive.

I open my eyes.

A brown-and-white knit afghan covers the back of a couch in my parents' living room. Disembodied voices come from a TV in black and white. Hawkeye Pierce is asking a nurse for something in the surgical tent, but there's a gag grenade on the tray.

Where am I?

My fingers dig into the shag carpet, sliding an inch deep across the thick threaded fabric. Something is cooking in the kitchen around the corner. Ginger. Chicken. Fish sauce. I get to my feet, then notice the rip across the knee of my pants—an injury I got while roller-skating with the neighbor kids when I was fourteen. A fresh wound is visible through the shredded jeans; it stings. My father snores, mouth open, on the worn armchair that would outlast every family pet we ever had, and I tiptoe past so as not to wake him—in my dream? Am I dreaming? I must be, because I was just somewhere else.

Where was I?

A quick peek around the corner confirms my mother is stirring a pot of soup. Bones rest against the lip of the deep pot, an animal's. Maybe one of the chickens we keep in our backyard that died last week and that my uncle came and plucked the next day.

My mother mumbles to herself. Not an unusual sight, as she often recites a recipe from memory while she prepares it. Her mother, my grandmother, was a healer back in China who knew every combination of ingredients there is to fix an ailment or sate a hungry belly. From what my mom told me, their house was always full of people seeking my grandmother's wisdom. And she was happy to give it. Even when she would tell visitors she was going to sleep and she'd talk to them more tomorrow, that's when the spirits used to pop in.

"Simmer for ten minutes until broth is murky," Mom says to no one. She stirs the pot, her other hand clutching her lower back. She's old, older than I think she wanted to be when she had me finally, her only child. If she's awake, whether she's moving or sitting, my mom battles an ache and pain that can only be cured with a special meal of specific ingredients. Like I said, something is always cooking in the kitchen.

This close to her, I can smell the laundry detergent of my childhood—the perfume of clean clothes: sweet and floral but stiff thanks to the spray bottle of starch my mom preferred.

I step toward her. She died over a decade ago, leaving an ocean-size hole in my heart—nothing can fill it, not my children or my wife. A ball tightens in my stomach at the thought of wrapping my arms around her waist. Hugging her soft middle and the knobby elbows that would remind me to stand up straight with a loving nudge.

"No." The word is a low growl, uttered just above a whisper. I pause moving toward her, withdraw my outstretched hand.

My skin is soft and smooth at this age. None of the scars across my knuckles that I will eventually earn during combat.

"No," she mutters, louder this time.

"Mom," I begin, not wanting to startle her. "What are you cooking?"

She whirls on me, spraying broth with the wooden spoon that she yanks from the boiling pot of soup. Scalding liquid sears my chin in the most realistic dream I can recall ever having.

"I said no!" she shouts, over my head. "Not my boy. You leave him alone."

My mother lowers her gaze to connect with mine. Chills undulate across my arms in my short-sleeved tee, like the caterpillar ride at the fair.

She hisses, "You don't belong here."

When she rears her arm backward, I know that's my cue to leave. I skip out of the kitchen, past my sleeping father, then nearly trip over the threshold of the front door.

Sunshine blasts me in the face outside. Cold wind gusts across my jacket, the sturdy trousers I chose this morning, and then I blink and the scene before me comes into focus.

A crack in the windshield spiderwebs across the length of the cockpit. Blood drips from the glass onto the Cessna's sloping dashboard.

5

FIONA

Pungent aromas of acrylic paint and varnish mingle together at the front of the gallery's open door. The Hughes Gallery, the location of my very first exhibit dedicated solely to my art, is hosting an art class. Students were told to BYOBB—bring your own brush and bottle—to paint along with the instructor, Quincy, the owner of the gallery. In the back of the deep, narrow building, black tarps cover the tile floors beneath a half dozen people furiously slashing at their canvases with sloppy strokes, trying to keep up with Quincy's practiced hand.

I've always admired art of any kind. But years ago, the idea of throwing myself into the rat race with the millions of other amateur and pro painters seemed like a nonstarter. If I was going to indulge in the effort, I would at least give myself a fighting chance to stand out by working in a rising genre: modern sculpture. Or as my art dealer likes to promote my pieces: the tangible manifestation of trauma using the very source of the trauma itself—nature. When my critics accuse me of exploiting my family's pain, Darleen likes to shoot back, *Isn't all art an exploitation of a hurt, a trauma, an unresolved fear?* She's good, my dealer. I'm lucky we found each other several years back when I was first shopping for representation.

"Miss Seng."

From the sidewalk, a man in a suit jacket and jeans stands beside a Mercedes. "Miss Seng, could I have a word?"

I step inside the gallery, then catch my tense reflection in the glass window. Brown hair that I keep elbow-length is swept up in a ponytail. Baby hairs that have never behaved stick out behind my ears, while the light makeup I applied is already smudged from frowning.

"Are you with the *Boston Times*?" I ask. "Someone named Nathan Wallace has been leaving me messages and I'm not interested in giving any interviews."

The man shakes his head. Dark-rimmed glasses frame bright-blue eyes beneath thick eyebrows. Clean shaven with a few deep-set wrinkles, he looks exactly like my type, like my last three ex-boyfriends. Or, I guess "guys I dated" would be a more accurate descriptor since I never had labels for any of them. That's the result of dating less time than it takes for a frozen pizza to go bad. Relationships have never been elusive for me, not really. Yet they've always ended when the guy decided I was withholding from him—believed that if I couldn't share every part of myself, I must not be invested. They weren't hangers-on, exactly. Not groupies, as I've discovered I have—people rabid for sightings and information on the "girl-survivors." But they didn't cope well with me keeping my secrets.

I hope to meet a man one day who doesn't think loving someone means having ownership over all her thoughts.

"Some guys don't know when to quit, huh," glasses guy says with an impish grin. "No, that's not me. Although I was hoping to talk to you—"

"Whatever it is you want me for, I'm not interested." I reach for the door.

"Hey, no pressure. I only want to discuss art. Something I think we're both passionate about. Could I buy you a drink?" He lifts his eyebrows in a hopeful arch. Then he smiles. "That sounds so lame—"

He scans the white, flowing peasant dress I wear. "Could I buy you a pinot grigio? There's a bar around the corner that specializes in Tuscan options that won't stain your outfit."

I hesitate. Of all the times I've been caught off guard by a "fan," few people have made the effort to approach me as if I'm a regular person. It's rare that someone is this thoughtful or—the more likely—this strategic. Maybe self-serving.

"No, thank you. Please stop following me." Without waiting for his reply, I kick the wedge free from underneath the glass door. Cool air ruffles the hem of my dress at my ankles as the door shuts behind me.

His voice carries through the window. "There's something you should know." I keep walking farther inside, ignoring the urge to glance behind me. He is cute. But only as attractive as someone barging into my private life could be.

My lace-up boots announce that I've arrived, and several heads turn at the sound.

Quincy lifts a hand to me. "Five more minutes?" he says, pointing to his wrist, which isn't wearing a watch. One of the women from the back row of the class rises. Darleen.

"Hey, there you are." She glances behind me, a spot of white paint on her neck. "Who was that?"

"No one. I mean, another journalist, I think. Is he still there?"

Darleen shakes her head. "He's gone. Nosing around for a quote? Let's get a glass and you can tell me about it."

Instead of returning to the back of the class, she plucks a wine bottle from beside her chair and we continue to the next room. Tableaux bearing thick acrylic paint in muted colors cover the walls. We post up on a bench beneath a six-foot-long seascape. Or maybe it's the sky.

Bright lights overhead illuminate the creases in Darleen's face. She's around the age my mother should have been, but they'd otherwise share little in common physically. My mom, Janet, was petite, Chinese and white, with a complexion that glowed and brown eyes that seemed hazel in the sunshine. Darleen shares the full cheeks Mom had, but she was a plus-size model before diving into the art world.

Violet was Mom's twin in so many regards—both in the way they each enjoyed quiet time and reading and, more significantly, in their appearance. Violet, as a seven-year-old, was our mother's carbon copy in mini.

Darleen pours rosé into two plastic wineglasses she brought from the tarped area, handing me the larger one. "What did that guy say?"

"Oh, I don't know. I stepped inside before he could really talk. Probably wanted a selfie for his socials." I sip my cup. Sweet floral notes hit my taste buds. It's good, not the cheap stuff that usually comes with the price of these paint nights. BYOBB might be onto something.

Darleen fiddles with the cork. "Is that pine cone behaving yet?"

She once told me she was a sketch artist in her twenties, after modeling. Then she took up painting, sculpture, and ceramics, and she loved each medium so much, she became an art rep to work with them all. Eventually, her focus narrowed to modern art—painting, performance, and sculpture.

"It's getting there. With some coaxing," I add. "And the other pieces are coming along."

Darleen is all smiles. "That's great. You've had such eager buyers in private, I can't wait to see what they do when they're together in public. We might even have a bidding war. I told you the heiress from Montana is flying in for the night, right?"

"Oh? I don't think I knew that."

Tension ratchets my shoulder blades. So much interest has been rumbling since Darleen sent out a press release. Dealers, buyers, magazines, and galleries all took notice in varying degrees: requests for press kits and photos of me with my art, and queries for interviews. Darleen turned the interviews all down, per usual. But I couldn't help feeling then—and now—that this could be big. If this show goes well and I sell a lot of pieces, this could set me up for a few years. Maybe even life, if I continue to manage the settlement money and donations. The pressure to perform and achieve reminds me of my mother's constant, quiet support—both expectant and worried at the outcome.

"There's my favorite artist!" Quincy steps from around the corner, arms open wide. We hug, having met two years ago, when one of Quincy's benefactors desired to buy a leaf collage I made from materials I scavenged in Temecula.

"How are things going? Are you okay? Getting some sleep?" Quincy holds me at arm's length, like an older brother might.

"Fine, I think."

"Good, good. And the work? That's going well too?"

"Yes, definitely," I reply. As friendly as we are, I'm fully aware of our roles to one another. I need Quincy to amplify the local art scene's anticipation of my pieces, and he needs me to further legitimize his gallery in the heart of San Diego's commercial art district, Little Italy.

Darleen and Quincy spend an hour discussing all the ways in which they're going to "knock this pitch out of the park"—Darleen's words—then I do my bit, reassuring them that I will deliver the moneymakers. It's a strange turn of events, to hawk the sculptures that I first created as a form of catharsis—of dealing with what happened—as commodities to be collected and valued at top dollar.

"Oh, I got a text," Darleen says. She holds her phone up, then swipes a finger along her screen. "Oh."

"What is it?" I ask. Darleen is never at a loss for words. I smooth out the bunched cotton fabric of my dress, worrying at a loose string. "Everything okay?"

Darleen darts a glance at Quincy. "It's . . . ah, a woman. She's claiming something about your family."

I frown. "That's not new. Lots of people try to cash in on our lives."

Quincy casually pulls out his own phone. He nibbles on a cracker, scrolling. "Oh. Honey, this is a bit more than that."

Heat flushes my chest. "Let me see."

He passes his phone to me. The biggest daytime television host in the country, Charissa, poses with a middle-aged woman I've never seen before. The headline of the article teases a big announcement on tomorrow's episode—New Untold Details about Henry Seng, Says His Mistress.

I clutch the screen closer. Chills crawl up my spine as I reread the headline. "That's . . . new."

Darleen pours me another glass. She examines me through thick black eyelashes. "Fiona. Fiona, are you okay?"

I scan the article. It's scant on information, likely saving the real bombshells for the show. Geri Vega, a freelance consultant—meaning, she's unemployed—says she carried on an affair with my father for the better part of three months before the fateful plane crash. Although she "begged him not to go," Henry insisted that he try again with his wife, Janet. According to Geri, the vacation was planned as the romantic and adventure-filled getaway that Henry hoped would reassemble his family—despite being madly in love with Geri.

I lift my absurdly full glass, then press it to my lips. A sharp urge to bite down, to shatter the plastic in my mouth, clenches my jaw. Instead, I take a long, slow drink.

"Fiona, babe?" Quincy says. "Even if this were true, the bright side here is that Charissa is covering you less than four weeks before your big show. If anyone comes looking for a quote or a response, you can just say, 'I have a showing at Hughes Gallery in November. Any quotes will be provided then, and you can confirm your attendance with the handsome yet capable Quincy Hughes.'"

He ends with an empathetic smile. Darleen watches me, waiting for my response. She, at least, knows me better than to pussyfoot around the truth.

"My father didn't know how to love anyone but himself," I begin. "So this woman's story is complete nonsense, with or without the extramarital affair. And it's not a good thing. Regardless of the extra publicity, it probably means my show will be attended by gawkers and tabloid affiliates. Not the art community that I so want—that I so need—"

My throat closes, forcing me to pause. Darleen extends a gentle hand to my knee. I'll never be more than one of the girl-survivors, and I'll never be allowed to work through my trauma on my own terms, via my sculptures. All they or I will ever be is an object of fascination and fear.

And worse, I can't blame anyone. Everything that happened has in some way or another been my fault. I'm the problem—even if I've never been to rehab.

"So, Fiona," Darleen says in a quiet voice. "What do you want to do?"

I exhale a breath. Pluck a cracker from the plastic tray. "Let's talk about the rest of the pieces. Then I'm going home. There's a sculpture on my dining table that needs subduing."

6

JANET

The Wild

Blood covers the cockpit. Cracked plexiglass shattered on impact, and a branch stabs into the back seat.

"Girls," I muster. My voice is hoarse from screaming when the earth rushed up to meet our tiny plane, whose nose collapsed like crumpled paper. "Girls."

But they're not there. No one is. Empty seat belts, discarded toys, Violet's journal. The blanket I packed for them on the floor. Glass everywhere.

Henry's door is ajar. A slick red handprint smeared across the beige leather of the upholstered armrest.

"Henry?" I croak. Fumbling for my seat belt elicits sharp pain that splits down my right arm in two directions. I pause, wincing from the effort.

Where are they? Were they ejected? I struggle to sit up, then notice my jeans were ripped in the crash landing somehow. "Fiona. Violet."

The branches, or bushes, in front make it impossible to see beyond the nose of the Cessna. I clutch the metal flap of my seat belt again, then succeed in releasing the buckle. Reach for the door handle and push. The door doesn't move. I press against it with all my weight as new pain shoots down my arm. Jimmy the handle and push. Jimmy and push.

A whimper. Someone is crying nearby.

"Girls? Fiona? Violet?" I call again.

Bracing myself for a new round of hurt, I launch my body into the door, and it swings open. I fall forward, onto a patch of grass. No, leaves. A bush. Tiny twigs scratch my face, grate existing scratches I didn't know I had. I push to my feet, eager to feel solid ground underneath.

More whimpers, but these I recognize as my own.

"Girls!" I shriek, as loud as my lungs will carry.

"Mom?"

"Mama!"

Footsteps come crashing through the trees, the soggy earth squelching with each movement, and my babies bound forward from the wilderness. Fiona throws herself into my arms, while Violet clutches my hips, my waist. I hold them with a fierceness I didn't know lay within me. Recognize it as the adrenaline rush that leads mothers to lift whole cars off the bodies of their children. Wetness streams down my face: rain—no, tears. All-consuming emotion that comes to those who share their entire selves for months on end, just to see one breath of life inhaled by a tiny face.

When my heartbeat slows, I kiss the tops of their heads, their cheeks again for good measure. Wings flap somewhere above, hidden among a canopy of leaves.

"Where's your father?" I ask. "Are you okay? Let me look at you. Are you hurt?"

The girls peer at me with tear-streaked, dirty faces. They wait patiently—probably still in shock—as I touch their hair, necks, arms, hands. They seem okay.

Fiona coughs. "We don't know where Dad is. We crashed. I woke up and he was gone."

"But I was awake," Violet adds in a small voice. "I didn't sleep. I—I saw—" Sobs interrupt my youngest and I bring her in close. Rub her back and the tiny space between her shoulder blades until she's able to speak.

"We crashed." She hiccups. "Then Daddy messed with the radio again and the walkie-talkie. Everything was broken, and then he left."

"He didn't say anything to you?" I ask. "He just left?"

Violet meets my gaze. Innocent confusion gives her the look of a baby deer scampering across a busy street. "He looked at me and did this." She lifts one finger to her lips. "Then he got out of the plane."

Shock prickles my skin, hearing the summary of my husband's betrayal. Another one.

"Okay. Let's get back into the plane."

"What?" Fiona asks. "We just survived getting out of it."

"I know, I know. You're right. But it's cold out here and the plane will offer some kind of shelter. It's starting to rain." Small puffs of white accompany my words, reminding me that we're in November, somewhere in the Pacific Northwest. Henry's genius idea to visit Canada for a long weekend before the weather "got bad" failed to consider us getting caught outdoors. Although bad is relative. Being outdoors for any stretch of time right now could be uncomfortable, but I'll be worried if a storm begins.

I scan our surroundings for the first time since tumbling from the aircraft. Tall fir trees reach to the sky, as if trying to extinguish the pin-prick of sunlight that already beats a retreat toward the left side of the forest. Sharp pain returns to my right arm. I clutch my upper biceps and smile, not wanting to scare the kids.

We're in a forest. In the middle of nowhere. "Your dad probably went for help. Everything is okay."

Fiona opens her mouth, likely to tell me off for my aggravating optimism—but she doesn't. "C'mon, Vi. Let's get back inside."

Violet takes her sister's hand. They climb into the back seats. The engine seems terrifically damaged from what I can tell of the metal parts scattered around the landing site. I don't smell any gas.

"I'll be right back, girls. Stay put, okay?"

Several steps away from the plane and my children, I search the adjacent trees for some sign of my husband. Where is Henry? Was he badly hurt and didn't want Violet to see him in pain? But where would he creep off to like a cat seeking a safe place to die?

A branch cracks several feet from the airplane. Someone, or some animal, is watching us.

"Henry?" I call.

The Cessna flattened twenty feet of saplings, creating our own clearing. Branches and green needles carpet the ground, insulating my feet in the casual sneakers I chose for the flight. I step forward, teetering along sacrificed plants, louder than a herd of elephants. "Henry!"

The forest is silent. Light filters through a thin copse of trees untouched by our deus ex machina arrival.

"God, please let us be near a town. A rest stop. A ski resort." I fumble in my pocket for my prayer beads, then grasp my phone. My cell phone. Of course. It takes forever to boot up—rather, the normal time of sixty seconds, but it feels like eternity.

"C'mon, c'mon." Anxiously, I watch the bars in the top right corner of my screen, hoping and praying for the miracle we need. A large X appears instead. "No service. Fuck. Fuckity fuck."

Holding my phone high above my head, I continue toward the light between slender conifers. Step over a panel of grease-streaked aluminum siding that was ripped from the tail of the plane.

"Girls?" I turn.

Their heads pop up in the cracked back window. "Yeah?"

"Just checking."

Birds warble overhead as the forest begins to resume its normal cadence—a comforting sound. A squirrel watches me from a thick tree trunk untouched by our intrusion.

The light I detected becomes clearer, brighter as I approach. Verdant, sloping hills lead into a valley below. The remaining rays of sunshine before night falls illuminate snow-dusted trees and a gurgling river like a scene from a Thomas Cole painting. Fat white clouds dotting the sky are moving away—pushed along by gray clouds. The kind that bring thunder, and which the pioneers of these parts might have said hold an ominous portent.

At the edge of the cliff where I stand, I scan the deep banks below for movement. An animal, a fox, darts along a path and then disappears into the brush. No humans. No cars. Definitely no ski resort.

No Henry. Only unadulterated wilderness.

"Fuck," I whisper.

On my walk back to the plane and my daughters—my arm extended as high above my head as it will go, searching for reception—I think of all the scenarios that could have drawn Henry from us. From his family. His children, flesh and blood of his own. And from me, his wife of thirteen years. But then I grimace at the answer: nothing could take Henry Seng willingly from his kids, and I know exactly who would lure Henry from me.

Snapping branches announce my return to the crash site. Two sets of eyes peer at me from the back seat of the Cessna as wetness pitters on my forehead.

Rain falls lightly, carelessly, turning the dial on this situation toward worse. Quickly, the volume becomes pummeling, soaking my thin shirt and jeans, as if each drop is burrowing toward my bones.

I make toward the plane. Beside it, a small grove of trees was knocked to the ground when we crash-landed. I grab a splintered branch—use my foot to angle it away from its last remaining grip on the fallen tree trunk—and yank. I throw it underneath the body of the plane, wincing through the pain in my bad arm. Grab another smaller busted limb and chuck it under the steel shelter. I continue until I have a pile as large as Violet stored away, then climb into the front passenger seat.

The girls stare at me, though they don't say the obvious: I'm soaking wet. Shaking out the wool blanket that was covering my legs during the flight, I unfurl the crumbs of my own sandwich, then strip off my shirt and the pants I'm wearing.

"Mom?" Fiona asks. "Are you okay?"

"Yes, honey, I'm fine. Where's the water bottle I gave you?"

Fiona hands me hers empty, along with Violet's half-empty bottle. I open them both, then set them outside on a rock that was showered in dirt when we landed. Rainwater begins to collect in each plastic container.

"Puke bucket?" I ask over my shoulder. The shallow orange drawer I took from Henry's tool set in the garage was my answer to Violet's concerned question when we first told them we'd be flying for six hours until we got to our first stop to gas up—"What if my tummy hurts? Or I have to pee?"

Fiona hands it to me. I place it on the ground outside, then wring my clothing over the open mouth. When I'm done, I wrap myself in the wool knit blanket.

In the reflection of an unbroken part of the windshield, I catch my girls watching me. "Everything's fine. Really."

"But . . . why did you do all that?" Violet asks. Her expression reminds me of when she was a toddler and genuinely perplexed when I would do something unusual, like wash the underside of the dining table.

"Just in case," I reply, keeping my tone light. "Fresh rainwater is delicious and good for washing our hair. This could be the last storm we have for a while."

Violet settles back into the seat, satisfied with my answer. Fiona peers at me longer than I'd like.

Thunder claps overhead. Then it does again. Lightning flashes across the area, illuminating the expanse of trees that stretches beyond our clearing. As if instantly contradicting my last words as wishful thinking.

7

VIOLET

A plump brunette named Geri Vega sits on a striped couch, discussing my father. Charissa, the daytime TV host, a person I spent hours watching as a kid, who always exuded a sense of safety and warmth to my twelve-year-old mind, leans in to encourage this liar for more.

"But I think what our audience really wants to know is"—hold for dramatic effect—"how was the sex?"

I pause the screen, grateful that I set the DVR yesterday when I randomly saw the headline: New Untold Details about Henry Seng, Says His Mistress. The "new untold details" part, I was familiar with—had seen countless empty articles attempting to milk the public's interest over the years. I knew not to let my emotions go wonky at the clickbait.

The "mistress" part took me off guard. Sent tremors down my limbs and made me reach for my phone to text my old dealer. My father had a mistress? The idea that my father had secrets from my mother didn't concern me. I knew that. Well, that became apparent extremely quickly out there. But a person coming forward after all these years with a seedy relationship to my dad—credible enough to merit a feature on a morning show that literally millions of people watch—made me sick down to my toes.

The nausea led me to draft a message to my sister, Fiona. Type it out, but not send. I was waiting to see the extent of the damage before I took that irretrievable action.

Frozen in place, Geri Vega's face shows surprise, shock, maybe a little embarrassment. Choppy bangs hide penciled-in eyebrows. Some contouring around a full nose. She's pretty. Or maybe she's pretty astute to the excited reception her revelations will have, and her expression shows hours of acting lessons over the last twenty-five years since she supposedly slept with my married father.

"Only one way to find out." I squeeze the stress ball I've made into a swiss cheese look-alike these last several months, picking out chunks of foam rubber each time the squeeze itself wasn't enough. Three hundred and eighty-two days without drugs or alcohol. And a lifetime without some needed therapy, but whatever.

I hit play. Audience laughter and a few gasps overwhelm Geri's stammered response. Then the noise dies down. She places prim hands in the lap of her long skirt and says, "Henry and I were intimate, it's true. I loved him. And I don't kiss and tell," she adds with a demure smile.

"Even after all these years, you love him?" Charissa asks, thirsty for sky-high ratings. Dark hair that has been relaxed and highlighted rests on pointed shoulders. Known for being both the consummate interviewer and an iconic beauty mogul, Charissa leans forward in a burnt-orange sweater that complements her unblemished, melanated skin.

Geri doesn't break eye contact yet still manages to appear wounded. "Always."

"Let me ask you this. Why not come forward with your relationship earlier? Why wait twenty-five years to reveal your relationship with Henry Seng, when something you knew may have helped locate the family? Maybe in time to save him and his wife?"

"Janet," I say, alone in my apartment. "My mother's name was Janet."

A class syllabus I haven't read sits on my coffee table, and I set a bag of Doritos on top. Wipe my hands on my pants. Before I played the episode, I did an assignment for my humanities class, cleared my schedule—of not much—and made sure to stock up on comfort items. Chips, chocolate doughnuts, and yellow-green-colored soda form a row of security blankets on the white particleboard surface.

When I went back to the Quick Shop down the street, I entered hoping to see that guy again. The weird one who suggested we eat our empty calories together. The cute one.

Geri Vega shakes her head. "I felt in my heart of hearts that they would be okay. That Henry would be okay. I didn't want to come forward and ruin anything for him, in case he was alive, when I didn't know anything to begin with. All he told me before that weekend was that he couldn't see me."

"Anymore? Or just that weekend?" Charissa asks.

"Anymore. He said it was over between us." Geri's big cow eyes brim with tears. "Then, the day that they left, a handwritten letter arrived in the mail. From him. It said, 'Meet me you-know-where.'"

"Really? Where was that?" Charissa practically salivates.

"I don't know. I've told the police this several times now. I spent years trying to figure out what he meant, but I've come to realize that I don't have that answer."

"Which is why you're coming forward to all of us now," Charissa deduces. "You no longer hope to be reunited with your lost love."

Geri sighs—finally, someone understands. "Yes. He said he was going to leave his wife eventually, and that we could start a new life together. I always wondered if he meant for us to have our own getaway that weekend. Whether he meant to cancel on his family and join me at the you-know-where spot, or—or otherwise, I don't know. But now there's a documentary being made about them. So it feels like the right time to go on record with my story."

Charissa peers at this woman. The camera zooms in on Geri's face. She chews on her bottom lip, revealing lipstick smeared on a tooth. "You know that Henry's two daughters are all grown up now, right?

And that your confessions will affect the people who are still living out this tragedy and trauma?"

The audience murmurs in appreciation. I nod along with them. "Yes. I do."

"Do you have anything to say to Henry's adult daughters?"

Geri turns to the camera, whose operator I guess was already anticipating this moment. "Fiona and Violet. I just want you to know how deeply I cared—continue to care—for your dad. Henry was a wonderful man, who I'll never forget. I know we could have been such a happy family together."

The frame cuts to Charissa, whose mouth purses in a straight line. Then to the camera: "Okay, then. We'll be right back after this break."

I freeze the recording. The show aired about an hour ago, and directly afterward, my phone began to ping from each of my social media accounts. I never post anything to my profiles, instead use nearly anonymous accounts to watch cat videos. Yet the deluge of message requests that have come in during the last thirty minutes tells me I've been found.

One message request in particular stands out. An account calling itself "VeryGeri" invites me to chat on camera for a dollar amount that could cover two months' rent. Seven other messages from this account date back to a month ago, though this most recent one is the first to offer money.

Without meaning to, I glance at the framed photo of my mom, with her sister, on an end table. Auntie Taylor was warm and caring, and she took Fiona and me in after we were rescued. She went to all our parent-teacher conferences, shuttled Fiona to therapy, and allowed me to read books when I refused to talk to anyone. But she never could replace my mother. Whereas my mother's mixed-race features could be described as "white passing," Auntie Taylor took after my grandmother, who was Chinese—olive skin that tanned well and showed our family were villagers from the rice fields, and jet-black hair that could never hold a curl. Auntie Taylor was a major source of stability for us—which is why I don't really know how we lost touch a few years back, although her house is less than ten miles from here. There is so much I don't understand about myself, even as a thirty-two-year-old woman.

Viewing the photo of my mom and her sister reminds me of the other relative I've lost contact with: Fiona. Only I recall the exact conversation we had when she said she was no longer willing to support my bad habits, when she dropped off a box of my things that she found in storage. A distaste for my drug use made sense. But once I got clean last year and told her I had been sober for several months, she only reiterated that she wasn't interested in a relationship with me.

"I can only take so much, Vi."

"I know," I had said. "And I'm sorry for stealing money from you and lying all those times. But that's behind me. I'm really done with the bad coping strategies and I'm ready to move forward. To finally start life, you know? I want to share more of that journey together."

Her expression hardened. "Right. But it seems we've both done well the last five years that we haven't talked. Better to let a good thing keep rolling, right?"

"Are you serious? I'm your only sister. After all we went through—"

She cut me off then. "Exactly. After all I know about you, all that I saw out there, it's best if we don't pretend."

"What . . . what do you think you saw?"

Images of dark clouds, shadowy woods, and glowing embers from a makeshift fire flashed to my mind then. Frames from a movie that I unfortunately lived, and desired never to recall again. The smell of acrid flesh filled my nose in a jolt.

"What do you think you saw me do?" I asked.

Fiona only shook her head. She wasn't angry, not anymore by that point. Just disappointed. Sad, it looked to me.

Next to the framed photo of my aunt and mother, a small handheld clock I bought from IKEA creeps down to the bottom of the hour.

I turn off the TV. If I don't leave for class now, I'll never beat the midday traffic in time.

———

The lecture hall empties as if a fire drill were underway, instead of the end of class. I reach the exit, then push out into the sunshine with my classmates, some of them already complaining about the midterm that was just announced.

When my humanities professor shared the requirements—a five-page essay—groans rippled across the seats. My first major assignment this quarter should feel intimidating—but I'm excited for it. It's a step toward graduation, then maybe a job I could actually stick with for a while. A career in writing, with any luck.

"Excuse me?"

A man in a blue button-up long-sleeve tucked into jeans waits beside a concrete bench across the walkway. The benches are found all over campus, each with some inspirational quote built into the backrest. Appropriately placed by the English department, this one says, NEVER WALK WHEN YOU CAN RUN TO THE LIBRARY. —UNKNOWN.

"Violet Seng?"

I pause to take in this stranger. Black wire-frame glasses make him seem closer to Fiona's age than mine. Is he a teacher's assistant? A professor?

"Uh, yeah. That's me."

He smiles, and I instantly regret replying. "Yeah, great. I wanted to talk with you about an opportunity to—hey, excuse me. Wait, please!"

"I'm not interested."

His footsteps follow as I dodge my classmates, who leisurely return to their dorms or the parking lots. From the corner of my eye, I spot a guy slouching along one of the quote benches. Something about him is familiar.

"I was just hoping—sorry, excuse me—if you had a sec to chat, we could—whoops, sorry—"

I push forward, now staring straight ahead. My car, a large purchase I made when my settlement money was still flush in my bank account, is parked in the back of the lot toward the exit. An hour and a half ago, it seemed like a life hack to take the spot right by the campus loop. Now, given over two hundred yards to cross with some kind of paparazzo on my heels, I own it was a mistake.

"Violet. Ms. Seng, my name is Daley Kelly, and I'm a filmmaker. I tried talking to your sister, Fiona, outside an art gallery, but she was—uh, she was busy. Anyway, if you would just pause a sec, I could—"

I stop so fast, he nearly runs into me. "You saw my sister?"

Daley Kelly nods. Blue eyes the color of a Cool Ranch Doritos bag brighten. "At an art gallery."

"Which one?"

The man hesitates. As if correctly guessing that I don't know her whereabouts and that I would be willing to concede something for the info. "The Hughes Gallery in Little Italy."

Dark stubble lines his chin and jaw in patches. No gray yet. I continue on toward my car, my short ponytail brushing my neck. "Please leave me alone."

"Did you see the interview?"

Just a bit farther. Another fifty yards and I'll be safely behind my car's steel door.

"The interview," he continues. "The one on *Charissa Today*, with Geri Vega. Your father's mis—"

"Yes, I saw it." I whirl to face him. He stops short and I know I've scared him. Good. People should be scared of me. "I don't have any kind of comment."

"That's fine." He lifts both hands in surrender. "I tried to warn your sister about it before it came out."

"Are you with the show? With this . . . Geri woman?" She'd already sent me a dozen messages on Instagram. Why not upgrade to sending a stalker?

He shakes his head. Black hair barely moves, sprayed in place. "No, I'm . . . Like I said, I'm a filmmaker. Documentaries. I heard about the interview through a friend and wanted to give your sister a chance to comment in advance. To stay on top of the speculation that's happening now."

"How nice of you."

"It's going to get worse. The coverage. The requests for interviews—"

"They never let up." I resume marching to my car, then break into a jog. I'm over this conversation, this harassment.

"Look, Violet, I'll leave you alone if you truly want me to. But other people, other platforms, newspapers, and gossipy daytime TV shows won't. Especially as Geri Vega is making the rounds."

"She's a liar," I say, finally at my car door. "And you can quote me on that."

"Vega was vetted by the police three different times, according to my sources. Her relationship with your dad happened, Violet."

I toss my backpack into the passenger seat, then slide inside behind the wheel.

"I'm sorry to say it, but if you don't give someone an interview," he continues, "other people will continue to dictate the story for you."

My door slams shut harder than I intended. I crack it open. Daley Kelly approaches my car.

"And what are you proposing?" I ask.

Blue eyes brighten. "I think it's time your story was told the right way, with your approval."

The button-up shirt that I initially wrote off as the uniform of a teacher's assistant is wrinkled along the forearms; the sleeves were recently rolled up. His jeans hug tight across tapered hips, and the fabric of one pocket is ripped. Although Daley Kelly gives the first impression that he's a polished individual, a closer look makes me like him more.

Geri Vega's interview with Charissa mentioned a documentary—his? I meet his hopeful expression. "I'll think about it."

8

Janet

The Wild

The kids fell asleep at some point. No doubt, exhaustion and fear, coupled with the soothing sound of rain everywhere, all around us, led them to doze off. Unconsciousness would be my choice too, rather than face the all-consuming terror of our situation. But as their mother, I don't get that luxury, nor do I want it.

We're stranded. Henry is nowhere to be seen, and he hasn't replied to my frantic screams, then dialed-back shouts after I noticed Violet starting to cry again. Dark clouds that appeared so innocuous while flying above them create a thick layer of foreboding on the ground. The rain has stopped at least. And the tiny sliver of sunlight we saw earlier poked a larger hole in the blanket overhead to bathe the valley below. Once I realized reception was not going to materialize where I sat inside the cockpit, I turned off my mobile phone to save the battery. That was an hour ago, at three o'clock in the afternoon. Night will fall soon.

I creep from the front passenger seat, not wanting to wake my kids and force reality on them. Not yet. Broken branches frame the Cessna in a circle, organic booby traps all around. I place my feet carefully, like that scene in *Mission: Impossible*, dodging invisible laser beams. When I reach the outside access door of the luggage compartment, I'm relieved to find it popped open at some point, saving me the trouble. Each of us packed a light bag for the four-day trip, but we at least intended to vacation in cold weather. I find my thick winter parka lying on top of a swimsuit I planned to wear in the hotel hot tub, then slip it on. Instantly, my mood brightens. A favorite Bible verse comes to mind, but with a stranded spin on it: *I can do all things through* warmth, *which strengthens me.*

The girls' jackets are likewise accessible and thick. We're going to need them.

Pawing through my bag, I find mittens, scarves, and some long johns for sleeping but none of the snacks I meant to bring. Henry's duffel bag is stashed at the very back of the luggage compartment. Did he pack them? I drag out his heavy brown canvas bag, cringing as aluminum dog tags scrape the metal floor. It's been ages since I've seen this thing, a remnant from his time as a marine.

I unzip the closure. "Please, please, please have packed food."

Shoved into the side, Henry's thick black snow jacket hides two long-sleeved shirts, two pairs of pants, and a sweater with reindeer across the chest. Underwear and long socks are all that's left because I packed his toothbrush and toothpaste with my toiletries.

"Fuck," I say, breathing the word into several syllables. Cold white air puffs from my lips.

I throw my hand inside the duffel, searching for anything I might have missed—a candy bar, men's multivitamins, a package of chewing gum—then scrape my fingers across the small aluminum hook of a new zipper. A closed interior pocket.

Inside, I find what I need: four protein bars, matches, a scented candle, a package of peanuts, eight Hershey's Kisses, and something else that stops my breath. Condoms. Five individually wrapped condoms.

New cold freezes my lungs. The wrappers are warm between my fingers, as if perpetually ready for use.

We haven't had sex in months. Not since I found out about her.

No, that's not right. We did sleep together that one time. After the apology dinner and the I-don't-know-what-I-was-thinking speech. The you-and-the-girls-mean-the-world-to-me speech. I fell for it then, in part due to the really delicious wine Henry bought at the restaurant, and because I wanted to believe him.

I turn the condoms over in my hand, twirling them around my palm like a ribbon. Magnum size, because no man can resist impressing the store clerk with the accolade. We haven't used this kind of birth control in ages. What was Henry planning this weekend?

Is he still seeing his girlfriend? Some woman he met through a college alumni association dinner—something I "wouldn't know about," as Henry put it, because I never graduated. I was close to getting a degree in sociology before I got pregnant with Fiona. People say they want a family, but rarely are the real consequences for the woman part of that discussion.

The chrome wrappers glint in the sunlight that still dapples the ground.

God, if this whole vacation is part of some scheme to cheat on me in a different country, I don't know what I'll do.

Violet begins to snore from the plane's back seat. She's just getting over a cold, and being out here, albeit underneath the plane's protection, can't be good for her. Fiona dozes peacefully beside her. The sisters—one with fair features, the other taking after me—snuggle together, Violet's head on Fiona's shoulder. My heart squeezes, wondering just how much more trauma my babies will endure before this is over.

"For heaven's sake, Janet," I say out loud. "We need to find help."

I traipse through the broken brush back to the edge of the trees. The valley below is as I left it. Serene and unbothered by humans. How we managed to hit the mountain's plateau and not fly straight into the face of the cliff, I don't know. An act of God, I guess. I'll have to hope He's got a few more for us squirreled away.

Crossing back by our crash site, I venture deeper into the forest. Thick conifers appear unbothered and unaware of our noisy entrance, nor the screaming that followed. Animals make their twilight sounds. The warblings and scattered movements would be a comfort—to know that we are not alone—but for the thought at the back of my mind. Where there are small creatures cute enough to merit their own cartoons, there are much larger creatures in the darkness waiting to prey upon them.

A branch snaps beyond my line of sight, somewhere farther in among the shadowy trees. I touch a wide trunk that must be well over a hundred years old. When I pull away, stickiness coats my palm. Syrup?

A beam of light breaks through the leaves, and I lift my hand to its warm rays. Red smears across my skin. Blood.

Another noise. Twigs and dead leaves crunch, sending chills racing along my spine.

Predator or prey, I have a feeling we will find out which role is ours sometime during the night.

9

FIONA

Tiny gray-and-white plumes form an unstable pile on the driftwood I found floating at Windansea Beach. The wood took a solid week to dry out on my back porch. Once it did, it was the perfect base for my next sculpture.

A trash bag of feathers that I collected sits open mouthed on my workstation slash dining table. Iridescent plumes shine beneath the dull lighting of this room, changing color depending on my vantage point. Brown, black, and gray from one angle—gold, green, and ivory from another. The feathers each had to be cleaned, then air-dried, a process that took several hours—enough time to reflect on the inspiration for this sculpture. Something I try to avoid.

Once I read the article that Quincy and Darleen showed me at the gallery, I was distracted. Anxious. It was difficult to focus on my plans for the remaining sculptures of my show, but I shared what I could—they're both excited to see the feather idea when it's finished. Although Darleen offered me more wine, I was no longer in the mood. I went home.

Generally, I'm not especially moody. But I shut down fast when people ask too many questions about my time in the wild, and that's been mistaken for angry. It's the opposite, in fact: I feel things so deeply that I turn off my emotions in order to survive. Probably a tactic that I learned while stranded out there with Violet. After a certain level of trauma is reached, the only choice we have is to either feel the pain in all its depth and depravity or choose numbness—ice to assuage the heat.

Therapists have suggested that by working through my experiences, I might be able to move past the numbness strategy and instead embrace my feelings and all that they've taught me. But in order to do that, I'd tell them, I need closure. And that's not coming anytime soon.

I unroll the chicken coop wire that I bought from a local feedstore, then bend and manipulate the cage until it forms a dome. Once I have it stapled and glued in place, I set about selecting the right feather for each section.

An hour passes, during which my confidence in the sculpture begins to slide. Does it look like it's supposed to? Or a lumpy wire tumbleweed? My hand starts to cramp, and I take that as my cue to break for lunch. Marshall dozes on his bed in the corner of the kitchen. The only person in my life who doesn't care to make a buck on my past. Including me.

I bend down to give him a scratch. "Hey, buddy."

He lifts his head with a whine.

"No, Marshall. No tomato for you today. You'll just end up playing with it."

A salad takes five minutes to prepare, complete with tomatoes, avocados, cucumber, and baked salmon that I bought in a pouch. Memories of eating roots, berries, and whatever protein we could find have been returning to me lately—tastes I haven't thought of, except during very specific culinary experiences. At a French restaurant, I selected the chef's menu without realizing rabbit was the second course. Instantly, I was transported to being wrapped in my mother's parka around a makeshift fire, the bone cracked open in front of me revealing the nutrient-packed marrow.

I gag in my kitchen. Marshall gets to his feet.

"I'm okay. Sorry," I add. My Great Dane trots past me to the dining room, not even a glance behind. "No, no, don't worry about me. I'll be just fine."

There's a knock at the back door. I peek around the corner, then spot someone cupping a hand to my screen and peering into my house.

"Can I help you?"

The person leans backward until I can clearly make out features I only see in my nightmares these days. My younger sister, Violet.

"Hi," she says. "Can I come in?"

I approach the screen door, wary of inviting her inside. Yet drawn like a fly to rancid meat. "What are you doing here?"

Violet pouts, the way she always did as a kid. Lower lip puckered, thin eyebrows stitched together. We haven't been in regular contact in almost six years, not since her twenty-sixth birthday, when things really went to shit between us. Prior to that, our aunt kept us updated on the other's activities and lured us home for the holidays every year with the promise of homemade dumplings. Then Violet stole enough money from Auntie Taylor that she finally cut us loose.

"Maybe more importantly," I tack on, "how did you find this address?"

Violet loses some of her disappointment. She stiffens the way I know I would in her position. The ramrod posture reminds me of our mom when she would read my report card. Every year without fail, Mom would heave a sigh reviewing my grades and their C average. Our dad would bark about how important education is to our family, that it's the reason we were able to thrive in this country. Then he would go back to placing bets with his bookie on whatever football game was coming up that afternoon.

"A filmmaker, actually." Violet crosses her arms. She looks good upon closer inspection, healthy. The hollows of her cheeks have filled in, the dark rings beneath her eyes from not taking care of herself and drug use have likewise disappeared. Though I wonder if all substances have been cut out. In a pinch, she would chug back cooking sherry if regular alcohol was scarce.

"Am I supposed to be impressed?" I ask, still standing behind the screen door.

Violet scans my street. My neighbor Lina takes the trash can to the curb. "It would be better if I could come inside and talk."

Tension knots my stomach at being so close to my sister again. Knowing what I do about her and the hell that we both lived through. The knowledge that Violet was responsible for some of it twists around my chest and tightens.

"Okay, I guess. Come in."

Vi steps into my home, wobbly on the landing. She scans the couch I've had since forever, probably recognizing the armrest that she once spilled vodka on. Despite any influx of money that I've seen for my art, I can't shake the old fears of being left with nothing, alone, abandoned to the elements. So I keep everything—like a frugal single woman. Not a hoarder, I hope.

Marshall growls, guarding the hallway to my bedroom. Violet ignores him. She takes in the half-finished feather sculpture. "So this is your art, huh? I heard you were doing well for yourself there."

I can't tell if her tone is mocking or appreciative, so I only nod. "Do you want something to drink?"

"No, I'm good." An awkward pause.

"So, the filmmaker?"

"Yeah, he approached me on campus. I went back to school, by the way. I've been sober now for over a year."

"Good for you." I wait. I've heard this song before.

Violet inhales through her nose. "Okay, well, I'm doing well. Glad you care to ask."

"Can we not do this, please? I'm kind of in the middle of something. And you surprised me, didn't bother to call or give any warning here."

She balks, her mouth falling open as if she's sixteen years old, instead of thirty-two. "You haven't returned my texts or my calls. I tried getting in touch over the phone but you didn't—"

"You know what? Maybe this was a bad idea, inviting you inside. Why don't I call you tomorrow and we can talk then?"

I step past her to open the screen door and she makes a noise. A sob. Tears fill the dark-brown eyes that she got from our mom.

"They're doing a documentary on us, Fiona," she whispers. "On the crash and what happened afterward. They're going to find out everything."

A breeze reaches through the mesh panel, encircles my neck. "What?"

Violet nods. "The filmmaker said he tried to tell you outside some gallery."

The man in the black-rimmed glasses. I thought he was another reporter, rabid for a new angle. "I remember him."

Violet stares down at the scratched hardwood of my floor. At a squeaky chew toy Marshall discarded. "I think we should do it."

"How—why—what would be the point in that?" I stammer. "That's not an option."

"But they're going to uncover more information. Dad's mistress—did you see that interview?—she's already talking to the media, and the police have questioned her. If they get it in their heads that something . . . something happened . . . the police will start digging."

I shake my head. "Geri Vega only wants to talk about sleeping with Dad. She doesn't care about us. Why would anyone think to accuse us of anything?"

Violet opens her mouth, then closes it.

"We agreed," I add. "It does no good to talk about it."

My little sister, now a grown—sober—woman, furrows her brow. Black hair spills from a messy ponytail. "I think we should give interviews to the documentary. Participate in some way so that we can control what is being said. Otherwise, they'll just write whatever is interesting. Sensationalize stuff to get ratings, and this woman's story is turning heads."

I lift an eyebrow. "You don't think our story is already sensational? If we were to consent to being filmed or whatever, anything that we say would be used as evidence against us in court. If it came to that."

Violet steps toward me. Marshall growls from the hallway. "Geri Vega's team has already reached out to me via social media. She's offering money to meet me on camera for some dumb news show. A lot of money."

Ah, here we are. My gut was right. She's here to ask me for a check. "Don't do that, Violet. Don't make this ugly."

"I'm not. I don't want anything to do with this woman. The fact is, she knows something about Dad. And if she knows anything about him, it's obvious that he would fight to the death to protect us."

I pause, feeling the weight of my sister's words. "We said he and Mom died in the plane crash. That could happen regardless of anyone's survival skills."

Violet fixes me with a knowing look. "All anyone has to do is get it in their heads that Henry Seng survived the first night. Then it calls into question our whole story. Motivates someone to go up there and poke around more. We can't allow that to happen."

I stare at the mound of feathers. It halfway resembles the bird of my nightmares. No matter how accurate the wing placement is or the color that I know my memory has warped, nothing visual can capture the sound of the animal's cries as we cornered it. Then pounced with our mother's fine down parka. Just two girls against the wild.

I meet my sister's gaze, eerie in the hollow way she looks at me. As if she is remembering the same scene. "I still don't know, Violet."

She nods. "Right. And that's okay. Because I do."

10

Violet

In a cramped interrogation room with bare walls, Detective Ashlee Hummel points a suspicious finger to the signature line. "There. That's where you confirm that everything you've said today is—to the best of your knowledge—the truth. It is, isn't it?"

Her strong jaw reminds me of a nutcracker's, while her grimace isn't far off from the painted expression either.

"It's exactly as I remember it."

"Because Ms. Vega shared with us new, interesting information. And since the case was never closed . . . Well, we want to look into anything that's relevant. That might help us finally locate your parents' remains, once and for all."

I meet Hummel's deadpan expression with my own. When the police called requesting a meeting, I felt vindicated in a perverse way. Ever the little sister, thumbing her nose at her big sister to say, "I told you so."

"Great," I reply. "We'd like that too. Maybe, if you tell me what she said—"

"We can't do that. Not yet."

"Fine." I shrug. "But I've never heard mention of Geri Vega until she started trawling for media platforms. I wouldn't put too much stock into anything she says. She's no better than other people hungry for their fifteen minutes."

At the bottom of my statement that Detective Hummel transcribed, I scrawl my name. I turn to Hummel's counterpart, Detective Molesley. An older man with ashen skin, Molesley seems to analyze my every twitch and each lie I tell. Across the chrome table, I can smell the pack of cigarettes wafting from his pores. "Are we all set?"

Detective Molesley retrieves the stack of paper I just signed. He taps my looping cursive. My writing has gotten me in trouble before, but I hope this time it sets us free. "I didn't speak with you all those years ago when you were found and returned to San Diego. But I worked underneath Captain Vo, who did."

I have zero recollection of any captain, lieutenant, or otherwise. I was seven years old, nearly eight, and horribly withdrawn into myself by that point. People spoke to me, fed me, bathed me, and I endured it all in a daze. But that's no longer the case—not when the dust on the past is being kicked up again.

"And? What did the captain tell you?"

Detective Molesley leans onto the forearms of his white dress shirt. "That there was more to the story than what we discovered. That these kids should be carefully returned to their family—into the care of their aunt—until the time comes that they're ready to share more."

"We've shared everything that we recall."

"Have you been in touch with your sister?" Molesley pinches bushy eyebrows together.

"Only recently. Yes." Last week in fact.

He nods. "We'll be reaching out to her next. It's in your best interest not to discuss anything with her that was said here."

I get to my feet. "Thank you. But I doubt that."

Exiting the police station downtown, I count back the number of lies that I told to the detectives. Count them back so that if—if, if, if—the truth comes out, I'll remember the ways I need to cover my ass.

Fiona is waiting for me on a restaurant patio in Little Italy three blocks over.

"Hey," I say, laying my book bag on the table. My copy of the *Odyssey* by Homer, which I have to read for my midterm, spills out.

"Hey," Fiona says. "I already ordered. Hope that's okay." The awkwardness of not knowing each other's rhythms anymore continues to appear in our conversations. We've met up a few times since I barged into her house—into her life again—but we're still learning about each other. About the sister each of us let go of six years ago, after another hardship too many.

Over a negroni—hers—and a seltzer with lime—mine—I tell her everything.

Fiona's hazel eyes are pinched at the edges. I've observed my older sister all my life and can tell whenever she's thinking really hard about something—as she is now. Weighing the pros and cons of an opportunity, the way she has always done, and I've never managed to do, before jumping into a decision.

"That's it, then?" Fiona asks. A bead of condensation slips down her glass. People hurry past on the sidewalk, separated from us by only the patio railing. "I'll wait for my phone call. Go into the station and give them the same account that I did back then."

I nod, recalling the scratch of my signature in the tiny room. "Yeah."

Pursing my lips, I scan the string of cars parallel parked along the street. There's some kind of bachelor party happening at a bar across from us. Normal people, behaving in normal, debaucherous ways.

"I know you already said you weren't interested," I begin. Fiona stiffens in her metal chair. "But the filmmaker I told you about asked to meet with the mistress too, as part of the documentary."

"Violet—"

"If we don't do it, she'll get top billing and a platform exclusive to whatever she comes up with. Plus, don't you want to know what the filmmaker knows? So we can maneuver around him?"

Fiona sips from a metal straw that came with her drink. "I really don't. To agree to interviews on camera seems like the opposite of what we should be doing: Stay the course. Maintain our silence. Let them all speculate, but never confirm anything."

"And it worked for so long. It did. But we're not alone in the conversation anymore, Fi. Dad's girlfriend, or whomever she is, just mixed things up. If we let her dictate the conversation, things could spin so fast out of our control."

"So let's wait and see," Fiona says, lowering her voice. "Why give up our advantage of the public, the world, believing us? I have so much riding on the gallery show in a few weeks. I can't have anything mess that up."

"But think about what could happen if Dad's mistress levels some bombshell the day before your show. This gets us ahead of whatever she might have planned."

Last night in a fit of masochism, I googled my name. Fiona's. And was deluged with headlines questioning everything we ever recounted. Questions about my previously reported drug use, essays on the ethics behind mass donations to some trauma survivors and not others, and—most concerningly—comparisons to *Lord of the Flies*. Anonymous keyboard warriors wondering whether we aren't as innocent as our lawyers would have the world believe.

Geri Vega may not mean us outright harm, if she loved our dad "so much," but that woman has ripped open Pandora's box. More platforms and conspiracy theorists are talking. I can't help the rippling sense across my skin that things are about to go sideways for Fiona and me.

Fiona stares at the cocktail napkin on the table. "If we do this . . ."

My heart leaps into my throat.

"When would we do the interview? I need to create another five sculptures. Deadlines are coming fast, so I really can't—"

"We make time. Look, I'm busy too. I have midterms coming up in two weeks."

"Why are you in school?" Fiona frowns. "You never wanted to go to college, said it was a waste of time and money."

"You did; you graduated. On time, even."

"Because I had to. Because Mom had already ingrained it in me that there was no other way by the time I was ten. You never got the full Janet Seng treatment."

That shuts me up. Fiona hangs her head, but she doesn't smooth over the slight. I didn't get the full experience of our mother mothering me because she died while I was still too young.

I push the metal straw to the side and sip my seltzer with lime. "I didn't. But that doesn't mean I don't want to make her proud. My point is we'll make an interview work, regardless of demanding schedules. I've already got it covered."

My sister becomes more rigid, if that's possible. "Meaning?"

"The filmmaker is meeting us here. Today. In five minutes."

Fiona's eyes nearly bug out of her perfectly shaped head. "Are you serious? Violet. I can't believe you would—"

"Ah, sorry. Is this still a good time?" Daley Kelly, with the Doritos bag–blue eyes, stands awkwardly at the entrance to the restaurant's patio. He wears jeans and a zipped hoodie this time. Less formal.

"Is it?" I ask my sister, then cock my head to the side. Although the moment Fiona opened her screen door a part of me instantly forgave her for ditching me all those years, a large part of me enjoys needling her now. Fiona would never have agreed to meet him. I had to ambush her.

"You're the filmmaker?" Fiona lifts a finger to Daley. "You stalked me outside the Hughes Gallery."

He turns a shade of pink. "'Stalked' is a little strong a word choice. Followed, yes. Because I was trying to help you."

Fiona scoffs. "An altruist." Then to me: "Violet, what do you even know about this guy?"

"I googled him—"

"Oh, thank God. A tried-and-true source."

"I dug around—I didn't just scroll on his socials."

Daley holds up a hand. "Could I sit down?"

"No," both Fiona and I say.

"Okay." Daley clears his throat. He continues to stand. A server pokes her head out from the restaurant. As if sensing the tension, she darts back indoors.

"That's the reason I asked to meet you both, and that Violet invited me here," Daley adds. "Let me pitch my film—and me—to you."

Fiona fumes, plucking a breadstick from a basket the server delivered with our drinks. I hold my palm flat in an invitation. "Go on."

Daley pushes up the sleeves of his gray hoodie. On a Thursday afternoon, the streets are beginning to pick up in anticipation of the weekend—laughter and conversations drifting to us from indoors, but Daley only has eyes for us.

"Picture this," he says, making a frame with his hands. "Twenty-five years after the fact, the girl-survivors are not only surviving, but thriving. They attract the interest of the art world at sold-out gallery shows, mingle among like-minded college students also looking toward a better future, and most importantly, they've held on to the bond that brought them out of the wilderness, despite all odds."

Fiona lifts a skeptical eyebrow. "So the entire documentary is providing a microscopic update on our lives. No, thanks."

"It's telling your story from the lens of today. It's shrugging off the labels that society gave you: circus act. Freak show. Public event to be ogled. It's asserting that you are more than your tragedy and you deserve a fair shot. You merit the right to use your tragedy however *you* see fit. Not however the next closest person to the crime decides to exploit it."

My sister sits up taller now. She does that thing with her jaw where she relaxes and lets her teeth unclench. "You mean Geri Vega? The woman calling herself our father's lover."

Daley hesitates. "Yes."

"But you plan to include her in your documentary? She mentioned it on TV."

"Yes. Well, no, not if you agree to do it. She sought me out after it was announced. She wants the story told in a light that's flattering to your dad. But my goal has always been to get your—the family's—blessing."

The server makes eye contact with me from the doorway. I shake my head.

"And who are you, exactly?" Fiona peers at him. "Why should we trust you to tell any of our story?"

Daley puffs out his chest. "I've been into documentaries my whole life. At age eighteen, I was accepted to USC's film school, then won a contest to intern with Amy Berg and was nominated for an Oscar for the work I did during the ten years that followed. Plus, I was twelve years old when you were both found alive. It stuck with me."

"It stuck with everyone, apparently," Fiona grumbles. "Why should we choose you, though?"

Daley casts his eyes to the empty patio tables beside us. "Honestly? It's not a pretty reason, but it's mine, I guess. My mother walked out on me and my dad when I was five years old. I know what it is to feel the loss of a parent. I often use that lens of loss to explore . . . I guess, unhappy families and their hurt. You can check out any of this stuff on IMDb," he adds.

Fiona tears her critical gaze from our prospective filmmaker. "What do you think, Vi? There's a lot we'd be opening the door to. For you, I mean."

"If you mean my drug use and the people I've pissed off along the way—yeah, I'm aware. I still think—" I nod to the corner at the end of the street, where I came from my interview with the police. "I still think it's the only way to get ahead of all this. Steer it in the right direction."

Fiona has, historically, done right by us. She brought us through the Alone Time. Told me how to act and what to say to get the reporters and police to go away and leave us be with our grief after we were rescued. She helped me find my path in the world without our parents, until I drove her off with my shitty behavior. It's my turn to help guide us forward. And . . .

And I also want to know what this Geri Vega has to say. I want to hear her "revelations" for myself and judge them to be true or false. Most importantly, I want to know about my dad. About the person he was when he wasn't being a lackluster father or failed husband. What Vega loved about him and hated in equal turns. Fiona doesn't care about any memories this woman supposedly harbors because she has her own cache of memories of both our parents. Not me. If we agree to work with this filmmaker, I hope he'll tell us whatever Geri Vega confided in him.

"Right. By sharing your story with me, you can get ahead of the media," Daley pipes up. "Because Vega has already been booked by everyone in the industry that has an audience for this kind of stuff." He winces. "For the fallout of this kind of . . . unusual event. It's only a matter of time before someone more legitimate decides to take her on and make some money off her memories. True or no."

Fiona's expression could burn the ice cubes of her negroni. "You mean like you're doing from ours?"

Daley faces her head-on. "I'm not after money, believe it or not. I'm after the truth."

With his chin lifted, he turns to me. "Call me when you're ready. You have my number."

He reenters the restaurant at a slow pace, as if anticipating—willing us to take—another jab at his integrity. Then Daley exits to the street and walks to the block's end, where he turns out of sight, past a middle-aged man with thinning hair.

Although the man wears dark sunglasses, we stare at each other. Something about him is off. Tense. Then he lifts a camera—a nice one that's handheld with a zoom lens—and snaps a photo of me glaring.

Fiona gasps. "Did that man just—"

Fight-or-flight instincts surge in my chest, urging me to do something—anything—to hide from the camera still trained on my sister and me.

Rather than run out of the restaurant and back to the safety of my apartment, and provide more intriguing images for this photographer to capture, I will myself to focus on the bachelor party drinking and shouting outside a bar. Watch as their group spills onto the sidewalk, oblivious to the line just crossed. Fiona fixes her beady eyes on me, expectant and accusatory—like they were so many years ago—but I don't meet her gaze.

Photographers have kept at a respectful distance over the years. Given Geri Vega's confessions, that invisible barrier is gone now. Just like I predicted.

And while I wouldn't call my sister a control freak, she's in her element when she's making the decisions for us. Maybe it's time that changed.

11

HENRY

The Wild

I hear them before I see them. My girls' shrieks of terror at something—a slug—that Violet sat on. Fiona swats at her little sister's bottom.

Where is Janet? Through the trees and the brush that got knocked down in our crash, I don't see her. It doesn't help that darkness set in over an hour ago, but they did figure out how to make a fire. Probably thanks to the matches in the plane's storage compartment, and dry kindling they found God knows where.

Janet was always capable. The kind of stay-at-home mother so many families dream about. Healthy snacks and meals for the kids, activities that enrich the mind instead of stagnate the brain and body—all while running a mile a day, in the morning usually, when the girls were at school. She messed up, of course, every now and then. Forgot to make dumplings in time for Lunar New Year or let laundry sit for a week if she was experiencing a bout of "the blues," as she called them. None of that really mattered to me, so long as the kids were taken care of. She could live her life and I could live mine.

"Fiona, will you come help me, please?" Janet's voice cuts through the girls' vocal disgust. "No, not you, Violet. You stay put. Stay there!"

"But, Mom," Violet whines, "why can't I come with Fiona? I don't want to be here all alone; there's *bugs*."

Bright orange-and-yellow flames cast dancing shadows on my baby's face. She's seven years old already, but I can still see the infant, chubby cheeks that haven't worn off yet.

"Violet, honey, you don't want to see this."

"Yes, I do!"

"Violet Esther, stay *put*," Janet barks. And the girl stays. Fiona walks off out of sight, into the darkness, but the reflective strips on the purple snow jacket she wears allow me to track her movement.

Violet pouts by a felled tree. She starts humming "America the Beautiful," already moved on.

Janet's whispers carry farther than I think she realizes. "Fiona, come here. Closer."

"Ew, Mom! I don't want to touch that," Fiona squeals.

"Nonsense. This is what your grandparents—on both sides—did all the time. Now, step on the neck."

"Ugh, come on. We can't be out here that long. You really want to carve up an animal? I just started being vegetarian, Mom."

There's a long pause, and I can just picture Janet's eye roll for her oldest daughter. I've told her to go easy on Fiona, but they've been so snippy with each other lately.

"Fiona," Janet says, and her voice is surprisingly tense. "There's a lot you don't know about me. About our situation. We don't know how long we're going to be out here. I have no clue where your father is and if he's okay, and my arm got banged up pretty bad in the crash—" A sob cuts off her words.

Fiona, stunned, doesn't reply. My wife rarely shows emotion in front of the kids. I don't either.

"This bird was injured somehow when we landed here," Janet resumes. "I heard it . . . kind of moaning a few hours ago. It just died and we can't waste the protein. We shouldn't, at least. Anyway, I need your help holding it while I pluck the feathers."

"Can't you do it by yourself?"

"Fiona Lang Fa." Janet's voice hardens. "I'm hurt, and—look. All you have to do is keep it still while I pull."

There's some rustling. Some grunting. Violet now sits on the log, bathed in the light of the flames, humming a bouncier song I don't recognize.

"God, this is totally going to stick with me forever," Fiona whispers.

Janet doesn't reply.

"Where did you get the big knife, Mom? Holy cow. How do you even know how to use that thing?"

"Like I said." Janet grunts. A crack rips across the forest, the sound of hollow bones submitting to her efforts. "There's a lot you don't know about me."

Instead of protesting, Fiona goes quiet. Ten minutes tick by while I assume my oldest and my wife tackle the plumage of some bird. Maybe a falcon like the one I saw hours ago, when I first stumbled from the plane.

My motivation in leaving them was to find help. At least I think it was. I was in some kind of daze after the crash, and when I stopped to focus, I realized I was all the way down the ridge by a mountain covered in snow. And hurt. I limped along the rugged hillside for around a mile before turning back. It was clear to me, as I checked out the valley below and discovered a waterfall farther beyond, that any campers or first aid station were too far for us to travel to on foot. Not yet. And then I couldn't help myself. A strange desire to hide from my family, from my life and the world we just flew away from, crept over me like a spell.

Fiona screams. "Mom!"

"I'm sorry, honey, it splattered." Another squelch. "I can hardly see over here. Go grab the flashlight that was in the emergency bag, will you?"

Fiona tramples through the brush back to the busted aircraft and the crackling fire. Violet watches her older sister intently. She takes after her mother—black hair, small stature—while Fiona is the opposite. Light-brown eyes, brown hair, and already as tall as I am, even though she's only thirteen.

The girl's sharp features soften as she takes note of Violet, who has stopped humming. "Everything's okay, Vi. We're just . . . we're making dinner."

Fiona stoops beside the Cessna, reaching into the cockpit. She pumps a manual flashlight, generating enough energy to fuel the bulb. A sphere of light swings toward me in the trees, and I dive to the ground.

Branches crack beneath my sudden shift of weight. I hold my breath, not daring to give Fiona another reason to investigate.

A long pause rolls by. It feels like we're flying overhead again and the engine just cut out, filling the cab with throttling silence.

Footsteps. "Here, do you want your journal?"

I peek my head up. Fiona offers the bound notebook that Violet brought along and was scribbling in during the flight.

"I've been collecting rocks and making pictures from them. But, for you, it might be nice to . . . I don't know, write down your feelings."

Violet doesn't reply as she takes the book, peering down at the relic from normal life—prior to us falling from the sky. She fixes her older sister with a stare. "I want Daddy. Where is Daddy? Why does no one care he's gone?"

That's my girl. I smile, recognizing the truth that probably Fiona was the first to sense: Violet is both Janet's and my favorite child. It can't be helped. No matter the bull that's fed to us by modern parenting magazines, every parent feels pulled one way or another.

Fiona sighs. "Look, why don't you write him a letter? That way you can tell him exactly what you're thinking right now, when he gets back. Okay?"

Violet stares at the baby-blue journal, which appears green beside the flames. Fiona tramples back to her mother somewhere behind a conifer, while Violet withdraws a pen from the elastic loop attached to the spine.

Another branch cracks underfoot. My youngest snaps her gaze across the clearing to the exact bushes where I hide.

12

Fiona

"Is here okay?" I ask from behind my dining table. Since the documentary will be released around six months from now—"If all goes well," Daley said—I've agreed to let them film me working on the mountain sculpture. Violet's insistence that the doc would grant us the control we need hit home after that photographer published his photos. Girl-survivors get happy hour just like us! was the headline I did not need.

Armed with the latex gloves I wear while using superglue, I add a few drops here and there to mimic my actual process. God knows I couldn't actually perform while creating a piece. The art requires that I be much more in my head, deep in my feelings, as Darleen likes to say.

Twigs form the basic structure of the mound, while green leaves coat the surface as lush grass. Once we were found, we learned that we'd crash-landed in a rainforest. We were lucky, despite the storm clouds that were a constant fixture in the sky. Only five miles west, we would have plowed right into snow country—an area that would have been nearly impossible for two kids from the city to survive twelve weeks on their own.

The peak continues to trip me up. Branches shift during the night, or the carefully arranged feathers dip to form a pyramid I didn't intend.

Beyond the details, there's something else that isn't working. I don't feel anything when looking at the sculpture. I don't care. And if the artist only sees a pile of discarded lawn debris when viewing the piece, no one else will care either.

I glance up at the roomful of crew. Daley whispers something to his DP, and then she adjusts the checkered kerchief around her neck. "Outside, B Team. We need an exterior shot," she says.

"Not of my address, though, right?" I look to Daley for confirmation. He had everyone on-site sign confidentiality agreements—the only way I agreed to my home as a filming location.

"No, definitely not," he says. "Any shots with location indicators won't make the final cut. I wrote that into the contract you signed."

I nod. That clause stuck out to me as the most important one, but it doesn't hurt to confirm while my guard dog is within mauling distance. Daley directs another trio—"A Team"—to the couch that belongs to Marshall for a different angle. Although the film crew was intimidated by a Great Dane sitting in the same room, watching their every move, Marshall has been well behaved. He only barked once before settling into the corner.

"Fi, you're getting a call," Violet says from the kitchen. "It's from a number ending in 4149."

"Don't answer it," I reply. Daley asks a man with a long blond ponytail down his back to adjust the spotlight trained on my face. Makeup that I applied myself feels like it's melting down my cheeks under the heat of three lamps positioned across the room. Violet arrived early to help me get ready, but I insisted I had everything under control. I'm always making the effort, at least.

"Who is it? Spammers?"

"It's that woman again. Geri Vega. She found my number last week and wants to meet me—us, I guess—on camera."

Daley stops what he's doing. Pushes the sleeves of his plaid shirt higher on his arms. "Really? Did you already speak to her?"

A brown-and-green feather that I found in Ocean Beach, shines under the intense lighting. It might be better used in my bird sculpture, the one inspired by a night hunting for dinner, just us kids.

"No. And I have no intention of it. She can keep up her lies, and I'll keep up—" I stop myself. Stare at my mountain rather than throw an incriminating glance to Violet. "She should know better than to reach out to me. Our dad was a war vet, and now she's rewriting his legacy to be something he's not. A cheater."

"Hey, uh—Daley? You should see this." A production assistant holds up his phone. "Geri Vega is live streaming right now. I found her on the hashtag for the documentary name we just announced. She's with that women's rights attorney. You know her? Sylvia something."

"Sylvia Jenkins," Violet supplies. "She's an icon. She investigates claims by women that are dismissed as untrue. I can't believe she's with the Vega woman."

The PA turns his volume up so we can all hear. Geri wears a pressed tweed suit, taking a cue from Chanel herself. Her team has been busy.

"Well, no luck," she says. "I wish Fiona would have answered. Then we could have talked things out a bit more."

"Right. Another missed opportunity for her. It's always disappointing when the people we want to help aren't ready to receive that aid quite yet." Sylvia Jenkins—famed women's and human rights lawyer and global poster child of successful women in male-dominated industries—shakes soft brown waves.

"Didn't she defend a case before the Supreme Court recently?" the PA asks the room.

Daley hushes him.

"To be clear," Geri continues, "I don't want anything from her. I'm only fifteen years older than her, so I'm not attempting to be anyone's surrogate mother. Really. I hope to, one day, you know, share what I can."

Sylvia nods emphatically. The movement doesn't register on the screen, the cell phone camera probably stationary on some fancy stand owned by Sylvia flipping Jenkins. "Of course," she murmurs.

"You know? I just want to meet with Fiona, and Violet, and tell them about their dad's last few months from a different perspective. What I think they deserve to hear from me first. Then, eventually, what the public deserves to know too. After all this time, anyone who has ever flown on a plane has a right to understand what happened."

"I am in complete agreement with you." Sylvia reaches out a hand that Geri takes with a grateful smile. "And I reject anyone's assertion that you're lying about your relationship with Henry Seng. That's why we're going to do a lie detector right now, live."

"That's enough." Daley frowns as the PA locks his phone. "Didn't Geri also reach out to you, Violet?"

"Her team did, whoever they are," Violet mumbles, shell shocked. "Not the woman specifically. Someone named Leslie. I never returned their calls or their messages."

"How did they even get our phone numbers?" I ask. "I pay a company to wipe mine from the internet."

Daley crosses his arms. "There are . . . uh . . . ways around that, actually."

"Did she ask you for ours, then?" I try to keep my voice measured. Nonaccusatory. "I know you were in touch with her before Violet and I agreed to be filmed."

Silence falls across our group. A twig on my mountain sculpture dangles from a lower hillside, then lands on my dining table with a dull tap.

"No, of course not. Everything you've shared with me is confidential. Including your phone numbers."

"Fiona. Let's get on with it."

Violet stands in the kitchen doorway, framed by pressed flowers that I've been drying for my next piece. Always short for her age, Violet stopped growing after she turned fifteen. With the strong spotlights facing me in the living room, shadows find the hollows of her cheeks, aging her beyond thirty-two years—appropriate, given the things she saw and did at a tender age that no grown adult would dream of enduring. Brown eyes appear black as they stare at me. For a moment, I'm returned to the campfire we made that first night, and the sense that someone unknown was watching us. That we were on the precipice of something terrifying. A shiver traces my neck, until I tear my gaze away.

"All right." Daley claps his hands. "We've got work to do, and plans to counter whatever story Vega's dreamed up for her own personal gain. Right?"

I nod, appreciatively. I believe him.

"I think we got enough footage of you working, Fiona. Let's move to your couch for the interview." Daley nods to the corner where Marshall sits. Hackles rise along Marshall's back as strangers approach him.

"Not sure that's a great idea. How about the front room? It's cleaner."

The crew transfers all their equipment—cameras, tripods, giant lights, and microphones on long sticks—while I settle into the stiff sofa. I never use it, so it's never needed replacing. The floral pattern reminds me of something my mom would like.

Once everything is ready, I catch Violet's eye. She leans against the counter of the kitchen island, tension drawing her shoulders to her ears. We're both feeling the pressure. Whether we can successfully spin the narrative back toward our version of events depends on this interview. The police made that abundantly clear when they asked me to come into the station to "catch up" about a week after they met with Violet. Their questions mirrored what they said to Violet, and I made no show of being surprised or bored by the interaction, lest they think she tattled. They asked if I had anything new to share, anything that I recalled now that there was additional interest in us, and said that

I should tell them first thing. I smiled and nodded, as if I had every intention of complying.

"Okay, Fiona. I'm going to start with some questions, to prompt you off camera. But you'll be all that the lens sees, okay? Fine to deviate a little from the topic at hand if you want." Daley checks his notes in a handheld spiral notebook.

I bet he'd like me to go rogue. Give him the gory details that have never been spoken aloud.

"Sure," I reply to the roomful of gawkers. "I'm ready when you are."

13

Violet

As the crew packs up to leave, gathering cables, boom mics, silver collapsible reflector discs, and the extendable spotlights nearly twice my height, my sister rises from the uncreased sofa in a daze. I wonder if that's due to the stress of itemizing her recollections on film. Or the number of people my reclusive sibling just allowed into her precious personal space.

Fiona finished her answers like a total pro, even ending the interview on a subdued half smile. Reflective, yet optimistic. There was one moment where she seemed a little distracted, but she managed to rein it in.

Brown hair that could be blonde in the sun glows against a window as Fiona makes conversation with the DP. On another person, I might compare the effect to a halo. But not my sister.

"Ms. Seng, there's some more coffee in the Starbucks box. Did you want it, or should we take it with us?" a production assistant with a nose ring asks.

"No, please," Fiona says, as if she's the party's hostess and the revelers are taking to-go plates. "Enjoy the rest."

I smile to myself. When did I become so bitter? Maybe around the time Fiona left me? Rather, she stopped returning my calls after I made a few mistakes, then straight up moved in the middle of the night. Still, I know I gave her solid reasons to disappear like a magic act. And I'm grateful she's putting them aside to protect us both now. If I'm being honest, I understand exactly why she cut me off.

"Violet, you ready?" Daley points two fingers at me like pistols. "If we're going to film at your college, we'll need some exterior shots before traffic gets bad."

"Yup. I'll see you there. Fiona, you coming?"

She shakes her head. "Deadlines. I need to make some progress. There's only three weeks left until my show."

"Sure. No problem." On my way out the back door, onto the curved driveway behind Fiona's house, I pass a red bucket of glass recyclables full of discarded beer and wine bottles. The scents of tannins and hops linger in the air. I flick my tongue from my mouth to taste them like a snake.

———

"Now, walk normally." Daley follows me with a skeleton crew of five people on the large tile pathway through the center of campus. Scores of students in the middle of the first quarter of the school year pause their conversations to stare at us. At me. If I was able to keep a low profile before, it's a lost cause now.

"Can we get a shot of you sitting on the bench there? Yup, right over there beneath that tree."

"The one with the inscription, NOT ALL THOSE WHO WANDER ARE LOST?"

Daley pauses. "Yeah, no, you're right. Let's go to that other one ahead. The one that says, KEEP CALM AND CARRY ON."

I'm on board with that. I take a seat, pressing my knees together. Students slow their walks to class beside our production, hitching their backpacks or book bags higher. Midterms arrive next week, but I'm not sure when I'll finish the *Odyssey*. Damn quarter system makes everything happen so fast.

With a wry smile, I recall saying that exact thing out loud the last time I was enrolled in college, then dropping a tab of acid.

"Look off to the right. There, that's it." Daley directs me from over his camera operator's shoulder. "Perfect. I think we got it."

A petite woman with straight dark hair that reaches her waist parts the crowd without a word. Professor Tran heads for the humanities building, the three-story lecture hall that is quickly becoming my home away from home.

Daley takes note of the onlookers as if seeing them for the first time. "Is there someplace we can go for your interview that's a bit more private?"

When Daley first pitched campus, my place of work just as Fiona's dining table is hers, as my featured location, I rejected it outright. Why should I tell the world where to find me three days a week? Then he suggested my apartment, to mirror Fiona's portion, and I liked that even less. *What other locations are pertinent to you—important to who Violet Seng is nowadays?* Daley asked. I pursed my lips then, resigned to filming at school. There were no other spots that could be good options. When I got sober, all my favorite haunts—where people knew my name and didn't care if I resembled someone-but-they-couldn't-put-their-finger-on-it—were lost to me.

"Yeah. Let's go this way." I lead Daley and the crew to the first floor of the humanities building. We find an empty classroom, where last week I met with a TA to discuss Homer's use of metaphors. A woman in a black vest slaps a sticky note that reads FILMING IN PROGRESS to the outer door, and then we slip inside.

Seated at a desk with an L-shaped wooden table that connects to chrome chair legs, I wait for Daley's crew to set up. For the camera's red light to begin blinking.

Daley checks his notes. "Let's start from the top. Tell us your name and what you do."

I go through the motions. Repeat the same story I've told over the years that should come as second nature, that Fiona gave only two hours ago. Yet during the course of this Q and A, the well-worn monologue starts to feel like a sweater that's shrunk in the wash—when I'm doing the laundry anyway. Constrictive, close to suffocating. As I stare into the black, reflective lenses of the two cameras trained on me, recording me for all posterity, the sensation that I'm going to vomit worsens. Apart from police security cameras and for the FAA, I've never recounted the details before any kind of recording device.

Was Fiona right that this was a bad idea? I lose my train of thought for a moment. Scan the dirty tile at my feet.

When I look up, Daley and the rest of the crew are expectant. Waiting for something from me.

Did I overshare, more than I was supposed to? Terror trips down my body as I try to recount the words that just fell out of my mouth. Were they the right ones? Did I stick to the script? Sweat forms under my arms while I try to smile. Act normally. The cameras continue to blink red. Silent admonishment that I wasn't focused while I was speaking, instead allowing myself to become distracted.

"Is there anything new you want to mention?" Daley asks with a sigh. "What about your father? Henry Seng. What do you think of the claims being made about him cheating on your mother?"

Daley asked this same line of questioning to Fiona, and she shrugged it off with a noncommittal answer. But Fiona didn't have the relationship with our dad that I did. And I doubt it would do any harm to set the record straight.

"Well, he was complicated. My dad had a brilliant mind that was pretty damaged during his time in war zones as a marine. Sometimes I would wake at night to his screams, and my mother hushing him back to sleep like a child."

The room stills. All eyes are trained on me at the front of the class-room, with the blackboard behind me as if I were a teacher imparting a lesson. Which I guess I am in a way.

All this information has come out before. My dad's record in the military became widely known: he was discharged after a second tour abroad, but whether it was honorably or dishonorably no one knows. He kept his secrets close. And he didn't confide in me when I was seven.

"I don't know, personally, if my dad cheated. But my parents loved each other. That's all I can say from my own memories."

Somewhere along the line they started to hate each other—or, maybe, at a certain point and intensity, love and hate in a relationship become blurred when extremes are at hand. But I don't say any of that out loud, not wanting to muddy the waters. I'll go to my grave say-ing my parents loved each other and therefore would never willingly hurt their marriage, or their children, by cheating. I adopt a bland expression, waiting for Daley's next question. Whoever in the San Diego Police Department views the final version of this documentary, and this interview, should get no surprises.

"Okay, I think we got it." Daley claps his hands together as the door to the classroom opens. Sunlight from outside overpowers the fluorescent lamps in the high ceiling.

Professor Tran marches down the broad steps to the floor of the classroom, where I sit. She slaps a thick manila folder on the desk behind me. "Sorry, everyone, but I have office hours here right now. Can you work on your project elsewhere? I saw some film students out by the quad."

Daley lifts both eyebrows. "Yeah, guys. Let's go join up with everyone."

The crew files out with Daley bringing up the rear. As he stands, he mimes a zipper closing his mouth. Mum's the word. Probably, he didn't ask the school for permission to include its campus in his documentary.

Asking for forgiveness rather than permission has been more successful in my experience too.

Professor Tran crosses to the blackboard and begins erasing an assignment from the previous class. "You're in my Humanities 101, right?" she asks over her shoulder.

I pause on the steps at the front row of seats. The door slams shut above, Daley exiting to the hallway outside.

"Yes. How'd you know? I'm usually in the back."

Tran continues to erase the board, jumping periodically to reach letters at the very top. "Because," she draws out, "I completed undergrad at the age of forty. And I always keep an eye out for students who are here for the work. Who actually desire to learn."

She turns toward me, chalk powder coating her cheeks like rouge. "That's you, isn't it? Someone who's here for the right reasons?"

"Yes." My automatic reply satisfies my professor, who resumes facing the chalkboard.

Yes. The easy answer to give. But is it true? I enrolled in courses again because I'm excited to start over, to actually use my brain and body that survived against the odds. But the way I drag my feet at completing assignments and doing the readings and the difficulty I have with paying attention to the actual lectures suggest the opposite.

Metal scrapes above as the door opens again. Students file down the steps for Tran's office hours, while I walk up and past them. I step into the afternoon sunshine. Panting for a reason I can't place, I breathe deep until the chill leeches from my skin.

———

We spend another hour walking around campus, enjoying curious looks from twenty-year-olds who are technically my peers. Daley assures me that he's got everything he needs for my footage—which only fuels the worry I've felt since I left the humanities building.

A strange daze hasn't dissipated during my drive home. Or while I scurry down to the Quick Shop for Twinkies.

Sometimes, I can be in the middle of speaking, or performing a mundane activity, and forget what I just said or did. I don't black out exactly. More like, I lose track of a moment. The sensations, the colors, the sounds of a scene, all kind of flitter away two seconds faster than I can grasp when I'm not focused on what's at hand. Oftentimes, it happens when I'm most stressed. Like today, when I agreed to be filmed talking about my trauma.

Bells chime as I pull open the smudged glass door. Ahmed rings up a customer at the counter while I slip to the right, past the soda pyramid.

"You again. I wondered when we would each have a craving."

I pull my gaze from the yellow sponge cakes to take in the guy who loves beef jerky. Smooth, unwrinkled skin. Barely any stubble to mar his clean jawline. A hardness that pinches the eyes and suggests he's lived on the fringe.

"Yeah, hard to resist." I pluck a package wrapped in crinkly cellophane from the shelf. Add a diet soda from an end display under my arm. "See you around."

"I hope so," he says. A wink to his words makes me look up. He smiles. He runs his hands through thick wavy hair, the requisite stick of beef jerky already tucked into a jeans pocket. He doesn't smell . . . good exactly—almost as if he doesn't wear deodorant. But his scent makes my mouth water.

"Do you go to San Diego College?" I ask. Last week, I thought I saw his slouch nearby the quad.

"Yeah, I'm a business major. Maybe see you there?" Another smile, and then he strolls out of the convenience store like he owns the shop. A bell chimes at his exit. Did he pay for the jerky? I don't remember any conversation at the cashier counter when I walked in, but I was also lost in my thoughts from the interview.

With my comfort food in hand, I hurry back to my apartment. The road beside me is jam-packed with cars on their commute home, but no driver watches me. Each person at the wheel I pass has their head down or peers straight ahead, no one caring what the lone woman is doing on the sidewalk. I feel only two eyes on my frame, from behind. From the man leaning against the building I just left, whose scent clears the haze from my brain and reminds me that I'm hungry.

14

VIOLET

The Wild

Dear Daddy—Fi Fi says to write you a leter. So Im writeing you a leter.

I don't no were you are. But I miss you. Im scared. And cold. And tired.

Ples com back to us at the airplane. Animuls are toking to us now. I think I saw one in the trees? Ples come find us again.

I love you.

Love,

Violet Esther Seng.

15

Fiona

Hughes Gallery occupies a busy side street of Little Italy, in the heart of San Diego's arts community. A poster board visible in the gallery storefront as I approach advertises my show less than three weeks from today. Hope stirs in my chest. This could be something big. Something worthwhile to wake up for each day. A new chapter to leave all the others behind.

"Fiona!" Quincy grins, meeting me at the entrance. Mismatched checkered print covers his soft frame like a gingham blanket. He pulls me in for a hug. "You are going to die when you taste the samples for our menu. Have you ever seen dim sum as an amuse-bouche course?"

Quincy leads me past an artist's sculpture of Nokia cell phone covers on our way to the restaurant in charge of catering. He fans his hands across the corner of the gallery, noting where two of my sculptures will be displayed.

We step into a hallway that connects to other restaurants and bars on this block. Plain white doors shoot off from the shared corridor, and Quincy slows beside the exit labeled TAN TAN EATS. We pass inside, and then aromas of basil, broth, sriracha, and sweet-and-sour sauces hit my taste buds. My mouth waters as I follow Quincy through the savory cloud to a window spot in the corner of the restaurant.

Small plates present food in bite-size portions. Dumplings are lined up on beds of sauce-covered, palm-size bread buns. Amuse-bouche dim sum banh mi.

Forgiving the fact that I'm Chinese, not Vietnamese, I slide into an old-fashioned hairpin café chair, suddenly starved for lunch and comfort food.

Quincy steps back toward the corridor.

"You're not joining?"

"Sorry, Fiona. I've got a marketing meeting right now. Ralph always does amazing with catering requests for gallery events, though. Let me know what you think when you're through. Looks delicious!"

I scan the six different pairings. Chicken, pork, and shrimp compose various dumplings, along with beef skewers sprinkled with what looks like roasted sesame. Although everything appears mouthwatering, I can't help the disappointment souring my appetite. It would have been nice to discuss more of the plans for the show with Quincy. More so, I was looking forward to this tasting lunch with him for the socialization—to get out of my house and enjoy conversation with a human. No offense to Marshall.

"Fiona?"

I lift my head to where Daley Kelly stands awkwardly by an empty table. A smile hits my lips. "Hey. What are you doing here?"

"Ah, well, I was looking for you actually." He dips his head, though he doesn't break eye contact. Black hair is styled to the side, while the plaid shirt and jeans that I've grown used to seeing him wear are untucked, more relaxed. "I saw your car out front of the gallery, and Quincy just directed me back here. Mind if I join you?"

"Please."

Although Daley and Quincy connected last week when we all signed paperwork for Daley to film the gallery show, I'm surprised Quincy suggested he join me. As I stare across the table at Daley's warm blue eyes, I suspect Quincy may be a better friend to me than I realized.

"Sesame ball?" I point to the center plate.

"Love one." Daley takes a bite, then moans. "So good, wow."

I use chopsticks to pluck a dumpling with orange seeds across the top. "This is kind of an audition for food we'll serve to guests at the show. Everything is local, and the ingredients are inspired by foods I loved as a kid."

"As homage to your family?"

Daley goes for the same plate of dumplings I just sampled, while a reply lodges in my throat.

What Daley suggests is true—by choosing the food my family grew up with to celebrate my art, we honor them in a way. But I am also hoping to keep questions about them to a minimum during the show. This exhibit is about me. About who I am today and my interpretation of the events that led me here—mine and no one else's. Strange contradiction, to acknowledge the people who made our success possible, while distancing ourselves from them and their sacrifices.

I settle on brevity, versus the complicated truth. "Kind of. So, you wanted me? I mean—you needed to tell me something."

Daley blushes as sunlight hits the window beside us. "Yeah, I did. It's just . . ."

I finish chewing a har gow dipped in spicy mustard. "Oh my God. This one wins. I want all the plates to be just this."

Daley places his phone on the table. He clears his throat. "Well, I had a question for you. Something isn't . . . I don't know. Sitting right with me."

"Oh?" I mentally scroll through the possibilities for what is about to happen. Was he dissatisfied with my interview? Did he realize my sculptures are not for the mass market—that some of them can frighten and others offend?

After another beat, Daley unlocks his phone. He lifts it between us, a new pinch forming between his eyebrows. "I have something to show you."

Footage of me sitting on my nice couch beside my front door rolls forward. Words I spoke only three days ago spill from my lips with confidence. My hair is brushed back and pulled into a braid that sits on my shoulder, and the lighting is good. I look fresh faced, hopeful.

"There," Daley says. He pauses the video clip, then leans onto his elbows. "You said, 'My parents argued from time to time, but they loved each other. They would do anything for each other, and they valued each other as equals.' Why did you say that?"

I tear my eyes from my own face to Daley's stitched expression. "What do you mean? I said that because it's true."

He sighs. "But is it? I've been doing more interviews with people related to your lives back then. Not everyone agrees."

"I don't get it," I reply, my chopsticks paused. "You sought me out, here, at a tasting for my show to tell me . . . what? That my recollection of my own parents is wrong?" Heat begins to climb my neck. People walk past the window quickly, unaware of the awkward conversation unraveling beside them over small plates.

"No, not—I came to ask you—to give you the opportunity to explain."

"But . . . what could I need to explain about recounting my own story? Why are you fixating on my parents' love for each other? Wasn't that the point of doing this film, to share my own version of the events?"

A server refills our water glasses. Daley waits for her to leave, and then he makes eye contact. "If your parents would 'do anything for each other,' why did neighbors say they often heard them yelling during the summer before the plane crash?"

For a moment, I'm stumped. I don't have that answer—at least, not one I want to share. Someone laughs, swearing on the other side of the restaurant.

"You see"—Daley leans in—"I was reviewing the timeline for your account of the plane crash, the days leading up to it. Checking public records for anything that might be relevant to your family and a documentary on their ordeal."

"Okay. But that's all you found. Some busybodies making a noise complaint." A statement, not a question.

"Not quite. I interviewed a first responder who treated you and Violet. He was a part of the team that went out to get you after those hikers noticed light reflecting from the hilltop. The first responder said you were stripping the plane of materials. Burning items in a campfire when he arrived."

"So?"

"So, that wasn't a part of the police report. And you said the plane was nearly destroyed in the crash."

"We were desperate for help in January. We burned everything we could get our hands on to make a smoke signal, and yes, had started ripping off the insulation from the plane."

"Was that all? Or were you burning something else—evidence of some kind—when you realized people were coming?"

The swinging door to the kitchen opens, and dishes clamor within. A fountain beside the entrance makes a gurgling sound like a waterfall or someone dying, choking on their own blood.

"What would that even be?"

Daley gives me a pleading stare. "Your parents' bodies were never found. What do you think happened to them?"

"Animals," I reply, automatically. Sweat begins to dot my hairline, against the window. "I moved our parents away from Violet to a field. When I found a rock big enough to dig a hole, the bodies were already gone."

"How much time elapsed between when you left the bodies in the field and when you returned with a rock?"

"Daley . . ." I shake my head. Realize the butterflies in my stomach that appeared when Daley sat down were a warning. "If we were trying to cover something up about the plane, and the first responder told you this, why didn't this come out before now? This doesn't sound at all suspicious to you, like someone else trying to cash in on our trauma?"

My chest tightens but I try to remain calm. In control.

"Fiona, you weren't up-front about the campfire. You're withholding. Which is a not-so-distant cousin to hiding something. What are you keeping secret?"

"Nothing." Nothing that concerns the public.

He sets his jaw. "I don't believe that. Like it or not, since you accepted money from donors and the settlement money from the plane manufacturer, you owe us—the world—the facts."

"Wow." I lean away from the table, my appetite shot. "You didn't come here because you were innocently thinking of me. Or seeking clarity for the documentary. You came here to trap me in what you think is a lie. You're just looking for the most exciting angle for your film."

"No, Fiona. I did—I do—hope you can explain some of the troubling details."

"You're sensationalizing a couple of minute—"

"Fiona, stop." He hesitates a moment, then hits the play button on the video clip. My interview resumes. My own self-assured voice rises from the speaker: "The first night out in the wild, my parents died. Almost instantly with the crash. It was—"

Daley locks his phone, cutting off my recollection. "Before it was 'instantly with the crash.' They died instantly. Now it's 'almost instantly'?"

"Nitpicking. They died—"

"It's inconsistent. As if your story is getting harder to maintain after all these years."

I shake my head. I no longer trust my words to free me, as they have in the past. Each defense I give only beckons Daley to attack at closer range.

"And they didn't both die that night. Did they?" His voice drops to a whisper. "That's not all that happened."

When I don't reply, he reaches across the table to grip my hand in his. "Fiona."

"No," I say, startled by the sudden contact. "There's more."

16

JANET

The Wild

Screaming jolts me awake. I flail about in the Cessna cockpit, kicking the blanket aside and falling from the passenger seat onto wet ferns.

My girls. I glance at the back seat to find it empty, then sprint out into the faint morning rays searching for my babies.

"Fiona! Violet!" I shriek. "Fiona, Violet!"

"Over here, Mom!" Screaming dissolves into laugher as I approach the edge of the cliff, where my daughters dance around their father. Henry. He's back.

Taking giant leaps, I launch myself into his arms. "Oh my God," I say over and over, as his hands tighten across my waist. "Thank God you're okay."

"Shhh," he says, stroking my hair. "Shhh, I'm here."

"Daddy, Daddy! Where were you?" Violet asks, jumping at his side.

Even Fiona, my mopey teenager, is brimming with excitement. "We made a campfire last night and ate some kind of bird that Mom barbecued and it was so gross—oh my gosh, so gross—but also really nice to eat something warm and it was good protein—"

"Daddy, where were you?"

Henry laughs, a big booming sound. Fresh color pinkens his cheeks, contrasting his black hair, which he keeps closely cut along the sides and long across the top.

"What happened?" It's my turn to ask. "We all woke up in the plane and you were gone. Or, I mean, Violet saw you leave. She said you were hurt."

I scan his frame for obvious injury. His shirt is torn across the midsection, a comfortable cotton tee he chose to fly in, but the leather jacket he wears looks undamaged. Slacks that he said made him feel like "a real commercial pilot" are dirty, layered in mud, and ripped down the side. A red scrape covers his thigh.

"I'm all right; I just cut my arm when I climbed from the cockpit. No big deal," Henry says. The ghost of a smile plays on his mouth, as if there's something funny about all our reactions. "Violet is right that I got out of the plane after we landed and inspected the body. Everything looked as expected, but I got disoriented and ended up walking about three miles that way."

He points off past the tree line to a sloping hillside I approached yesterday as I searched for kindling. Henry is ex-military, so it makes sense he found a place to set up for the night, that he emerged appearing in good spirits. But—he got "disoriented"?

After thirteen years of marriage, I shouldn't be surprised. Henry has woken up confused and alarmed in the middle of the night several times, reliving things from war that I doubt I could stomach myself. He's been off and on medication for the gamut of conditions: anxiety, hallucinations, low appetite, depression. I never judged him for any of it—least of all my old friend Depression—until now. How could he have become so disoriented that he disappeared when we needed him most?

The rain came in droves all night long. I was grateful for the shelter the plane provided and for the rain, as it kept animals at bay. Still, as

I stand in Henry's arms, concern washes over me as if it were another deluge.

My husband pulls back to look at me. Birds whistle their morning melodies overhead, as if all is right in the world. Henry lifts a hand to stroke my cheek. "I missed my girls."

His touch is soft, warm. I begin to tremble, so riddled with adrenaline the last twenty-four hours that the relief Henry brings almost feels painful. Suddenly I'm so grateful he's alive that even the last three months fall away, a distant, anguished memory. I can forgive him if it means we get out of here alive.

When she first called the house, it felt like the air had been punched from my torso. Like I'd been kicked in the belly—the place where I had grown his children, cared for our legacy every moment of every day for nine months. Twice.

I sputtered, asked, "Who is this?"

She only replied, "Where is Henry?"

His name rolled off her tongue with such ease. Presumption and intimacy.

Had she called before? Had she already spoken to my children? How had she identified herself to them? "A friend of your father's"?

I mustered, "Don't call here anymore."

She replied, her voice full of pity, "Do you think he still loves you?"

Rage swelled my chest then. And hurt. This woman believed she knew my husband—the man for whom I quit college in order to travel around the world to wherever he was stationed. If she was bold enough to call and speak to me, his wife, in such a way, I had to assume it's because Henry himself had given her permission. Henry, the proudest and most arrogant person I've ever encountered, would otherwise cut down anyone who dared attack his family in such a way. This woman was dangerous. She threatened our lives, the beautiful path we, Henry and I, had forged together for our kids, for our marriage.

"Don't call here again. I mean it." I hung up the phone, certain of several truths: Henry was cheating on me—with an awful woman, apparently—and she'd have to be dealt with.

"Daddy! Come see what we did!" Violet shouts, breaking through my painful thoughts. Henry allows our girls to tug him over to the plane. Turning back to me, he takes my hand so we form a caravan. An unbreakable chain.

"Coming, darling?" he asks.

I smile, pushing the dark thoughts from my mind. We're beyond all that. We're in a much worse position right now, as it happens.

Still, as we near the remnants of the campfire I made last night and Fiona encircled with rocks, the three syllables that have haunted all my waking hours for months refuse to be quiet—the woman's name: Alicia.

17

Violet

The metal doors of the lecture hall slam shut as I exit the humanities building. Professor Tran's midterm required a five-page essay analyzing Homer's metaphors and how they might be received in today's social and political climate. Mine was pretty solid, I think, but Homer makes it easy. Fear of the unknown, self-destruction, and observing how people elevate themselves above others are themes I know well.

As I head to my car, my classmates gather in twos and threes along the concrete walkway. Conversations about the Humanities department and the next midterm on their minds all drift across my path. I'm relieved I didn't add the pressure of another class to my already fragile, sobriety-filled plate. Today it seems like a good idea anyway.

Traffic is light before lunchtime on a Tuesday morning. I approach my block and my favorite comfort food dispensary, the neon glow of the Quick Shop flickering hello. I park in the tiny parking lot, forgoing the added effort of returning here on foot in ten minutes.

Ahmed, who usually works the early shift on weekdays, is texting on his phone when I enter. "Welcome in," he says without raising his head.

"Morning," I reply out of habit. Breezing past my usual choice of a treat that could survive the apocalypse, I pause before the jerky section. There are foot-long and longer ropes, a Cajun-style version, a five-alarm version, a sweet-and-sour kind, a variety pack, and a teriyaki style. My mouth waters at the thought of teriyaki flavor, so I grab two.

Turning to the counter to pay, I stop short by a pyramid of soda. Jerky guy walks in. Tall and sinewy despite his slouch, he brightens when we make eye contact.

"Well, what do you got there?" he asks, smiling.

I blush, without any reason to. I can buy jerky. I can buy all the dried, seasoned meat that I want and not have it be because I was thinking of him. Even though I was.

"Seemed like a good choice." Is our snack schedule aligned? Has he been waiting for me, trying to grab a pic of me for his socials? He's not in my Humanities 101 class; I looked for him.

"I'd say so. Can I join you?" He grabs two foot-long sticks from the salty aisle, then approaches Ahmed at the counter. "Hers too," he adds.

Heat flushes my chest, as I haven't had anyone buy me a gift in ages. It's not worth the hassle of missed communication and confusing expectations to allow it, when I still have settlement and GoFundMe money to support cravings.

Ahmed raises both eyebrows but rings up our items together. "Fifteen seventy-six."

The guy pays with cash from a tattered wallet. A pang of guilt hits me as I reflect that I could have bought our snacks. I know what it is to be hungry, though not what it is to be poor.

We step outside. Both of us slide onto a latticed table with connecting seats, an unspoken agreement to sit and talk for a moment.

"Thanks . . . ," I say, feeling as awkward as I'm sure I look.

"I'm Wes. I've been meaning to say that for a while now." He places his jerky on the table on either side like a knife and fork. A smile lifts his narrow mouth. "This is the part where you say your name."

"Oh. I'm Violet."

"Violet," he murmurs, hitting the *t*. "My favorite Willy Wonka character."

"Really? You're into demanding women with no sense of boundaries?" I return his grin, feeling like the version of me who used to drink all night and sing karaoke with the regulars at my four favorite bars—lighthearted, something I've had trouble grasping over the last year.

He cocks an eyebrow. A scar runs along his cheek down to his collarbone. "The best kind."

A school bus starts and stops at the intersection beside us. Children press their noses against dirty windowpanes, staring at our impromptu . . . date?

"Why are you following me?" There, I said it.

He laughs, ducking into his shoulders. "I'm not. What makes you say that?"

"I don't know. I've only seen you here several times. And I saw you on campus."

The teasing smile stays put. "Do you have many stalkers, that you assume people are following you?"

I take in his playful expression, the open posture as he tears into his jerky. A car honks across the street and he turns toward the sound. The scar is pink along his neck.

"You would be my first." Thankfully, though many people tried to seek us out after we were rescued, our aunt was fierce about protecting us from media attention. We were lucky in that small way. After I turned eighteen and certain information about me was leaked, unwanted "fans" found me, but none of them made it a habit.

"I do feel drawn to you, though," Wes says, from beneath dark eyelashes. "You know what I mean? Like there's this strange connection between us, without knowing anything about each other."

I want to laugh, to scoff and get up to leave. Instead, I hold his eye contact. Try to make sense of how his words could echo my own thoughts.

His jerky is long gone, both sticks, when I finally open one of mine. The meat is salty and sweet on my tongue, as expected for teriyaki flavor—delicious. A moan slips through my lips. I haven't had jerky in ages, not since camping trips that my family took in the Before Time. Wes watches me intently, his mouth working as if imitating my own.

"I was going to walk around Downtown right now. You should join me."

I stiffen, unprepared for the invite. "Oh."

"Or you can call me when you're free." He taps out a number on his phone, then reaches for my cell, which I placed on the table.

"What are you—"

With a swipe left, he opens my camera app. He snaps a photo of his screen. "Now you have my number."

"Uh, thanks. I think." I'm so out of practice—at everything—and I haven't met anyone with whom I shared a lasting romantic or platonic relationship in over a decade. "Oh, wait, I can't. I totally forgot—I have to go see my sister."

He grabs the plastic wrappers, all three. "You could just say no. You don't have to make an excuse."

"No, it's true. I—I meant to stop here and then run home before leaving for her place. She needs my help with something."

Wes doesn't speak, as if he's waiting for the full story. He scans my face with dark-brown eyes. "Do you put her first in your relationship? Does she prioritize you the way it sounds like you do her?"

I lean away from the table. "That's a forward question."

Wes mirrors me, pushing back from the wrappers. "I think it's fair to ask, since you were having so much fun you forgot about your plans with her. Tell me if I'm wrong—when is the last time you really indulged yourself?"

Indulged. The word alone sends a tremor down my midsection to my thighs.

"Do you actually want to go to school? Or is that something else your sister thinks you should do? Each time you mention it, you look like you're gonna be sick."

My jaw falls open. I sputter for a response but none comes. Wes continues to peer at me, flinging his words and accusations of self-esteem issues in full view of a trucker stopped in traffic. Does he know who I am? Was our chance meeting by the soda pyramid more calculated after all?

I stand to leave. "This has taken a weird turn. Thanks for the jerky, but I'm going to leave now."

"Fine." Wes walks with me to the tiny parking lot beside the Quick Shop. He approaches a black Charger streaked with dirt but that otherwise looks brand new. "If you change your mind, you can find me along Fourth Avenue. You have better boundaries than your movie counterpart, Violet."

With no time to go home now, I start driving toward Fiona's house. She asked my help with a sculpture. Only two weeks remain until the gallery show, and she's been stressed about getting her art pieces just right. The black Charger turns left when I turn right, and I don't bother searching for him to wave goodbye.

Screw Wes. And his implication that I've pushed my own needs to the edge of my plate to accommodate Fiona's. He doesn't know anything about us or our dynamic, or the fact that we have only gotten back in touch recently. I'm allowed to desire to help my sister, considering I was such a screwup for years. Back then, she said she'd had enough of my antics and that if I wouldn't stop, she would have to cut me out of her life.

My eyebrows pinch tight in my rearview mirror. The memory of that conversation still stings, as if I haven't learned to live without her in the interim—but I have. And Wes is wrong about me being a pushover.

As the freeway announces a junction to Downtown that veers west instead of my route south to Fiona's house, I hesitate. Consider what might happen if I were to hit my blinker left and merge toward Fourth

Avenue, where Wes is heading now. I haven't felt the kind of instant understanding with someone that I did with him, maybe ever. Although most of what he said was presumptuous at best and hurtful at worst, he was spot-on at each turn.

I hit my blinker. Merge to the far-right lane across the thick dotted line of the exit ramp toward my sister.

18

FIONA

A car pulls up into my driveway, Violet's blue gas guzzler. She exits, hitching up her pants, which slid down during the drive. Violet said she would be coming from her midterm exam, but based on her expression, it doesn't look like it went well. Her face pinches toward her nose, the usual worry she wears when she's dwelling on something.

Years ago, when Violet turned eighteen and came into her share of the settlement money from both the civil and federal lawsuits that our attorneys won, she went out and bought a giant box on wheels, one of those Range Rovers reeking of machismo. She loved it. When I asked her about the choice—"Why not a sports car?" "How about a second-hand hybrid car, a Prius?"—she gave me a look.

"Really?" Violet had replied. "If anything happens to me near this car, I want it to serve as shelter and shield, and maybe contain hidden features like a computer that will resuscitate me when needed. A Prius can't do that."

"Fi?" Violet says, tapping on the screen door. She cups a hand to her face like the first time, then leans against the mesh. "I'm here."

"It's open."

Violet steps indoors as Marshall bounds down the hall to greet her. He pauses just short of a friendly hello. A low growl bubbles in his throat.

"Hey, cut that out." I put down a brown-and-pink pebble that I found at Dog Beach. A whole treasure trove was buried underneath an adjacent piece of driftwood, and I greedily scooped up as many as a plastic poop bag for Marshall would allow.

"How was your midterm? You want something to drink? I've got sodas in the fridge." I wipe my hands on a towel dipped in acetone that I keep close whenever a project requires superglue.

Violet wrinkles her button nose. "Smells like a nail salon in here. Do you have Diet?"

"Nope. That stuff will kill you. But there's flavored seltzer waters if you like those."

Violet sidesteps my furry roommate to head into the kitchen. "What are you making? Today's sculpture."

"You tell me. What do you see?" The pink and brown that I loved in the first rocks I found mix with gray- and blue-hued stones collected during walks in Balboa Park and farther inland along hiking trails.

Violet joins me at my dining table, a can of seltzer in hand. "Is that the waterfall?"

"Oh, good. I'm glad you recognize it." Colorful pebbles form a border along a waterfall that feeds into a shallow pool of water. We discovered it during a long, ultimately fruitless effort to find help after our parents died. Heavy rainfall that winter made the water a fire hose spraying onto the pond below, and I try to make the chute of water wide enough to convey its majesty.

"It's like some scene out of *The Blue Lagoon*," Violet murmurs.

I nod, not caring to comment further. "You remember when we went to Oregon, and Multnomah Falls? Mom nearly lost it, she thought it was so beautiful. 'Some ethereal exhibit of God's creativity,' she said."

Violet scrunches her nose. "No. And nothing in nature feels as divine as all that. It's much more menacing."

I pause adding a tiny pebble to the hillside across the edge of the foot-long base. The chicken coop wire I used for the feather sculpture created great structure for the waterfall, expediting my usual process of forming a foundation that's solid all the way through. Considering I promised two other sculptures for the gallery show and the mountain piece is still not complete, I was relieved by the shortcut.

"Some of it feels that way for me too, still," I reply. A nook lies between a curve in the chicken wire and the next rolling hill. The pebble I chose fits snugly in the valley, as if it were always meant to be placed just so—kind of like life, I think. We experience terrible things, and in hindsight, our paths seem to drive us toward our individual narrow valleys, where we either push through to reach the open air of the other side or become stuck forever, pressed at all angles by our faults and sheer bad luck.

I chose to push through. Sensed it was the only way to survive and carry on in my parents' memories. After we were delivered to our aunt's doorstep, often the only thing I accomplished in a whole day was waking up and getting out of bed. It happens less often these days, with the purpose I found through making art, but I'm still no stranger to a morning in bed.

Violet continues to glare at the waterfall and its placid pool beneath. As if the pulsing water source were the faulty gas reservoir that allowed our plane's fuel to slip through the clouds midflight.

For years, I tried to help Violet leave the Alone Time behind us. To move forward and to find some kind of purpose—anywhere—rather than waste away on dizzying substances that numbed all reality.

I cast a sidelong glance at her. Sunshine has begun to slant behind the arbor vitas of my neighbor's yard, sending shadows stretching across the driveway. "You really don't remember the Oregon trip?"

"Why did you ask me here, Fiona? Was it to grill me on my lack of long-term memories?"

"I wanted your opinion on the waterfall. I needed to know if it resembled the actual place. Why are you upset?"

Violet huffs. She leans onto her heels away from me. "I guess I didn't realize you were going to ask me to revisit this . . . image. It's perfect and it looks just like the real thing. But I . . . I don't know, I was planning on supporting your gallery opening by showing up. Not analyzing each scene for accuracy."

Neither one of us speaks. A trash bin is rolled behind my neighbor's gate, audible through the screen door, though not visible. Children—from the house on the corner—laugh, screaming about some cartoon blue dog.

"And I was . . . I am . . . kind of frustrated by something a guy told me."

"A guy? In your class?"

Violet hesitates. "He's a student on campus but not in my class. I don't know, our interaction today is making me second-guess myself."

Donning a latex glove, I begin applying superglue to the center of the valley on the hillside, careful to hold it above the plastic tarp that I set on the dining table for good measure. This stuff is a death sentence for clothing and wood varnish. "I wouldn't do that, Violet. You have great instincts."

She smiles. "No, I don't."

"Yes, you do," I insist. "You've shown good gut feelings for several important moments in our lives."

I can feel Violet's heavy eye contact but I don't meet it. "Before the flight, you got in trouble, grounded by Dad for hanging up on some woman named Alicia. You remember that?"

She shakes her head. "I seriously have a hard time recalling anything before we boarded the plane. I was only seven."

"Nothing at all?"

"I mean, bits and pieces of events. Christmas morning when I was probably five years old. The year that I got that red bike."

"Yeah, you were five, and I was eleven."

"And another time when we kayaked in Big Bear Lake. Songs Mom used to sing us. But not much else."

The waterfall is three inches across, and probably accurate to scale. But it needs more. The locale was larger than life for Violet and me, one of the sources of fresh water from the snowy mountain range nearby, and a place where we could bathe when we were absolutely willing to risk hypothermia. "Hand me that bucket?"

"Which one? You have three."

"With the blue rocks."

Violet leans closer, as if intrigued. Using only the smallest pebbles and rocks to simulate the undulating chaos of the heavy water stream, I broaden the cascade.

"So, do you remember who Alicia was?" I ask. "You didn't say much then. You just said you didn't like the woman's voice over the phone."

"Really?" Violet smirks. "What a sassy little thing."

The chute begins to resemble an opened dam for the wide spray that showers onto the pool. I can almost hear the roar of the massive volume of liquid passing from the mouth, the cacophonous splash as it blends into the still body beneath, indistinguishable from one another within seconds. It's getting better.

Violet shifts her weight to one foot. "Can I ask you something?"

"Of course. Anything, Vi."

"Why did you leave me?"

I startle, nearly dropping my tube of superglue. "What?"

"After I turned twenty-six, you just dropped off. Stopped returning my calls and refused to give me your new address when you moved. You only came to my apartment a year ago to get rid of a box of my stuff that was taking up space."

The superglue feels like a weapon, given the shift in conversation. I place it behind me, to the far corner of the tarp. "Violet, I didn't just cut you off out of nowhere. Surely you remember that at least."

She winces. "I think you were just sick of me. I had screwed up one too many times—gotten high and embarrassed myself one too many times—and you were sick of it. You didn't want to deal with it anymore."

I don't reply right away. Violet's open face, the guilt and self-loathing written across her small features, reminds me of when she was seven and raving about that Alicia woman.

"You think you drove me away?"

Violet purses her mouth. She nods.

"No. That's . . . that's not what happened. I stopped contact with you because I thought I was enabling you. I thought putting up some boundaries between us, asking you to only come around when you were sober, would help."

"You didn't think to reach out? To request a check-in or update on how I was doing? You didn't worry I was dead in a gutter somewhere down by Fourth Avenue?" Violet's voice rises.

"I keep in touch with Auntie Taylor. You would have called her if you were in really dire straits."

"And that was good enough for you?"

"Look, Violet. I didn't ask you here to rehash old hurts."

"The hell you did; *look* at what you're building!"

"Okay, you know what?" I yank off the latex glove. "You showed up high to everything I invited you to, you stole from Auntie Taylor even though you didn't need the money, and you *poisoned* my cat by leaving your pills around my apartment."

I'm breathless, my chest rising and falling, but I can't stop now. "Not to mention what you did out there all those years ago. I didn't keep in contact with you because I couldn't. Because it was too painful on a lot of levels. Not the least of which is how much you resemble Mom."

Tears fill my eyes, the angry truth of our relationship laid bare.

Violet swallows hard. Her hand flies to her mouth and stifles a sob. She takes a sip of her seltzer water. "Well, I'm sorry. I stopped taking those pills because they weren't working, and I should have kept better track of them. And I'm sorry for all the ways I hurt you. And disappointed you. At the very least, I remember what you're describing. Most of it anyway."

Without another word, my sister grabs her phone, then steps around me to reach the screen door. Marshall growls as she passes, but Violet doesn't turn. She pulls out of my driveway, then leaves.

As much as I felt relief in speaking my feelings, my stomach twists. The way Violet's brown eyes widened, then narrowed, then glistened with unshed tears. Just like my mother's face. Like the last expression I saw on her before she died.

The waterfall's roar returns to my ears. Rushing, violent, and determined. A signal that I am plunging back into the past, and I might not come up as easily this time.

19

JANET

The Wild

Henry hacks away at an adolescent tree thicker around the middle than anything I would have attempted myself, but there's my husband for you. Using the bowie knife he always takes on trips—a remnant of his military days, he'll tell me—Henry has been stubbornly abusing the poor pine for around fifteen minutes, doggedly refusing to quit until he cuts through the ten-foot conifer. He's slashed into the exterior layers of bark, but he's only about halfway done.

At first, the girls watched in curious awe. Then it began to rain. I took shelter with the girls beneath the makeshift tent that Henry constructed using a tarp he found in the plane's cargo hull. With the tarp linked from the wing of the plane to one of the felled trees beside it, our lean-to gives us more room to move around and stay dry at the same time.

"I had no idea it rained so much—anywhere," Fiona grumbles. "My shoes and my socks and my toes are wet."

"Go put on your waterproof boots that you brought for the snow," I reply. "You were supposed to do that earlier when Violet did."

"Ugh, but they're the ugly green ones you got on sale last season."

Teenage angst knows no altitude. "They were a good deal, and you loved green last year."

"That was a whole year ago." She groans but digs around in the rolling suitcase she brought in the back seat of the plane.

"The Amazon," I reply.

"What?"

"In the Amazon, in Brazil, it rains a whole lot more than here. It only seems like a lot because we're outside."

Fiona slips the green, fur-lined, waterproof boots onto each foot. My shoulders relax an inch as I watch my oldest make a good choice without too much protesting. There's hope for her—for us—yet.

"I hate these boots. They're ugly. They're stupid, just like the idea to take this godforsaken trip. This is all your fault, Mom."

Or not. Maybe there's less hope than I opined. How many more years until college? Almost five?

I scan my daughter's face, round and full like mine, but more angular in the nose and chin. She's beautiful and the most gorgeous thing I had ever beheld in my life until Violet was born. Then they were tied for the most exquisite creature on Earth.

Fiona waits for my biting reply—seems to brace herself for a slap or some stinging rebuke from me. But I hold my tongue.

The last few weeks have been hard on everyone, even before Henry and I decided a trip together as a family was just what we needed. Ever since that woman called our house, Henry and I have been at each other's throats. I've been battling my own insecurities, trying to feed everyone, keep the house relatively clean, wondering if I can or want to move forward with Henry—my philandering-narcissist spouse—all while the girls have been soaking in our petri dish of anxiety. Children are resilient, I tell myself. But as Fiona began to lash out more frequently, at me in particular, I realized something was up.

Violet was the one to show me the notebook filled with printed images from horror movies that Fiona had hidden under her bed. My seven-year-old seemed concerned, though not disturbed, by the pictures she'd probably riffled through on her own before presenting them to me. People frozen in terror, blood dripping down their bodies, blood splattered on walls, images of monsters crawling from beneath beds and from sewage drains, and ghostly silhouettes wielding weapons in doorways. Once it was clear to me that Fiona had been collecting a mishmash of really bizarre content cut out from magazines and printed from the internet, I closed the book. Looked at my youngest and said, "Why were you searching through Fiona's room?"

Violet's perfect little face went blank, as if I'd caught her in some lie. "Well, I . . . I was just . . . I had thought that . . ."

"The truth, please," I prodded.

Violet blushed, then hung her head. "Fiona showed me her scrapbook after Halloween."

"Why would she do that? You're not allowed to watch scary movies." And Fiona is allowed to only watch PG-13 movies, but her best friend, Sandi, has parents who allow her to watch whatever she wants. I scanned the pages more closely then and realized these were all movies with Fiona's favorite teen heartthrob movie star. That explained why she would compile such gruesome cutouts in one spiral-bound collection. And I found out later that Sandi and Fiona had a falling-out, which explained why she was being so moody.

Violet mumbled into her chest.

"What's that? Speak up, honey," I said, still unaware of the bomb that was about to drop in our kitchen.

"I said, I like them." Violet met my gaze with steady eye contact then. Clear and confident in her words, with a crispness to them that caused me to shiver. "I like looking at that kind of stuff, Mommy."

Rather than dismiss the comment, or diminish the idea as something everyone can be curious about, I was mute. I didn't know how to reply until Violet shifted gears and asked about dinner that evening.

"Spaghetti and meat sauce," I choked out. She only nodded her little pixie head, then went outside to play in the backyard.

Staring at my girls now—at Fiona already battling the high stakes of adolescence and womanhood, and at Violet with her mysterious dark eyes that seem to carry untold secrets—I wonder how well a mother can know her children once they leave her body.

Fiona toes the ground with her waterproof "ugly" boots. "I'm sorry. You're not to blame for all of this, Mom. Not totally, at least."

"I appreciate that. Thanks."

A crack rips from across our clearing as Henry tips over his tree. The young thing lands on a pile of branches that have begun to rot. It's only been two nights since we crash-landed, but already it feels like a month.

"Success!" he shouts, triumphant. Rainwater drips down his jacket to the soggy earth. "Now we just need the rain to stop for a day or so. We need to keep piling up logs for a fire."

Last night, we heard yipping over the ridge. Coyotes or wolves, I don't know which. Henry said the wolves were all extinct up here, but the cries of a pack on the hunt made me worry otherwise.

I throw my hood over my head, leaving the girls to occupy themselves under the tarp shelter. My footsteps are silent across the wet terrain—a very bad sign for any campfire tonight. Anxiety twists the muscles in my back like needles as I approach Henry and his bowie knife.

"It's getting dark."

Henry wipes the giant blade on his water-repellant jacket. "Yeah, we're going to need to all sleep inside the cockpit tonight."

"Definitely. I think that's best."

"Will you look at that?" Henry lifts up his knife, water glistening on its edge. "The damn thing got chipped."

"Henry, I think we should form a plan. What should we do to get help?" Ever since Henry returned to us after getting lost the first night, he's been evasive about next steps. Where we should go. Whether he has any clue of where we are in the Pacific Northwest, based on our mid-flight coordinates when we started the descent. "Do you think maybe air traffic control actually heard our location?"

Henry shakes his head. Beads of rain drip from his hood, down his nose. "No. I really don't. Let's get under the tarp. It's going to be hard to warm up with no fire."

He doesn't smile, doesn't laugh or show any outward sign of enjoying our desperate situation. But somehow I get the sense that he is—reveling in being stranded out here, where he's the only one among us with any wilderness expertise. Before he left for Operation Desert Shield in the Gulf, he was as carefree as they came—a little head-in-the-clouds. When he returned, it was clear to me that something in him had shattered overseas. Something that caused him to occasionally stare off blankly into a solid wall, then other times to scream during the night about someone named Brian.

Brian, no. Brian, please. I would wake up the next morning and ask him who Brian was. Each time he appeared surprised to hear the name on my lips, bordering on angry. The response was always the same: "I don't know any Brian."

"C'mon," Henry says again, this time more forcefully. "The rain is coming down harder now."

I shake my head. "We need dry wood, Henry. And to gather all the food we can. Mushrooms, flowers, berries, anything. We shouldn't just resign ourselves to a sopping-wet night. We have the girls to think about."

"You think I'm not always thinking of them?" Henry grabs me by the elbow. "And of you?"

"I don't know," I say, louder than I intended, wresting my arm free. "We need wood—that's all I care about."

"It's dangerous to go walking around the mountain when everything is slippery."

"I'll be fine."

"Well, I'll come with you."

I whirl on him. "And leave the girls alone? Are you crazy?"

"Who's going to hurt them out here?" Henry's tone and volume now match my own. If Fiona and Violet can't hear us, they can definitely tell we're fighting by our jerky movements and hunched shoulders.

"Stay with them." I continue walking, seething from Henry's comment about "always" thinking of us. Was he thinking of us when he slept with his little girlfriend? The woman sounded like an idiot—and self-important to call the house line—so I can only hope she's young and naive, and not an asshole. But aren't all home-wreckers—aggressive and myopic toward the lives they're destroying—assholes?

Henry grabs my bad arm, turning me back toward him with such force I nearly topple over. I didn't tell him about the injury since it isn't broken—just badly bruised, tender, and scraped.

"That hurts."

He glares at me, suddenly towering from above. His grip on my elbow tightens. "If you're not back in five minutes, I'm coming to look for you."

Defiance rears in my throat. "Don't threaten me, Henry. I know too much for that."

I yank my arm free, adrenaline surging through the pain, then trudge forward, bristling. At the edge of the clearing, I turn back, hoping to confirm my girls are engrossed in some stacking game using flat rocks we found yesterday, oblivious to our marriage in turmoil.

They're watching me. Fiona and Violet cower together, clutching each other's thin little shoulders, beneath the tarp. Shivering from either the cold or the silent sobs that rack their bodies, my babies return my gaze, wide eyed, mirroring my own.

Henry has already returned to hacking at the tree he felled with the knife, paying none of us any mind.

Rain continues to pelt my jacket, my skin, but new heat flushes my cheeks. Fresh tears fall as I continue to scan my children, unwilling to break eye contact. Not yet. I wish I could tell them so many things. How proud I am of them, how they have impressed me beyond measure with their composure and patience the last forty-eight hours, far above anything I could expect of a grown adult.

Fiona and Violet. My perfect girls. The people who gave my life meaning.

Rather than burden them with any of that, I narrow my gaze—adopt my best "Mom look" and touch my earlobe. "Listen to your father," I say, though I doubt they hear me.

Raindrops wipe tears from my face. Then I turn and pass into the forest.

The canopy of leaves overhead that creates such a nice patchwork of light when the sun is out and smiling appears endless underneath. Shadows envelop the path I've taken to walking, following the curve of the steep face of the mountain, south of me. Thick air dips down my throat as if the darkness itself is trying to worm into my chest.

Rainwater soaks each branch I pass. Nothing on the ground remains sheltered and usable for a fire later on. The berry bushes I feel confident eating from along this route have been picked clean. By me, and I'm sure by certain forest animals.

"God, give us something to eat," I murmur aloud. Praying has become second nature in the last forty-eight hours. If anyone had told me a week ago that would soon be my norm, I wouldn't have believed them.

After growing up incredibly Catholic, thanks to missionaries who were kind to my parents in China, I've adopted a more basic belief system: be good to others, believe in God, and teach my girls to do the same.

Whether Fiona and Violet will follow suit is their decision to make. But I know my Maker. And I know His plan is a good one, even if I no longer force the kids to church on Sundays.

"God, please, please. Give us something to eat," I say again.

Rainfall ticks up into a more consistent rhythm. Tap, tap, tap into a puddle that formed in the deep roots of a tree I pass.

Tap, tap, tap.

Tap, tap, tap, tap.

Tap, tap, tap. Snap.

I pause. I haven't seen any animals out since I began my lone walk. And it's been more than five minutes since I left the camp. Did Henry follow me, like he threatened?

Turning around, I scan past the low-hanging branches that obscure the hilly trail. Saplings bend in the rising wind but no other movement registers. I press on, hoping the meadow where I discovered a family of rabbits this morning has some edible flowers.

"God, please give my girls something to eat."

Verdant green peeks through the dark curtains of foliage. The field, lush and thriving at the beginning of winter, lies just beyond the fringe.

I step along small, flat stones that seem as if they were placed here, like in a curated garden back home in San Diego. Water gathers on the surface of each, and I plant my feet with care.

Thunder claps overhead. Lightning flashes across the meadow and nearly covers a new sound. A branch that breaks behind me.

Hair rises on the back of my neck. I whirl to face the predator, but a body crashes into mine.

My eyes adjust in the near darkness, then shock spools through my core as my attacker's identity becomes clear—before the earth shifts. Tilts. Pivots hard, out from under my feet, as I fall backward until black clouds consume my vision.

Sharp pain cracks across my skull.

Then darkness converges above, and the sound of crashing waves fills my ears.

20

Violet

Bright fluorescent lights illuminate the lecture hall as I stare at my graded midterm essay. The first line I wrote seems to vibrate in my hands: "The heavy, hindered dreams of modern readers, upon consuming Homer's works, are his greatest achievement."

Heavy, hindered dreams.

A week has passed since Professor Tran's midterm, but my thoughts slide back to long before then. To the edge of an open meadow I remember as if it were half-real, half-imagined—blurry at the periphery like a dream. I remember rain and shadows. And the feeling of eyes on me.

The paper I'm holding slips through my fingers to the concrete floor. Professor Tran looks up from the stack on her desk—essays graded with red pen.

"You okay?" she asks.

My throat closes as I recall the dusty scent of rain that filled my lungs when I fell to my knees beside her. My mom died. I mean—I knew she died when we were stranded in some insane stretch of wilderness in the Pacific Northwest. A place I wouldn't have thought existed in the contiguous United States. But I think I saw her die. I think I was there.

Professor Tran continues to peer at me. The oversize brown knit sweater she wears resembles a sleeping bag. "Do I need to call someone?"

"For me? Oh. No, I—I'm sorry, I'm just . . . I'm . . . having a moment." I stumble through a response, not really hearing myself or this woman.

The lights seem brighter here. Burning with heat. "I need some air. Can I come back later?"

"Sure thing," Professor Tran says as I'm already bounding up the flat steps to the exit of the lecture hall, dodging other lingering students. "Remember, if you want to discuss ideas for the final exam prompt, I have office hours on Monday."

My classmates dispersed to various parts of campus or the parking lot after class, I gulp deep breaths of fresh air alone, until I only feel dizzy instead of nauseated.

She was lying in a bed of tall grass on her stomach, crawling away—from me?

It was nighttime. My legs were cold and wet, though I remember I was wearing these fur-lined boots that kept my feet perfectly warm.

Moonlight was almost nonexistent, but a tiny sliver broke through the clouds. My mother turned onto her back. She was alive in that moment, her eyes blinking, her chest rising, then falling. Her lips moved to form a word. Several words.

"On your left!" A bell dings. I turn as a bike zips by me in the hall-way, inches from crashing into me or some other student lost in resurfacing memories. Professor Tran exits the classroom, then walks toward the quad. Three guys in matching lederhosen march in synchronized steps, shouting a drinking song at max volume.

I was with my mother in part of the forest, a meadow, where the trees weren't so thick overhead. I was with her, and somehow I know that she died shortly afterward. Did I see her final breaths?

The earth tips, and then the concrete rises up to smash my face. Pain shoots down my frame, the right side of my body aligned with the ground.

"Whoa, did you see that?" someone says.

"Hey, girl! Er—lady, are you okay?" Cold hands touch my shoulders. My cheek.

"Someone call the campus first aid office!"

More memories rush forward. Then I taste blood. "No, no. I'm . . . I'm fine."

I pull myself up to a sitting position. My jeans are ripped, and the hoodie I grabbed from my closet this morning has chewing gum stuck to the elbow. But I didn't split my head open, so I'll call it a draw. My cheek feels hot to the touch.

"You've got a—a scrape there." A guy I've never seen before touches his own cheek. Thick wavy black hair is cut short on the sides, revealing a scalp tattoo in Sanskrit.

I get to my feet. Aside from bruises that I know will appear in a few hours, I feel okay. Elated, even. I remembered something about my mother in the wild.

A woman in blue scrubs wearing a lanyard with a dangling badge approaches. "Take it easy there. What happened?"

An image becomes crisp in my mind like a frame from a movie. My mother stared up at the sky for a period of time that felt like forever. Her skin was pale, bone white, beneath the clouds. I made some sort of movement that caught her attention, and she startled like a feral animal, still flat on the ground.

Then someone grabbed me and I fell backward—hard to the ground.

A crowd of people forms along the perimeter of the lecture hall, around the scene I created. The woman—nurse—continues to stare at me, expectant. "Are you okay? We should get you to lie down somewhere. Check out that skull, if you dropped five feet from standing. What caused you to lose your balance?"

I peer past her toward the straight shot to my car, toward the direction of my laptop at home. "The topic of my final exam."

Walking in a straight line is more difficult than it appears at first. But with each step forward, I become more confident, more determined to write down everything that I remembered, and then some. The prompt of the final exam of my humanities class is to write about a time in our lives that echoed Homer's metaphors—using either the Cyclops, the sirens, or another example from the *Odyssey*. Using Homer's imagery, make a connection between his text and our modern, complex issues.

Complex issues I have in spades. I'll be able to hit the five-page minimum without missing a beat. I've also been writing more since reconnecting with Fiona, and I think the poetry has begun to dust off the cobwebs of the more interior parts of my brain. Considering I haven't had a concrete image of our time in the wild in years—let alone an idea of what my mother resembled while dying—writing more must be the key.

For the final exam, if I surpass the five-page minimum—and more fully explore what happened, at least for my own peace of mind—I could turn in a portion that fits the prompt without divulging the bulk of the details. I doubt Professor Tran would consider the scenes anything more than hyperbole anyway—an imitation of Homer's imaginative style. Maybe I could write my memoirs.

I lift my phone to my ear, almost arrived at my car. "Fiona? I just had an amazing idea."

———

My sister walks through my apartment door with a fury. "Why would you even think of writing your memoirs, Violet? It's a terrible fucking idea."

"What? You were so receptive while I was driving home."

Fiona slams her purse, a smaller version of a fabric messenger bag, on the counter. "Yeah. Because I didn't want you to hang up before telling me everything. I'm so happy for you that you remembered something about Mom, but please—please don't do this."

She holds up her hands in a prayer, resembling our mother in a new way.

"Okay, I think you're overreacting a little bit. This is the perfect way to finish out the quarter, and I'll only turn in a tiny portion. The rest of my writing can be strictly for me, for us, if I remember anything else."

Fiona rubs the bridge of her nose. "Look, I was waiting to tell you this. Daley Kelly knows something. He . . . he basically said I was lying about Mom and Dad dying the first night."

I pause, waiting for the elephant in the room to be released from its cage. "Well. They didn't."

Fiona shoots me a look. "I know that. But he's suspicious of us, Vi. Which means he might not use our recorded—filmed—interviews in the way that we intended. This is bad, Violet."

What Fiona says holds water. If the documentary takes what we said, what we so carefully crafted and have repeated for decades now, then twists it against us, we might find ourselves in a worse position than when we started. Geri Vega continues to disrupt my daytime show routine with platitudes that bore even the most saccharine TV hosts: nonsense regarding our dad—*If you love something, you let it go; if it doesn't return to you, then it was never yours to begin with.*

"So that makes writing my memoirs even more important," I muse. "It's the only way to retake control from Daley and from that Geri woman, and the rest of the media that has decided to run with the story that earns the most reads and likes."

"Violet—"

I pop open a can of soda. "I'm writing down our story—from my perspective, and what we want to share, exactly how we plan it."

Fiona's eyes glisten in the light from my apartment's ceiling fixture. She begins to speak, but her hand flies to her lips, as if she might cry.

"What's wrong?" I ask, softening my tone. "I would have thought you'd be happy about this. Excited."

Fiona shakes her head. "I . . . I'm not. I'm sorry, Violet, I really am. I can't stress to you enough what a bad idea this is. I'll help you in whatever way I can—whatever way we need to deal with the documentary and that woman—but I can't support you writing anything new to share publicly."

I take in my sister's anxious expression, the resolute point of her chin. She's not going to budge on this.

"What are you doing? Are you . . ." Fiona points to my right hand. "I thought you stopped doing that?"

My fingers pause midgesture. For years after the Alone Time, I rubbed them together—my index finger and my thumb. Anytime I felt stressed or anxious, I would do it subconsciously. It became such a constant act that the gesture extended to moments when I felt unease in any capacity. Hunger, fatigue, longing, disappointment, guilt. The pads of my digits began to wear from the consistent pressure until sores developed. Infection set in as I continued to rub them together despite wearing gloves and, at one point, a removable cast meant to block the impulse.

I had become addicted to the gesture somewhere during my childhood. The act was part comfort, part compulsion that I couldn't and didn't want to quit.

"How did you stop?" Fiona asks in a quiet voice. "Why did you do it for so long?"

I stare at my hand. The fleshy pads of my fingers are back to normal width and fullness. But the color is off. A dark-red hue glows beneath the topmost layer of skin. Scars from years of abuse.

"I don't know why. And I stopped a few years ago, when . . ."

Fiona struggles to speak. "When we stopped talking."

I nod. A cold sheet rolls across my body as I remember the pain of abandonment a second time. "Yeah. I guess that was it."

She clears her throat. "Well. I always wondered if my interaction with you—me being so involved in your life—served as some kind of underlying trigger. Or catalyst somehow. I don't know."

"I don't either. But that's not going to happen this time. I'm going to keep my bad habit under control, I promise." The words come out pleading, as if I'm still a child, begging with the last representative of my immediate family to choose me instead of themselves—instead of anything that takes them away from me, even death. As illogical as that is.

Fiona takes my hand with the scarred tips. "Let's keep an eye on it while we work on these other problems. One thing at a time."

"Okay. Sure. First things first."

My older sister offers a warm smile. But she doesn't swear to stay by my side this time, and the omission stings.

Fiona throws her keys on my already-scratched coffee table. She plops onto my couch, probably sending up a cloud of Flamin' Hot Cheetos dust. At least she's getting comfortable.

"Number one. Convince Daley Kelly to use our interviews the way we want." Fiona kicks up her socked feet. She pats the cushion next to her. "Ideally as soon as possible, before my gallery show. The documentary was supposed to celebrate my event, but now it might derail the whole thing."

She groans. "Number two. Figure out what that woman's deal is. If we discredit Geri Vega, dismantle whatever claim she has to our story, we can reframe the details and ensure the police leave the past alone."

"Right." I notice Fiona leaves out my memoirs, and I don't push the issue. I know where she stands, and she knows I'm going to forge ahead. Stopping isn't an option—not now, when I'm beginning to recall scenes in more depth, more clarity, from our time in the wild. Scenes with our mom.

"If we can do those two things, I think we're golden," Fiona continues.

Wet pine trees and the sound of dripping rain return to mind. "Hey, did we ever learn why the Alicia woman called the house and I hung up on her?"

My mother's lips parted beneath the nearly full moon in the dark night sky. I think my mom mentioned her during . . . then.

Fiona gives me a blank stare. "No. At least no one ever told me. Did you remember something about that call?"

"No. Not yet."

"Where's your laptop?" Fiona asks, already moving on from my oddball question. "Geri Vega has a head start on us of two and a half decades, if she knows anything at all. We need to get digging."

21

HENRY

The Wild

"Violet!" I shout into the darkness. "Violet, where are you?"

An animal flies past me, grazing my head with its wings. A bat.

"Violet!"

The forest is quiet now that the rain has stopped, as if the animals are watching me, waiting to see when I'll let my guard down. "Violet!"

A whimper sounds from the brush beyond a curve in the mountain. "Violet?"

Renewed cloud coverage overhead makes it near impossible to see more than three feet in front of me, but the reflective stripes on my daughter's waterproof snow jacket make her adolescent shape clear. "Fiona?"

She startles, then jumps to her feet. "Dad. Dad, Mom—she's—"

Fiona stumbles backward, her young face frozen in horror. Janet lies splayed out in the grass, legs akimbo, beside a jagged rock that's smeared with blood.

Janet, my wife of thirteen years, the person I have taken for granted more than once, is . . . gone. She's clearly left this world, her eyes wide open and empty of warmth. And if her eyes weren't an obvious indicator that she's departed, the concave void where a portion of her skull should be confirms it. Pain ricochets through my body at seeing my spouse—seeing her damaged shell. I double over. Dry heave into a bush.

Fiona takes me in with a blank expression. Tears streak her cheeks, though she makes no other sign of crying. No contorted features, no anguished sobs. Strange.

"Fiona, get away. Get away from your mother." I lurch toward her, and she matches me in steps backward.

"We have to find your sister," I add, breathless. I might vomit. Dead bodies used to be part of my life, and a more common occurrence than any civilian might experience. But not anymore.

Fiona stiffens, her eyes wide on high alert. "Violet? Where is she?"

"I don't know. When I came back from looking for your mom, both of you were gone from the camp. You can't walk around here at night, it's not—" I stop short of saying the most obvious phrase with the poorest timing imaginable.

"Violet was napping when I left her," Fiona whispers. She moves farther down the hillside, keeping to the patches of moonlight.

Here the woods are thick. Rocks like the kind it seems Janet slipped and smashed her head on are rampant on this path-that's-not-a-path. Trees and bushes, plants and flowers containing untold nettles, and poisonous berries flank us on all sides.

"Violet!" I shout again. Something moves, feet from us, rustling a leafy plant that reaches my shoulders.

Fiona stops short. "Violet?" she whispers.

Dirt covers small cheeks as she lifts her head. Crouched in a ball as Violet was, I never would have found her. I might have stepped on her. Hair the color of darkness camouflages her head, and even the skin of her hands is caked in mud. The purple jacket identical to Fiona's is covered in discarded leaves shaken loose by the rough winds of this altitude and the heavy rains that formed a creek that wasn't present two days ago down the mountain. She sits in a bed of white flowers.

"Vi? What are you doing here?" Fiona asks.

Violet regards us with a hollow stare, ghostly in the semidarkness. A spirit-child from centuries past who never found her resting place, just like in the stories my ying ying used to tell me. "I was looking for Mommy. I found her."

"Oh, honey . . . ," I start, then trail off.

"She was saying something. Doing something. Then she . . . she . . ." Violet bursts into sobs, the dam broken, and Fiona swoops down to hold her. The pair of them shiver, crying, hugging each other tight. Wailing across the mountaintop echoes after the onslaught of rain quieted the forest. Now even the trees listen to us.

"Shh." I hold up a hand. "Did you hear that?"

The girls freeze anew, little ivory statues. "Hear what?" Fiona whispers.

Branches sway in the constant wind that twirls up here. Leaves scratch together, creating ambient noise that pricks my ears. A twig snaps.

"We should return to camp." I lead my daughters back through the woods, continuing first in the direction that we were headed, then circling behind a copse of saplings. No sense in returning past Janet's body, and retraumatizing the girls all over again.

"What about Mom?" Fiona asks, apparently the spokesperson for her and Violet.

"Don't worry about her right now."

"But what does that mean?" Fiona pushes. Always, she's been a pusher, but that quality seems on turbo drive out here with high stakes surrounding every question and answer. Asking for more information than we have, wondering if there are more snacks and favorite treats than what Janet asked me to pack for the flight and in anticipation of snowy hikes.

We arrive at the small clearing and the carcass of the airplane. Rocks that served as a campfire barrier and that contained the small flames I coaxed from nothing are scattered. The tarp I tied from the plane to a tree is flapping in the breeze, untethered. Wrappers that were corralled into a makeshift trash bin that Janet made from a reusable shopping bag and bucket she found in the cargo hull tumble across the small arena that we've made our home in the wild. Our campsite has been disturbed. Someone was here.

Turning back to the girls, I bite back the fear scrabbling up my throat. Try to project calm, stability. "I'm the sole parent now. And I'm going to do what's necessary to protect you."

Instead of appearing to be comforted by that, Fiona and Violet shrink backward. "And Mom?" Fiona pushes.

"I'll take care of Mom. Now, help me clean all this up. Please."

Violet takes a tentative step forward. Sniffling back tears, she reaches down and begins the task of chasing down our trash.

"Right. Because that's so important. We wouldn't want to leave the mountain in a worse state than we found it, right?" Fiona scoffs. "God knows that's more important than figuring out what the hell happened to our mother."

I grimace. A sharp, shooting pain throbs behind my eyes. Rolling pinpricks that I haven't felt since my army days. Flashes of light splash across my vision like meteors from heaven. "You're not being fair, Fiona."

"Aren't I? Look at you," she continues. "You're not even upset."

She jams her hands on her hips, resembling both her mother and her former toddler self gearing up for an epic tantrum. At least that's what I imagine Fiona looked like. I was on active duty and abroad most of the time, from when Fiona was a year old until she was five, but Janet was plenty descriptive of the screaming episodes.

Janet. My wife, the mother of my children. Did she have a life outside of that? Did she have friends, even? I've been a terrible husband and, I suspect, father. But that's all going to change now.

Fiona steps away from me. "You don't care. Do you?"

Violet pauses at the edge of the clearing. An empty package that came with a handful of crackers dangles from her hand. She looks from me to her sister. "Daddy?"

"I care. And I'm doing my best to process the loss of your mother, while thinking about what needs doing next—"

Fiona claps her hands over her ears, eyes shut tight. "Stop it! Don't say that!"

"Fiona, your mother is gone." My voice breaks. The truth stings worse than any splinter from this mountain. Emotion tightens my chest, and I can feel myself drifting into the bottomless void of grief that I've entered a few times in life—while I was deployed, when my father passed from heart failure, then my mother from an accidental overdose of OTC pills. I focus on Fiona's anguish—the arch of her eyebrows as they press in a prayer above her nose. Struggle to stay present with my girls.

"I wish things were different," I resume. "But there's nothing—"

"Stop it! I said, stop! Stop talking!" Wild eyes lock on my face, equal parts rage and fear. She's nearly hysterical, and for good reason. But I recall she had a similar reaction this summer when she learned that my girlfriend was calling the house; I caught Fiona listening at the door to the main bedroom, after a particularly loud fight between Janet and me, but I didn't punish her, not wanting to make things worse. The following night, Fiona screamed at Janet for making the rice too sticky—asked her, "Can't you do anything right?"—then threw the rice cooker at Janet from across the kitchen. We were all so stunned that only Janet had the peace of mind to calmly reply, "Go to your room."

She wasn't a punching bag, Janet. But she somehow managed to regulate her own emotions despite the tornado of hormones—mine and the kids'—swirling around her. Fiona hasn't yet learned that skill. Though she has grown taller than her mother and has reached my height. Does she possess the muscle to match?

Fiona kicks the Cessna's broken tail, damaged in our crash landing. Again, and again, with not even a whimper. Did something happen this morning, before my fight with Janet about gathering wood—before she stormed off into the forest to her death? Did Fiona and Janet have an argument that escalated in this stressful setting?

Fiona huffs, turned away from me. Rather than approach while she's so volatile, I move toward Violet. Help her grab one of the travel-size tissues that blew into a tree branch out of reach of this seven-year-old.

Violet accepts my gift. She places it in our trash bag. "Finished."

She crosses to the log beside our muddy campfire. Retrieving a different plastic bag, Violet withdraws her journal from the protective covering, along with a pen. She starts to write.

"Sweetie," I say, approaching my girl. "I know you have a lot going on in your head right now. But I want you to know that I loved your mother, and I love both you and Fiona. Everything is going to be all right."

Violet doesn't look up. "Will it?" She writes something on the page but tilts the book away from me.

"It will. You just have to believe in me, that way you did when you were little."

Ink-black eyes flit to mine. She crooks her finger, beckoning me closer. I hesitate for a moment, as some instinct warns me against underestimating this child. This cherub with full cheeks and whose warm gaze could make a seasoned killer offer up his final meal on death row.

In spite of the internal bells pealing within me—the ones that have lain dormant since I was dishonorably discharged from the military—I lean forward into her confessional bubble.

Inches from my face, she says, "I'm still little, Daddy. But I know enough."

I pull back, but it's too late. I saw the words—will never unsee the phrase—that might be my undoing.

At the top of the page on which she was writing, in unstable script, the words are stark:

Mommy told me the truth.

22

FIONA

Holding the dozen instant camera photos in my hand, I fan out the images like a deck of cards. At the top of my pile, bright colors on snack wrappers reflect the camera's flash in sharp patches of white. Labels of food products are manipulated to compose a greater image of a landscape. Sourcing enough green items was hard, until I explored the candy aisle. Then Jolly Rancher Bites were the obvious solution.

"What's next?" Quincy approaches from the back corner of the gallery. He just directed a lone shopper, a man, to a series of watercolors in the next room.

"*Convenience Store Wrappers.*" I turn the mini photo toward him. When he first suggested I borrow his camera to take snapshots of my work, I thought it was a cute idea. A little retro for the sake of being retro, but I was happy to indulge him rather than take photos on my phone. Seeing the clear, sharp images of my pieces, set against the white walls of the gallery, I can see why he insisted.

"Right." Quincy walks past Darleen, who sits on one of the benches placed against a wall. She pores over a magazine.

"How about here?" Quincy asks. He pauses at a narrow wall that bisects the room. "I can change out the filter on that light overhead for a softer white, a cream gel."

I lift the photo to the wall. Knowing it will be opposite my mountain sculpture—the middle of the room—the collage can act as a foil to the more natural elements. "I like it. Darleen, what do you think?"

"Hmm?" Darleen snaps her head up.

"My collage piece. *Convenience Store Wrappers.*"

"Oh, yes. Yeah, that looks great right there. Good choice."

Quincy looks from my face to Darleen's distracted expression. "Should we move on?"

"What are you reading? You've been deep in those pages ever since I arrived."

"Oh, nothing." Darleen closes the magazine, then flips it over.

I lift both eyebrows. "Should I look at that?"

She sighs, handing it to me. "All right. Yes. Here. The middle section."

I open *Art Lover's Magazine* to a spread of Benny Zimmer, a well-known benefactor and gallery owner himself, sitting beside a curvy woman with dark hair and heavy eyeliner. Geri Vega. "What is this?"

"Apparently, Geri Vega is an art collector and old friends with Benny Zimmer." Track spotlights above cast Darleen in a harsh glow that makes her appear too pale.

"Oh. Wow."

Darleen nods. "Right. The interview just came out. She will not be ignored."

I purse my lips. Scan the storied white walls of one of the most respected galleries in the Southern California art scene. Work to subdue the outrage percolating beneath my skin.

"Well? Does she mention us?" I step beside a recent installation of a video in the center of the main room, in the place of honor. The camera focuses on the nest of a bird—a bluebird with brilliant feathers whose colors seem to ripple beneath the sun.

"She does—you. She says in the article that she doesn't want much. Just the chance to speak to you. Preferably on camera in the coming months."

I lift my eyebrows in surprise—although nothing about this woman, or her timing, should surprise me at this point. "So far away from my show that's scheduled for almost a week from today?"

"I know, right? She's so obvious." Darleen scoffs. "I can't believe Benny Zimmer agreed to support her. The guy has enough old friends. He owns more Picassos than Italy."

"Why not Violet? Seems like Vega's focusing more and more on me. Attacking me in my safe spaces."

Darleen shrugs. "Yeah, you're right. Violet's name isn't mentioned anywhere in the interview."

I purse my lips. "Okay. Well, thanks for telling me."

"Are you feeling okay? You look pale."

"Yeah. Yeah, I'm fine. Listen, Violet is going to be here any minute. Is it all right if we talk about this later?"

Preferably never again.

"Of course, go. Go ahead, I'll be here," Darleen adds. "And Quincy and I will figure out the best spot for your feather installation."

"Already on it," Quincy says from along the back wall.

My footsteps echo, loudly announcing my retreat. An audible finger wag that I can't handle this Geri woman's incessant presence. She's everywhere. The ubiquitous theme of my year that I probably should have seen coming. Every time things begin to go right—I land a spot in a new biennial, a favorable review is published, or I score a coveted spot to visit a gallery opening—it feels like a hiccup appears to offset the balance. A flat tire on my drive or a hair baked into the cookie I'm eating at the event when I've already wolfed down two.

Outside the gallery, the sidewalk teems with weekday shoppers. I skip across the road to the man-made park, to the safety of the pond that I know will never overflow and trap me in its environs.

As I walk the path beside the water, waiting for Violet, I focus on the bubbling fountain in the middle. Water spits from a tube that probably serves some mechanical purpose but whose sound is calming in an urban world. Instead of car doors, people saying goodbye or hello at the surrounding restaurants and bars, the soothing sound of tumbling water fills my ears as I plant myself at the farthest point from the gallery. Even when the rain was a deluge out there in the wild, from beneath the protection of the airplane, the steady thrum against metal was comforting. A sound that I recognized and associated with growth and rebirth. A reminder that this storm would pass. Eventually.

My phone vibrates in my pocket. Violet's name scrolls across the screen: *Vi Vi Mui Mui.*

"Hey," I answer. "You here?"

"At the corner."

I spy Violet's blue, boxy SUV in the shadow of a café awning next to the gallery. When I cross the street to her passenger door, she narrows her eyes. The door is unlocked and I slip inside.

"What were you doing over there?" Violet asks. "I thought you had more installation stuff to do."

"I just needed some air. Geri Vega is now talking to print publications in the art world about me."

She pulls forward, then flips a U-turn back toward the freeway. "Anything new?"

"No."

"Great. The same tired story, we can handle. Good thing we're going to Mira Mesa today."

In the days since Violet and I agreed that we need to go on the offensive against the woman harassing us, we've learned her basic résumé: Geri Vega worked as a social worker for a few years in Orange

County before she got her master's in clinical psychology from a college in San Diego. She moved to Del Mar around the time that Violet was born, then set up an office in North County, near Carlsbad, where she seems to have held an address until one year after our plane crash. She let her state license to practice psychology lapse nearly twenty years ago. From what Violet and I could find on the internet, Geri has been doing consulting work for oddball corporations, across a variety of white collar–company needs: team building, trust seminars, "Bringing Your Whole Self to Work" workshops, and goal setting for personal and professional objectives.

When we discovered an old archived image of Geri's former website that was shared on LinkedIn back in 2012, I contacted the person who posted it. A man named Phuong Nguyen, the small business owner of a paper supply company. All these years later, he still had nice things to say about Geri Vega, especially to a "prospective client" of hers like me. When I asked if he'd be willing to discuss his experience in person, he offered his address.

The freeway moves us inland and away from the ocean view in minutes, thanks to light Thursday morning traffic. Violet turns down the radio, quieting the twang of country music to a low percussion. "So, I wanted to . . . ask you something."

I stiffen, anticipating another bomb. I fumble for the oh-shit bar on the passenger door. "What is it?"

"I was just thinking. Well, that is, I spent the morning writing."

My heart sinks into my stomach. "Your memoirs."

She pauses. A yellow sports car floors past us in the fast lane, and Violet checks her mirrors. "Bingo."

Instantly, my mind jumps to the night our mother died, the strange empty shock across young Violet's face, and the disturbing events that followed. "Violet, I don't know how many ways I can tell you this: please, don't. It's a mistake. Don't put anything in writing that you don't have to. Us signing new statements with the police is already enough."

"I know you think that, but—"

"No buts. Literally, everything in writing *will* be used against us." That woman—Geri Vega—and her false concern pictured for that interview with one of the great benefactors of American art, seems to underline that possibility as a probability.

"Why is the documentary okay, but not my memoirs? That's ass-backward."

"In the doc, we'll each have twenty minutes of screen time, while Daley splices in other interviews with rescue teams and experts on aviation and weather patterns. You're talking about putting down details to paper for public consumption."

"The public likes us, remember? What's the big deal?"

"What if they stop liking us, Violet? What if Geri Vega convinces them there is more to our story than what we've shared? The millions of people who donated to our GoFundMe could ask for their money back." I shake my head, nearing my boiling point. Why doesn't Violet see this?

She heaves a sigh, casting me a quick glance. "Fiona, my memoirs will mostly be for me. For us—and the final exam of my humanities class. Let's not freak out about putting the cart and the horse together."

"The cart before the horse. Look, would you really write all that, then keep most everything to yourself?"

She hesitates and I have my answer. Violet probably likes the idea of submitting her side of the story for the world to consume. Certainly, she was too little to form her own account of what happened when we were rescued. Plus, the money.

"Okay, I'm not going to repeat myself here," Violet says. "I just shared because I think I'm remembering more, and . . ."

An ambulance surges from the slow lane, and Violet steps off the gas in the middle of the freeway as it peels past.

"And? Spit it out, please."

"Fine. I think I was alone with Mom while she was dying."

I suck in a breath. The ambulance makes a sharp right onto the next exit ramp, nearly clipping a concrete divider. "Okay."

"Why would that be the case?" Violet asks. "Why would a seven-year-old have been with a dying person? I wasn't screaming, or begging for mercy from her attacker. I wasn't shielding her from a monster or animal surging from a bush. Why was I there and calm and alone?"

All good questions. Ones I have tried to ignore for years. "Some things are better not known, Violet. I don't have any answers to share."

"What does that mean?" She sucks her teeth. "None you can share. Do you have answers that you're keeping to yourself?"

"No. Look, I am as confused and concerned by your memory of sitting with Mom as you are. But I don't know why you were . . . what you were doing there."

Violet is silent the rest of the drive into Mira Mesa. Thankfully. When she parks at the curb of a nondescript commercial building, I'm relieved someone else will be in the hot seat for the next half hour.

We enter a beige tiled lobby, then turn left into a glass-walled shop. A literal pyramid of paper occupies a corner dedicated to printing products. A square sign hangs above a shelf display, advertising CREAM MATTE REAMS beside the front door, while a copy machine in the window is ready with "classic white" reams, according to the laminated page on the control panel.

An older man with graying black hair lifts a hand from the back of the shop. "Fiona?"

"Hi, yes. Thanks for meeting us."

Phuong crosses pilled blue carpet to the edge of the copy machine. The starched collar of the white dress shirt he wears could double as cardstock. "Any friend of Geri Vega's is a friend of mine. Should we sit?"

Violet and I exchange a look. We follow him to an alcove set up with folding chairs.

"Coffee?" Phuong points to a makeshift coffee station on an end table, motioning with his own paper cup. "We have real sugar and all the fun imitations."

Violet shakes her head, while I get settled. "No, we're good," I say. "Thanks for agreeing to talk with us. Has your company been here long?"

"Oh, about fifteen years. I hired Geri right before actually. Business was booming prior to the paperless movement, and I had a staff of twenty-five people."

Violet casts an eye behind him to the empty shop.

"Yeah, there have been a lot of changes. But we're still hanging in there." Phuong smiles.

"Of course," I reply, genuinely meaning it. If I weren't an optimist after all this time, I couldn't be an artist.

"So what did Geri do for you back then?" Violet begins rubbing her fingers together, her anxiety showing. I pass her a wooden stirrer from the coffee station.

"She led a goals workshop for us. It was all about helping us brand our respective groups—I had a marketing team, wholesale, finance and ops, and a strat planning team—and then helping us transfer that vision to tangible goals with milestones."

"Sounds pretty helpful," I offer.

Phuong smiles again, revealing a chipped yellow front tooth. He sips his coffee. "It was. I invited her back for another workshop after that— team building to better foster relationships among my employees."

"Geri seems like she was pretty effective. You didn't have any complaints?" I ask.

"Any concerns about her character, or her integrity?" Violet adds. I nudge her knee with my own.

Phuong slowly shakes his head. "Well, not initially. Geri and I became friendly over time."

"Romantic?" I ask. Phuong has a tan line on his ring finger, evident when he raises his paper coffee cup. Maybe Geri Vega has a history of seducing married men. Any detail that paints her in an untrustworthy light—rather than the lovesick, remorseful schoolgirl she's been playing on camera—would be a bull's-eye for me.

He chuckles. "No, no. Nothing like that. Just friends. We often had conversations about the future of our respective businesses and strategized about new tactics to gain more customers, or clients. Geri was all in on that. She was always coming up with wacky new ideas to generate interest."

"Like handing out flyers?" Violet asks.

"Or renting billboard space?"

Phuong lifts both eyebrows. "The zaniest thing Geri suggested was meeting with a psychic. Apparently, she had one that she visited every month, who gave her some pretty good advice."

"Oh. Well, that is . . . zany. Did you go with her?"

"I did, a few times actually."

"Learn anything interesting?" Violet asks, barely concealing her amusement.

Phuong smiles. "No, I did not. A total waste of money the two times I went. But Geri was deeply invested there, so the next time she suggested we go together, I made an excuse. And the next, and the time after that."

"What was such a waste about it?" I ask. Violet turns toward me, ever so slightly, in my peripheral vision.

Phuong sighs. "I mean, I feel bad saying it, even today. I haven't spoken to Geri in years, but it was clear to me then how much she needed the psychic sessions for emotional support. And that wasn't my thing."

"As in, Geri treated the psychic like a therapist," Violet offers.

"A little. When I visited with her, there was some time spent on our business endeavors and what the psychic saw for our futures. Said my business would expand into a megacorporation—" Phuong rolls his eyes. "But the rest of the visit was spent trying to contact someone."

"Who?" I lean forward. Violet resumes rubbing the pads of her fingers, the wooden coffee stirrer forgotten.

"I don't remember. An old boyfriend, who I guess died."

"Henry? Was it Henry?" Violet asks.

Phuong shrugs. "Sorry. It was a long time ago."

"Would you remember the name of the psychic? Or where they were located?" I whip out my phone, ready to type myself notes.

"Not the name, no. But the location, yes. It's on the corner of Garnet and Ingraham in Pacific Beach. But why would you want to meet the psychic, to vet Geri for work?"

I glance at Violet, who has always been a better liar than me. "We're very thorough in all our hiring decisions," she says. "You said you didn't have any integrity concerns initially. What changed?"

Phuong exhales a big breath. "Yeah, she—uh—stole from me. I loaned her two thousand dollars for a new business venture, something about hosting seminars in a dedicated workspace, and she took the money, then ran. I called her and drove by her office, but she packed up and went someplace else. Never heard from her again after that, and honestly, I never tried to contact her."

"Why not?" I ask.

"I mean, I needed the money," he says. "Still do. But I think she was much worse off than she let on. Probably in the hole with that psychic too. And anyway, I've been there—down on my luck. Rather than dwell on it or hire legal counsel, which would cost me more money in small claims court, I decided to call it a business expense and move on."

Violet and I exchange a look. The white paint is beginning to chip on Geri Vega's perfect veneer. I stand, then shake his hand. "Thanks so much for your time. And the transparency."

As we walk toward the shop's exit, Phuong clears his throat. "Hey, uh, if you get a chance, let Geri know I said hello, will you? I always felt bad about how things ended between us. And she still owes me money."

23

Henry

The Wild

Bright, twinkling lights cover the sky overhead. I've never seen so many at once before. Thousands—tens of thousands—blanket the black canvas. The night sky could be a mirror of the river down below so that if I allow my mind to wander free, I could lose my sense of direction, whether I'm up or down. I've never been this far from civilization in the US before. Even in Yosemite, the lights from campfires and a small grid of official buildings cast a glow across the park.

After the girls settled down, I went back to Janet and laid a tarp across her, weighting it with stones I grabbed from the mountainside. Then I went looking for help. Again. I walked probably three miles in one direction, then at an angle forty-five degrees opposite, bisecting my return route to camp so I was only gone about two hours total. When I arrived, Fiona was fuming and Violet was licking a wrapper from the trash bag. My girls were hungry. And I wasn't about to let them starve.

"Stay here, girls. I'm going to go get dinner." As I withdraw the knife from my pocket, the handle glints brown instead of black in the moonlight. For a moment, it resembles the government-issued knife I used back in Kuwait.

Fiona eyes me from where she sits beneath the tarp on an overturned bucket, her arms crossed. "What are you going to do? Play Whac-A-Mole with a gopher? Mom was the cook."

"Where are you going?" Violet asks. She leans out of the passenger seat of the cockpit. Small legs dangle from the side, hitting the hull of the plane. Straight, dark hair falls across her face as she hunches into her shoulders the same way my wife did. I wasn't able to protect Janet from the elements out here, but I'm going to do my best by our kids.

My stomach growls, reminding me that I need to eat as well. Distorted memories return—of hunger gnawing at my insides while hiding in the Iraqi desert—of strange episodes that caused my superiors to stare at me sideways. Ultimately those uneasy glances led to my dishonorable discharge; I know that.

"Your mom was able to find that bird the first night. I'll bet there are more where that came from."

"But what are we supposed to do here?" Fiona whines.

"Take care of your sister," I answer, starting off toward the darkest part of the forest, up the slight incline and away from the path that Janet took—where Janet still lies.

"How? And what about . . ." Fiona looks at Violet, then stands. She crosses to me, out of earshot from her sister. "What about Mom?"

"Your mom will be okay. Just stay here."

Fiona's eyes nearly bug from her skull. "Okay? She's—what are you—she's dead." Fiona adds, lowering her voice, "She's not okay."

"I know you're worried. We're all worried, Fiona. But we have to stay calm."

"We don't even know what happened to her."

"She slipped. It had just rained and—"

Fiona shakes her head wildly. "No. No, that's not what happened."

"What? Do you think I—or your little sister—had something to do with—?"

"I don't know!" she shouts. Her palms fly to her forehead. "I don't know, I don't know."

The pulsing continues behind my eyes, sending white spots across my vision. I need to eat something. Starting off at a wobbly gait, I reply, "Stay here. Just—I need to go."

Up the hill, away from the crash site, conifers grow more densely together. I walk as quietly as possible, though conscious of the noise I'm making. I'm probably scaring off any wild game nearby, but I push forward. For my girls. For Janet's memory.

She would laugh if she knew I was motivated by them all now. She'd say my actions didn't reflect it, that cheating on her seemed to disprove that notion handily. Janet was always my guiding light, even if I ignored it from time to time. Without her, without the stability I never received from my neglectful parents, the success I yearned for in the military, or the recognition I feel owed in my current job as regional director of mall security, the world seems off-balance. It's only been a matter of hours, but the moon has dulled—smudged at the edges.

Fiona is right to be upset. Both girls are. However, the idea that anything violent happened to Janet is laughable, and not something I want to think about—could think about, considering the only suspects would be my children.

Meanwhile, Fiona's emotions have pivoted from sobs to anger within seconds. Violet has remained stoic even through quiet tears. Which reaction is the more appropriate one, given the horror scene we all stumbled on? Could one of my kids actually be responsible for their mother's death?

Using thick tree trunks for leverage, I hoist myself up a sharp incline to the summit of this peak. The view is pristine. Clouds part before the stars to illuminate the valley below. The river currents shine in undulating sparkles, like something out of a wildlife program.

Movement across the river, on the back end farther away from us, catches my eye. Small dots that shift in tandem with one another, a hunting formation. One dark shape takes the lead until the dot behind relieves the first at the head of the pack. A half dozen animals sprint between trees, in patches of moonlight, before they leap into the narrow neck of the river where it curves away toward the snow-capped mountains. Wolves.

Branches nearby scratch together, though no wind twists through the leaves. Someone is close.

I crouch down into a defensive position instinctively, then back against a tree trunk. Watching, waiting for what happens next. The animal on this ridge stops moving, as if it does likewise.

A small noise reaches my ears. Dull clicking. I scan the neighboring bushes, the darkness that inks between trees, until I see it. A hunched body. Covered in thick fur, the animal could be a beaver but with a bushy tail, or a small bear with a long face. A word slips forward from a documentary I must have watched sometime in the past. A . . . a marmot?

The marmot stops. It glances around, as if sensing it has an audience. What must it feel like to constantly be on the lookout for a threat? To know that each second in repose might lead to your neck getting hacked off in the next minute?

But I do know that feeling—the state of war. All veterans who have been in combat zones are acquainted with the ticklish occipital lobe, on nonstop alert and ready to fight or fly from a scene. A wry smile stretches my mouth. I would have made a pretty good marmot.

I take a step forward. My feet find the space between a log and a soft patch of grass that cushions my weight. The marmot continues cleaning his paws, clicking his claws against his teeth. Moonlight seems to spotlight my quarry, the stars in the cheap seats eager to see how this will go.

The ground shifts. Then the knife vibrates in my hand, becoming the weapon I need for this exact moment, elongating another six inches. With the added reach, I part the tall grass that separates me from the animal, giving myself the perfect avenue to dinner. The branches sway in a new breeze, then lift their leaves to remove any visual obstacle. I crouch, not six feet from where my adversary licks his claws—blades unto themselves.

My grasp becomes slippery. I reposition my fingers tighter around the leather handle as the dry scent of desert stings my nostrils. I close my eyes. Raise my hand. Then flex my quads and leap forward through the brush.

I stumble as a piercing war cry rips overhead. Feathers erupt, flapping wildly as the marmot grunts, howls, and shrieks, and I startle backward into the grass. The marmot whirls to the owl, biting, snapping at the white-gray tufts, but massive talons clamp down on the animal's fatty coat. More cries of pain and fear ricochet off the mountainside as the owl flaps its imposing wingspan, lifting the weaker fighter to its nest.

I fall onto my back. My heart beats a drummer's solo, adrenaline pulsing in my limbs. Blades of grass make tiny cuts on my skin where my jacket folded up beneath me. They struggle to resume their original positions, bending and straightening to stasis. Images of ants crawling across my skin, of the scorpions I encountered over a decade ago, march across my mind.

Stars twinkle overhead in laughter, having watched my attempted attack before a stronger, more strategic predator took action. A reminder that in war, often the first strike is best, when the prey is still unaware of the imminent danger. Sharp grunting echoes from the owl's nest, where the marmot continues to struggle. Then the owl screams again, and all goes silent in the forest.

Little by little, insects begin to buzz. Other animals move about, resuming nighttime routines.

I lift my palm. Twist my hand this way and that in the moonlight. Red drops of marmot blood spatter my skin, confirming this wasn't another mirage.

Laughter slices against the rock face of the next incline. Fiona and Violet. They're feeling better at least.

But the noise changes, shifting as it does to reach my ears. The sound of their giggles reaches a new pitch and stretches into a long moaning howl. In a snap of clarity, I remember what I first noticed from this vantage point, down by the river: the pack of wolves. They're getting closer. Judging from the increase in yips, barks, and howls, they are closing in fast on some unsuspecting victim.

24

Violet

The Wild

Dear Mommy—
Fi Fi said I shuld write you a leter. I wrote one to Daddy to.
How are you? I am good.
Sorry. That's not tru. I'm very tired.
I'm sorry I didint lissen more to you. I love you.
The wuman is back again. I don no how she got here. But I don like
her. She is mean mean mean. More mean than Felix-kitty after forth
of july. She stares at me.
I love you and miss you.
Your mini,
Violet Esther Seng.

25

Violet

Rustle hustle muscle
The wind urges sleet
Cold clear care
Merging in the peat
Bodies mounting slowly
Never what it seems
Over under blunders
Heavy hindered dreams

Alongside the curb, bar patrons emerge from the restaurants and patios that populate Pacific Beach. Neon lights illuminate the neighborhood's banner overhead, ready to welcome Thursday night revelers.

I sit quietly in my car, not yet ready to join the fun. After I got home from visiting Geri Vega's old client, I knocked out another chapter of my memoirs. Though I've only tackled a few, the experience has been like opening a faucet—memories gush forward, along with new creativity that has probably lain dormant for some time, probably suppressed by substances I was taking. Poetry comes with ease and in ways I haven't attempted since high school, and I've been cooking more—like, actual meals. Instead of settling for a packet of Top Ramen like I do so many weeknights, I managed to make my own shoyu recipe, using pork belly from Costco and hard-boiled eggs I bought from a farmer I passed in the Walmart parking lot, and then I topped it all off with everything bagel seasoning. The result was better than any food wars photo on social media.

Despite what Fiona insists, that writing any of it down is a mistake, I feel a shuddering certainty that the opposite is true. Collecting the fragments of memories that still remain to me is all I have. And each fleck of dirt that I brush away from the covered mound results in more clumps of earth falling away, revealing distinct details that should have been clear to me all along. The same details that I'm beginning to suspect Fiona has always retained, since the day we were rescued. My sister doesn't want me to recall them for some reason, telling me to shut them down and push them away whenever the memories begin to take shape. It's time I did more to counteract her efforts.

My phone hums in the center console. A text from Fiona reads:

We have a problem. A new one. She just posted this.

"What now?" I push through my teeth. Sadly, I already know who "she" is without Fiona saying so. In a video featured on Geri Vega's stories, she sits with her back to the camera, facing a man whose eye color only makes sense on a bag of polluting chip packaging. Daley Kelly. Geri Vega is having or just had a meeting with the documentary filmmaker who suspects our version of the truth isn't as accurate as we've claimed. A self-described truth devotee.

I stare at the frame, pressing my thumb to the screen to hold the image in place. Geri wears a kind of suit jacket—light blue—that complements the gold highlights in her dark-brown hair. Her shoulders are rounded, and then they taper to a small waist where she sits on a wooden stool.

"You're not the only one who can dig up the past, Geri."

I exit the car. Walk the half block to a small shop on the corner of Garnet and Ingraham. College kids scream laughter from the adjacent open-air patios. But I'm only focused on one kid in their twenties. Wes. I spot him lingering beneath the awning of the corner shop. My stomach tightens with first-date jitters, and I recall it's been years since I went out with someone sober. Maybe never.

After our last interaction, when we ate our salty snack together outside the Quick Shop, I was annoyed that Wes suggested I wasn't prioritizing myself. Who did this guy think he was? Some Freud acolyte? Then Fiona made it clear how against my memoirs she is, and his suggestions started to make more sense. It's not that I've been submitting to all Fiona's wants and needs. It's that I've been doubting my instincts—my thoughts, my actions—since I reconnected with my sister out of fear of losing her again. With that fresh, enlightened lens, Wes seemed the right choice to invite along on tonight's task.

Strange that I'm still thinking about him. On the surface, he seems like every other man I've casually dated until I abruptly end things: attractive, and perhaps attracted to me the more aloof I am. The guys who approach me always seem to enjoy the chase—something I offer in spades.

With Wes, though, when he first spoke to me, something felt different. Magnetic. As if an invisible tether connected us and was pulling me toward him then, to that teasing smile and his flop of dark hair. He's quirky in a way that sets me at ease. Blunt but not awkward. Reassuring, that he doesn't want anything more from me than to chat about school and GMOs in Twinkies. Refreshing, in that I can be my naturally direct self without offending him.

"Hey, stranger." Wes removes his hands from deep in his jeans pockets. "Ready to see the future?"

"Only if it's the good kind."

He holds the glass door open for us, and then we pass through a beaded curtain that announces our arrival. Clairvoyant chic.

"Welcome in, you guys. Looking for a couples reading?" A woman with tight curls and deep lines around her mouth offers up two seats in the tiny one-room shop. She steps behind us to the door and flips around a sign with a clock that reads, BACK IN 10 MINUTES.

Wes shrugs, throwing me a smile. "Your call."

I told him I was looking for information on a friend and that the psychic shop was one of the last places I remembered her frequenting. A total lie for my part, but true for Phuong Nguyen.

The pads of my fingertips itch. I pinch the skin of my other hand to resist the gesture. "Yeah. That would be great. Let's do it."

We settle into two chairs opposite a small table covered in a knit shawl. The psychic sits behind the shawl and a deck of tarot cards.

"On y va," the woman says, cracking her knuckles. "The rate is twenty-five dollars for a ten-minute reading. Does that suit you?"

I nod. "I'm looking for—"

"No, no. Don't tell me." The woman lifts the first card, then places it on the table. "You and this man met recently."

Ah, the couples reading. "Yes. That's true." Obviously. We can't stop grinning at each other, and Wes has almost put his arm around my chair twice before removing it each time.

"Good. Good." The woman hums, then removes another card from the pile. Two people entwined in each other's arms, facing away from where I sit. "You each have things you don't share with the other."

I almost roll my eyes and get up to leave, and then she clears her throat. "And yet, you have those same secretive things in common."

She peers at us, narrowing brown eyes heavily rimmed with liner. The woman plucks another card, then lays it face up on the table. A man hanging upside down on a tree. "You will each stubbornly refuse to tell the other until the time is right."

Another platitude. Great. I'm back to stifling an eye roll, but Wes doesn't seem to mind. He leans forward, as if eating up each empty phrase. Give me a break.

The woman slides a new card face up before us. Two people holding goblets, again facing away from us. "That's interesting. I haven't gotten the two of cups in a while."

"What does that mean?" Wes asks. The rips in his jeans hit just above his knees, and scratches on his skin are evident.

The woman taps the deck of cards but doesn't withdraw another. Not yet. "You're experiencing a lack of communication. An unwillingness to share between you. It also means you two were destined for one another but you may be experiencing some difficulty."

I laugh. I can't help it. "Really? We just met. You don't want to start small and suggest we might have a second date but we'll need to return to your shop to find out what happens three months from now?"

The woman scowls. She's no better at hiding her emotions than I am, apparently. "I said you were destined for one another, meaning you were meant to meet at this point in time. Twin flames collide in life because there is something to be learned from the relationship. Oftentimes the fire dies out. But there is always, always an explosion."

Cold air sends the hairs on my neck upright. As if the spirits of the room agree with this woman's prediction. The memory of first seeing Wes slouching through the Quick Shop returns to mind, tightening my stomach into a ball. Without even speaking to him, I felt the tension coiling in my core as if already in tune with the words this psychic would speak weeks later.

Wes clears his throat, shifting in the barely cushioned chair beside me. "Violet, did you—uh—want to ask about your friend too?"

He wants to leave. The novelty of this outing has worn off for him, and as soon as we cross the threshold to the sidewalk, he'll be gone from my life faster than a package of Corn Nuts.

"Yeah, thanks. I'm also looking for someone. Geri Vega. Does the name sound familiar to you?"

The woman fixes her gaze on the ceiling, which is decorated in paper fans that I recognize from Chinatown celebrations. "Lunar New Year" is written across several in both Chinese characters and English. "Geri Vega . . . you know, it doesn't."

I unlock my phone, scroll to a screenshot I took from a recent live stream. "What about this woman?"

The psychic leans forward. "Geraldine. That's a longtime customer from years ago. What is she up to?"

"That's what I wanted to ask you, actually. Do you keep in touch with her? Does Geri still visit you?"

She folds her arms, sitting back in her wicker chair. The tarot cards are forgotten for the moment. "Gosh, I haven't thought about her in . . . five or so years maybe. She was an amazing client. Consistent, and so sweet."

"Yeah. Look, I'm considering . . . hiring her for a job." I try to appear relaxed, like I'm not retooling the same story from the paper supply store.

"What kind?"

"As a psychic," I blurt out. Both Wes and the woman turn to me. "Yeah. She's . . . Geraldine comes highly recommended, but she said you were a mentor. I wanted to confirm for myself."

Both penciled-in eyebrows lift sky-high. "That's interesting. But the Geraldine I remember was no mystic. I've kept this sweet corner spot in the middle of one of the busiest beaches in the world because I am, and I know the difference between a fake and the real deal."

I shift uncomfortably in my seat. I hope not. "So you're saying Geraldine can't divine the future . . . or whatever?"

The woman taps the discarded cards already on the table, face up. "When she was visiting me regularly, about once a month, she was always asking the same questions that everyone asks: What do I do to kick-start my career to the next level? And how do I solve such and such romantic issue? Geraldine's career, I could talk about for days, but her love-life problems—those weren't going away. I'm surprised she would suggest she's clairvoyant now."

"What kind of love problems? Did she have a boyfriend? Two boy-friends?" If this woman, Geri Vega's secret confidante, spills the dirty details that contradict Vega's innocent image in the limelight, Fiona and I could use them to our advantage. We could discredit her grabs for attention and put this chapter of public excitement behind us.

"Only one." The psychic shakes her head. "The same one, over and over. She would always ask me to contact him and see if he was okay. If he still loved her. If Alicia was okay."

I still. Someone runs past the shop outside, footsteps and music passing in a blur. Voices argue in a huff, and then laughter follows. "Alicia?"

The psychic waves her hand, a set of rings across long fingers. "I think, someone younger than Geraldine. Someone she felt protective over."

Wes's sneaker touches mine, but I don't move away. I can't. My heart tightens in my chest, as sweat forms along my hairline. "And who was the dead boyfriend that Geraldine kept asking you to contact? His name."

She stares at the ceiling again, as if listening or searching the paper fans for a clue. "It starts with an *H* . . ."

"Harold?" Wes volunteers.

"No, not that."

"Hector," he tries again.

"No."

"Horatio?"

The psychic smiles this time. "No, not Horatio." She snaps her fingers. "Henry. Geraldine's boyfriend's name was Henry. And without fail, each time she came to visit, she would ask about him."

My mouth is dry as I reach for the words. "And what did you tell her about him?"

"The truth."

Car doors slam along the curb. Feminine voices rise in a drinking song. "Which is?"

The psychic drops her eyes from the ceiling. She places both hands on the shawl tablecloth, bookending the discarded tarot cards. "That there are many spirits I am in touch with and they help me to seek out the answers my clients want. But this boyfriend never came to me. Not in the dozens of times I called out to him and asked other spirits to seek him for answers. I told her what she didn't want to hear, sadly. And I always wondered if that's why she stopped coming back."

"Tell us."

Brown eyes pinch at the edges. "The boyfriend didn't desire to connect with Geraldine. If he ever loved her on Earth, he certainly didn't in the afterlife."

A lamp fixture covered by a red scarf glows in the cramped space, adding to the eeriness of the psychic's revelations. I pause, absorbing her words. The petty, smug part of me that doesn't get to play in the sandbox very often is eating this conversation up. My dad—even in the great beyond—wanted nothing to do with Geri in a public setting. Serves her right, disrupting our home.

"What about you? Is there someone you wish to speak with?" Wary yet compassionate eyes lock on me from across the table. "I'm sensing there's something missing for you. Whether it's a person or something else. It's a lack of . . . purpose. Does that sound right?"

I glance at Wes, embarrassment replacing the smugness from seconds earlier. "No. I'm fine exactly where I am."

"Are you?" he picks up. "We talked about you doing more things for yourself, instead of prioritizing your sister."

"Nice to know everyone cares so much." I shift in my seat, creaking the legs.

"I'm serious." Wes nods to our spiritual tour guide. "She can sense it after only a few minutes with you."

"Well, what about him?" I throw a thumb at Wes. Adopt an awkward smile. "Doesn't he have some void that needs filling?"

The psychic takes him in a moment, scanning his face. His aura? "No. He's fine. He's fulfilled in whatever his life's vocation is. Very at home in his bones."

I look back and forth at these two people whom I don't know well or at all. Suddenly, this spontaneous visit feels like an intervention. "Good. Glad to hear it. I think I'm ready to leave."

Standing, I pay the woman what I owe her. "Thanks for your time."

"Come back when you're ready. I'm here," she adds, hitting a button on the wireless payment screen of her touch pad. "And I would urge you to do away with whatever isn't serving you—isn't fulfilling you, or moving you toward your goals. Cut away the fat. Whether that's a relationship, an activity, or a job. Make sure to choose you. As Geraldine's boyfriend would probably say, life is too short not to."

Wes and I rejoin the world on the busy sidewalk. In one direction, the pavement leads directly to the ocean. The other leads to my car, my apartment, the art gallery where Fiona invited me to join her for the dress rehearsal tonight, and a few miles farther inland, my college campus.

As we pause outside a crowded bar with open walls that allow music to bleed into the night, Wes takes my hand. He surprises me by touching my index finger, the one whose prints have long since been scarred. "So, should we get a drink? We can toast to you choosing yourself. What will you quit first?"

I smirk at his quick presumption. Then the answer pops into my head faster than I can quell the decision. My smile drops. "School. Let's toast—a mocktail—to my quitting school."

When Professor Tran opined I must be there for the right reasons; when Fiona accused me of never getting the full Janet Seng treatment that included pushing college; when I share in conversation that this is my third attempt at an education—during each of those moments, a nagging suspicion in me pokes its head up: school isn't the answer. Not mine anyway. It was always someone else's expectation that I've been trying to meet. Trying and failing.

Writing came to me before I ever took a college course, and it will be there after I formally withdraw from another. The exploration that comes with writing has already provided more clarity, paying in dividends, than any experience in a lecture hall filled with other confused new adults. And all the realization cost was another wad of cash thrown at the California school system—and a lunch of beef jerky to figure it out.

Maybe now I can finally start feeling as "at home in my bones" as Wes does.

He grins, as wide as when I found him waiting by the psychic's corner shop. "Deal. I'm buying."

Without waiting for an invite, he steps into my personal space. Snakes a hand beneath my hair, then kisses me. Heat flushes my body as his tongue finds my own. I reach from his chest to his neck, tracing his skin with my fingertips. He tastes salty. Delicious. Then sharp pain pierces my lower lip.

"Ow." I jerk backward. I touch the soft flesh and drops of blood come away. "You bit me."

Wes lifts his eyebrows as a slow smile curves half his mouth. "Did I? Sorry."

"Are you always such a—"

He leans down to kiss me again. Softer this time. "Really, sorry. Let's get you a drink to ease the boo-boo."

"With a shit ton of ice."

"The whole bar's worth." As we reach the entrance, Wes holds the door for me to pass inside first. His hand slides to my back. Through the light fabric of my shirt, his fingers caress the vertebrae of my spine.

"What are you doing?" I turn, now unnerved by his touch. I have to shout to be heard over the music.

"You know. Just admiring the latest edition," he says.

"Of my skeleton?"

He smiles. "Your newfound backbone."

26

HENRY

The Wild

Dry leaves twirl in the air, teasing the flames above our campfire. It's been two days since Janet died, and five since we crashed. Two days since the hope left our family, squeezed into the ether like the tube of toothpaste that I've started considering a viable meal option. Two days since we ate the last of the cooked bird meat that Janet kept in the waterproof backpack—emptied out and packed with snow from higher up the mountain. Two days since Janet was snatched from us by some sick plan of Mother Nature. The cruelty of the act has only begun to set in at night when Violet wakes screaming, begging for her mother to save us all and take us away from here.

My mind is going too. Not in an elusive, dementia-diagnosis way, but in the sense that it's wandering. It hasn't done this much exploring, pushing along the boundaries of my consciousness, experimenting with new ideas and images that I know aren't real, since combat. Yesterday, I thought that same snowy owl that attacked the marmot before I could had perched on our log next to Violet while she was writing in her journal, taking down notes from the day. I began to creep toward them both, the knife gripped in my hand—eager for fresh protein—when Fiona shouted, "Dad, what are you doing?"

The moment her shrill voice pierced the scene, the owl disappeared. And I knew I had imagined it perching next to my youngest.

"Dad," Fiona says, softly this time and right next to me. We all three sit beside the fire. "Should we go to bed?"

An animal howls. I stare toward the sound, past the path that we've begun to walk each day when the rain isn't going. Along the rocks that hug the cliff face and climb farther up to reach the summit. Every day, we tried the cell phone's reception from different spots until the battery finally died.

A chill nips the air at moonrise. Birds, turtledoves that Violet seems captivated by, dance back and forth from the tops of two trees within view, and their repetitive melodies spool in five-note loops.

Tremors rip across the ground, an earthquake rumbling from deep beneath my feet—no, an explosion. An enemy blast meant to take more of us out. Where's Captain Perris? He was supposed to radio for reinforcements.

"Dad. Hello?"

I blink. Focus my vision on Janet's smooth, unlined face. She's younger than she should be. Her hair is brown instead of her usual black, her eyes a lighter shade of hazel. I blink again. Fiona's worried expression becomes clear.

"Dad? Are you okay?" she asks. "Is this one of those . . . episodes?"

The recurring bouts of PTSD after I was discharged were brutal. They didn't let up for a solid year, while Fiona was running and giggling around the house, nimble on five-year-old feet. I had trouble discerning whether a kid was racing around the halls or if a dust-covered soldier—American or otherwise—was gasping for air, begging for help. Falling to the ground. The latest casualty of a war led by fully fed men in cushioned offices. A war of rations that had long since dwindled to nothing.

"No," I reply to my daughter. "No, those haven't happened in ages. How's your sister?"

Violet hasn't moved from the passenger seat of the cockpit for hours. She's wrapped in the blanket her mother wore during the flight. I saw her burying her face in it and at first thought she was crying, using the fabric as a pillow or tissue. Then she inhaled down to her toes, breathed in the remnants of her mother's scent.

My heart splintered again then, for the umpteenth time out here. Geri would say I was demonstrating how much I love my girls. But the heartbreak was for myself as much as for the kids. Janet handled everything regarding their needs—our family's needs—and I was an asshole to disregard all she did for us. To take her for granted and bitch and moan about how she doesn't wear lingerie anymore to other younger women who do.

Another rumble unfurls along the ground. "Did you hear that?" I ask Fiona.

"No." A single-word reply. I'm making her nervous. I recall the same anxious glances from Janet back during the heyday of the episodes—from my military superiors in the desert.

Violet stirs, swinging her legs over the side of the plane. "Daddy?"

"Yeah, Vi."

"Are you leaving us too?" Violet nods to the knife and the tarp in my hand. I found another, smaller version of the one we set up as a lean-to against the metal body of the Cessna, behind a spare wheel in the storage compartment.

"Yes. But I'll come back soon. With dinner." I smile but she looks unconvinced. "Have you been writing in your journal?"

Violet has been scribbling, doodling as any seven-year-old might in the notebook Janet gave her. But she's also been writing letters, apparently. Fiona suggested it, and Violet seems calmed by the act.

Violet nods. "My pen isn't working, though."

"Oh yeah? Let me see."

She hands me the black clicking-style pen. I give it a good shake, wet it with my tongue, then hold out my palm for the notebook. Violet hesitates, but she passes it to me. I open to the last page, which is blank. A quick scratch across the white page produces a solid dark line.

"There we go. I think it's working now." I hand the pen back to Violet. A small smile lightens the heavy grief she wears. "Why don't you write down today's date? Keep a log for us. So we can look back on this and see how far we've come once we're back home."

"Okay, Daddy."

"There's a girl." The note I read in Violet's journal—*Mommy told me the truth*—is seared into my thoughts. Yet without a moment alone with the girl, I haven't been able to question her. What could Janet possibly have told Violet that was otherwise secret? What did Janet know? Was it about me?

"So, where are you going?" Fiona starts again. "It's almost nighttime. You shouldn't go walking around out there in the dark. You could trip on something and fall, or—" She stops short. "You shouldn't go out right now."

"We need to eat something. I didn't get anything yesterday, but I know for a fact there are animals out there and close by. I just need to be faster. Cleverer."

I brace myself for a biting comment from my teenager, something about how we don't have *that* kind of time, but Fiona is silent. She hugs her elbows—which seem pointier in less than a week. "I'll be back before long."

Instead of taking my usual route—which the animals probably all watch with amusement at this point, from the safety of their hiding places—I climb up. The incline is steep, not at all easy for this desk-job junkie, but natural footholds in the mountainside make the climb doable. After about thirty feet, I reach a narrow plateau along a cliff's edge that winds around and then drops me from above into the wooded copse I stalked the small bear—marmot—in.

A thicket of grass grows on the curve of the hill, shrouded by tall conifers that provide additional coverage. I set the tarp on the ground, folding it so that a square will separate my pants from the saturated earth, then drop down with my knife in my lap. I wait. Night falls quickly, just as Fiona said it would.

Something chirps nearby. A deeper, more clipped noise than what the birds make. There's a frog up here hidden in the brush. Do I know how to cook frog? You just eat the legs, don't you? No, for the effort it would take to hunt it down and then the minimal payoff of two scrawny meat pops, I'll pass.

More time goes by while the dark clouds of the week shift, allowing moonlight to shine on the valley below. I saw the pack of wolves yesterday, prowling in a southeast direction for prey, but there was no sign of them this morning. Are wolves nocturnal?

Grunting rises from below, its source hidden by thick trees. Whining reaches my ears. Hope swells in my chest, and I grip the knife more tightly. Dinner.

It's been five days. That's 120 hours since we lost contact with the tower. There must be a search underway for us, but how much has weather stymied those efforts? Rain has pummeled this area, making a search on foot a nonstarter and any aerial views completely obscured.

The time to act is now. Now, while I still have the energy to wrestle whatever is necessary to the ground. While I still have my focus and my perspective clear, unconstrained by the episodes that came to me in the desert.

I don't know why they've returned to me here, when I need to be focused for the kids, more than I need to breathe. Though I haven't always been a good father—so far from it, the opposite idea is laughable—I can provide the basics for my family, what's left of it. As long as no one goes walking across slippery rocks in the rain, I can keep everyone who remains safe.

Rising to my feet, I step through the grass carefully, slowly. Almost into a pile of logs—bones, I note—but I sidestep them just in time.

When we get back home to San Diego, I'm going to do everything differently. I won't leave Geri—not exactly—but I'll put a pause on our romantic relationship. With any luck, she received my note that I sent at the last minute in the mail, inviting her to meet me up north—like the brazen, self-involved jerk I am. Hopefully she's a part of the search for us. Maybe she will offer some help there.

Whimpering continues as I approach the meadow. Growling. Jaws snap when I reach the edge of the clearing. Animals tussle with something hidden behind their pack of bodies and the raised hackles of fur. Wolves. The largest one barks orders to the rest, while it circles something they all seem entranced by. A smaller wolf, the runt of the pack, backs up out of the fray, then lifts its snout to the sky. A howl reverberates against the mountain behind me, silencing the forest.

Fear trips across my skin at seeing these beasts so close—and so near my kids, who are not two hundred yards behind me. My breath hitches, and I know I can't attack a pack. I'll be done before I raise my knife. So much for dinner options. Even if I were to sneak away and attack another marmot, the scent of blood is likely to bring these dogs quickly.

I'm screwed. I'll be three days without food tomorrow. My girls are already lethargic, the snappy comebacks slower from Fiona and the listlessness amped on Violet. We're going to die out here. Either the next time one of us wanders too far from camp when the wolf pack is in hot pursuit of prey, or from hunger. More likely, from hunger.

White dots flash across my vision. I shield my eyes as if the sun beats down across my shoulders. The green landscape turns gray, then yellow, in the moonlight, until sand dunes take shape.

Enemy soldiers flank a wounded member of their squad. Words I don't understand are exchanged, and then an explosion hits their base. All heads turn toward the sound, away from where I crouch. They disperse. They left their compatriot behind.

White dots flicker, the sun relentless. Heat douses my shoulders; then—curiously—cold air winds across my neck. I shiver as I approach the body.

He's dead, likely by a day or two. His leg was nearly severed by one of the IEDs lurking across the region, lying in wait for either a local soldier or American enemy. Better him than me.

A patch across his shoulder in English reads "Bahrain." I speak the word aloud. "Bahrain. Bahrain." It sounds like "brain," or maybe "Brian" in my American accent.

Since I was separated from my unit, the minimal rations I kept on my person are all that I've had to sustain me. The soldiers who just fled, or the wild boars that keep harassing my unit's camp, seem to have the same food problem. An arm of the cadaver has been stripped to the bone.

I find my government-issued knife already clutched in my hand, as if it had the idea before me. Hunger pains cramp my stomach, forcing me to double over.

———

When I wake, the campfire flames lick the soles of my shoes. I feel strangely sated. Calm. Refreshed. Instead of the blazing sunshine burning through my clothing from every angle, sharp cold hugs my back where I'm seated on a flat tarp on the ground. I'm at the crash site. Did I ever leave?

Movement across the logs draws my attention. Fiona and Violet. They look away from me, as if I just said something awkward. Or I reprimanded them. Shame seems to draw their young faces long—or maybe that's the shadows dancing across pale skin beneath the moon. Violet fiddles with her pen in her lap.

The forest is silent all around us. Did the wolves leave?

"Girls," I begin in a gravelly voice. I clear my throat. "What happened?"

Fiona narrows her eyes, though she doesn't turn toward me. "What do you mean?"

"I mean, how long was I away? Is the pen giving you trouble again, Violet? Here, let me—" I reach for her, but my youngest jerks away like I slapped her.

"The ink dried up," she whispers. "My pen is dead."

I pause. The journal was the one thing that was keeping Violet occupied—keeping her from panicking as I think Fiona and I have a few times. "How long have I been sitting here?"

At this, both girls stiffen. Violet continues to stare at her hands, while Fiona's upper lip curls. "Long enough that we watched you eat that."

She nods to my lap. Meat sizzles on a stick like a prehistoric kebab. Moisture sits in visible droplets across the seared top layer. My mouth waters, despite the obvious bite marks along the edge of the meat suggesting that I've already consumed a good amount.

"What is it?" I ask.

Fiona dips her head, holding my eye contact in an ominous stare. A breeze rolls through the clearing, ruffling the hair of my neck.

"That's what we'd like to know."

27

FIONA

My living room is overcome with art, suffocating from it. Each of these pieces has been painstakingly reviewed and adjusted, then glued into submission. I don't know if it will be enough to please the critics and to earn me a few more fans, but I'm proud of what I've created. Our time in the wild will always be with me, in three-dimensional—four-dimensional—memories that cause me to sometimes sweat at night during my dreams.

Even the mountain piece evokes the awe I felt, once down in the valley below, surveying the strange ridge that encompassed our whole world. I layered twigs and leaves across the base, achieving the sense of mystery, serenity, and foreboding that twisted together when I stared up at the spectrum of its majesty. The pine cone that seemed like such a good idea earlier still refuses to line up exactly parallel as the summit, but perfection is the enemy of progress. I'm almost there, at least.

Tomorrow, the Hughes Gallery will feature my work. Darleen will be charming anyone who shows interest over wine and small plates of dumplings. She's said that the New York art scene has begun to fly in today, a few of the reviewers and art collectors reaching out for one-on-one meet and greets. Right now, she's eating in a rooftop restaurant in the Gaslamp with Benny Zimmer, telling him how there's already a proverbial line around the block to snatch up a "souvenir of the girl-survivors." I wish she would stop using that phrasing, but Darleen insists on it. She says once we reach a certain echelon in the art world, we can start dismissing the direct link to my time in the wild, and my talent can stand on its own. Until then—until the Venice Biennale comes calling—I should indulge the rubberneckers. Considering one of them called me out for lying on camera, I'm not too fond of them these days.

I stand at my dining table, fiddling with the mountain installation for the hundredth time. A small branch that seemed to draw the eye perfectly, near the peak, now appears obtrusive.

Daley Kelly's angry expression when he confronted me at the restaurant behind the gallery almost three weeks ago has lingered in my head. It was difficult, nearly impossible, for me to keep a straight face as he interrogated me—made it clear he didn't believe my story thanks to some first responder's offbeat detail that we had a campfire going when we were rescued. When Daley touched my hand, I was so startled I blurted out a truth I've managed to keep tucked beneath my tongue for years: there's more to the story than what I've publicly shared.

My parents didn't die the first night. And while he doesn't have any proof of it—only my verbal admission that details from the ordeal remain hidden—if Daley is half the truth hound he said he is, I don't think he's going to stop until he gets it.

I inhale a deep breath through my nose, then release it slowly. Marshall lifts his head from the couch. "I'm fine. Really," I add.

Although I would feel better if Violet hadn't stood me up last week at the gallery for the dress rehearsal. Ever since she decided to write her memoirs, instead of focusing on school and getting through the current media blitz, she's been MIA—physically present, though not emotionally sometimes.

She called me an hour after she was supposed to show. The noise was so loud in the background, I could barely hear her. She was in a bar. As a man's voice leaned in and said, "Everything okay?," Violet imparted the gist of it: she went to the psychic that Phuong Nguyen told us about and saw for herself what bought Geri's trust and confidence. The fact that Geri tried to reach out to our father through the psychic and that she never received a response didn't give me any satisfaction. While Violet seemed pleased, almost gleeful that Geri was left hanging by the afterlife, the whole thing just struck me as sad. Odd, that anyone would place such importance and power on one specific person, or medium, or whatever. Probably, Geri Vega was seeking out any emotional support that could be gleaned from a perfect stranger. It made me wonder about her family—about my father, for the way she seems so heartbroken in all her interviews, each of which I've watched. Whether Henry Seng could have actually loved someone more than himself.

Marshall lifts his head, then whimpers toward the door leading to my driveway. No one is out there, at least not visible from the window beside my dining table. The door is open but the screen door locked, per usual.

"You okay?" I ask my roommate. Marshall continues to stare outside, as if seeing something that I don't.

I cross to where he sits perched. Together we watch the back door to my house. A long pause passes between us. "There's nothing there, buddy."

After ensuring the pine cone is secure—that it won't topple to the base of my mountain—I grab my car keys. I slide into my driver's seat, leaving Marshall at home to tussle with a rope chew toy he prefers during happy hour.

Violet and I have made serious progress in uncovering just who Geri Vega is and why she would want to upend our lives again. The other part of our plan—to convince Daley Kelly to tell our story sympathetically and not accusatorily—has gone less well. He's avoided each of my calls, but texted that he'll clear his schedule for me when I'm ready to tell "the whole story." I owe it to the adult I've become—the artist, who's worked her ass off to be something more than a hashtag for oglers—to try again, one last time before the gallery show, which takes place tomorrow.

The route to North Park and Daley's editing studio is jam-packed with afternoon traffic and bustling sidewalks. I pass a to-go tent set up in the parking lot of a taco shop, a singer busking on the corner, and a group of schoolchildren advertising a car wash in the middle of November. My mother used to love University Avenue. She would say you could walk down the length of North Park and find everything your heart and stomach desired, often bringing us here for the farmers' market on weekends.

Wedged on the second floor of a commercial building with a walk-way balcony, the business logo on Daley's website—a camera and a trio of birds flying overhead—is evident in the clear front door. Daley Productions, Inc.

Weeks ago, when Daley asked, he got express permission from Quincy, as the gallery owner, and me to film my show. Termination clauses were watered down in exchange for me getting final approval of how my art is featured on film. Pages of paperwork were signed before trust was broken between us—on both sides. I have to be ready for Daley to join and capture the culmination of my artistic career on camera for whatever purpose he decides.

I climb the steps.

A small front room is empty, save for a black leather love seat and, above it, a framed panoramic-style photo of the San Diego harbor. Water bubbles in a dispenser tank opposite the love seat, beside a no-frills coffee machine on a small end table. Written in black marker, a sign is taped to the next door and reads, EDITING IN PROCESS. PLEASE TAKE A SEAT.

Part of me hesitates—doesn't actually desire to screw up anyone's morning, knowing all too well how the artistic process can be hampered by a single interruption. The other part of me knows down to my Doc Martens that Daley is planning something for my show that I won't like.

I rip open the door to the next room, taken by surprise at how lightweight it is. Daley sits in a computer chair before three large monitors, each illuminated and frozen on a scene of Geri Vega midsentence. Because, of course.

"Fiona? What are you doing here?" Daley squeaks.

"I need to talk to you. Are you still planning to film the gallery tomorrow night?"

Daley glances behind me. "I am. Did you just come here to ask that? You could have texted. I'm kind of in the middle of something."

He does a double take, then clicks on a laptop and makes the screens disappear. "Look, if you're getting cold feet about having my crew there for your show, you already signed release forms. We've got notices that we're going to put up to notify attendees that they may be recorded. This is happening, with or without your enthusiasm."

"But you don't believe my story—my account—anymore."

"No, I don't." Daley doesn't blink. "And since we last saw each other, I met with Geri Vega."

I pause. "I know. You said you wouldn't do that. When Violet and I agreed to film with you, you said—"

"And you said you'd tell me the facts." Daley scoffs. "I think it's clear by now that we both fibbed. Plus, Geri has information that puts your experience in a totally different light. I think you'd benefit from having a face-to-face—"

"On camera, right?"

"Right." He grimaces. "I'd be happy to record you telling the *real* details of your story without her, but neither you nor Violet is willing."

"What did Vega tell you? Why believe her over us?"

Daley leans forward in his wheeled computer chair. "If I told you, I'd have to film you."

A sneer lifts my upper lip. My fists tremble. "So . . . you won't be coming to the gallery with a positive perspective. As a fan. You'll be filming to prove . . . what? That I have been profiting from my parents' deaths, just like the online trolls suggest?"

My chest tightens as I speak my greatest fear about presenting my art alone, without any other artist to act as a buffer. I've worked so hard for this, forgoing relationships and friendships in order to reach this point in my career. Although, if I'm being as honest as Daley keeps insisting I be, I've probably used my work ethic as an excuse to avoid forming bonds with others. Darleen, my art dealer who has a monetary interest in my productivity, is my closest friend.

The chair creaks beneath Daley's weight. "Once initial filming is complete, I'll use all the footage I have to create the best, most factual narrative as I know it. My duty is to my viewers, and everyone else who considers documentary film as the last sacred space of storytelling."

His glare softens until he merely looks disappointed. I'm reminded how charming he seemed when he first tracked me down during the gallery's paint night—and how I've fallen so far in his graces. Under other circumstances, I might have asked him out.

"I get that. But if you really are after the truth about our experience for your viewers, you also have to present the facts about Geri Vega." I nod to the now-dormant screens.

Daley straightens. "And what does that mean?"

"Have you done any background checks on the woman?"

"I've checked out her version of the events—"

"Or has all your time been spent sniffing out inconsistencies in my story? There's little difference between my parents dying on impact and succumbing to their injuries twelve hours later."

I inhale through my nose. The emotions I've kept bottled up since I was a teen, trying to preserve myself, begin to bubble, percolate in my throat, pinching the space behind my jaw.

"I disagree," Daley says. "There's a big difference if, during those twelve hours, it means someone facilitated one or both of those deaths along."

Shock spirals down my back. "What are you trying to say? That I—that Violet—"

Is he actually suggesting that two children could kill their parents—and under such unique circumstances as ours? Why would he think that?

Daley tilts his head to the side, watching me. "I'm saying that Geri Vega has been up-front about everything that she knows—just twenty-five years later than she should have been transparent. Including her extramarital affair with your dad. You haven't been as clear, and that calls into question everything you previously shared."

"Only if you're seeking out the drama." I shake my head, still reeling from this man's implication. "If you're here for the views, the likes, the fifteen minutes of f—"

Daley gets to his feet, pushing his chair into the desk. "What is your problem, Fiona? You know you lied on camera. You lied to me. I thought we shared something, some—I don't know. I liked you."

His words are a gouge to my heart, echoing the emotion that's been simmering in me from the moment he appeared on the restaurant patio to pitch his film to us. I haven't stopped thinking about his hand on mine since the catering tasting. Just after he dropped his investigatory bombs. "I felt it too."

"But all that's changed—if what I suspect is true." Daley spreads his feet wide.

"Which is?" I speak slowly. On the cusp of dangerous territory.

My interview. That must be what has Daley so convinced I'm hiding more. He can't be jeopardizing the cooperation of the girl-survivors based on the slight admission that there's more to my experience than what I've shared. Or whatever nonsense Geri Vega is offering up.

The experience of filming should have been mundane for me, in my living room, recounting what I've rehearsed and performed dozens of times. However, clearly I said something unusual to Daley. Off-putting. And I really don't remember sharing anything different from the most recent interview with the police—who, come to think of it, were also intrigued by what Geri Vega was shouting from the media rooftops. I'm off-balance.

Right now, I would kill to review the full footage myself, rather than the snippet Daley allowed me to watch at the restaurant.

Daley purses his lips into a tight line. "Geri said your father hasn't been given his proper due."

"More riddles."

"She said . . . She shared something that changes everything." He pauses. "And if you knew this and you didn't tell me, you didn't tell the police—you're not leaving me much choice, Fiona."

Sweat dots my hairline. My chest. He knows. She knows. "Geri Vega is not some innocent, reporting the news in a snap of altruism. She hurt people. She stole money from a friend and business partner."

"Did she?" Daley nods too fast to suggest he believes me. "Well, I'll look into it. If you don't have anything else to say for yourself—about *you*, Fiona—then I'll thank you for stopping by."

"I'm serious. She owes thousands of dollars to a man we spoke with, and she spent at least that amount with a psychic. There's another angle for your film that's worth exploring."

"Maybe. But Geri wasn't stranded in the wilderness with your family. And she didn't walk out on her own two feet when two people, your parents, died."

I stare at Daley. A man I don't really know at all. "What are you going to do with my interview? With Violet's?"

"I'm not concerned with Violet yet."

"Then what are you planning to do with mine?"

Daley narrows his eyes. "I've got work to do, Fiona. Please leave."

"Are you—would you go to the police with it?"

"I don't know. Should I?"

"You—I—I'm not." My words come up short. Running water whooshes through a pipe in the wall beside me, the only noise in the editing room for a moment.

I lick my lips. Steel myself to appear convincing. "I told you every-thing that I already told them. Many times."

Daley shakes his head. "If only that were true."

"What did I say?" I finally blurt out. "Why do you think whatever it is is so incriminating? Why are you doing this?"

Daley punches the air. "Because this is the story I always dreamed of telling! It's what drove me to study film. I believe in this documentary down to my bones and that some good can come of it. I believe in it so much that I fronted most of the money when my investors wouldn't cover the rest. And *now*, now that the girl-survivors have pulled their support of my doc, those investors have withdrawn."

Bright-blue eyes are wild as he pauses. "If I don't have the fam-ily's blessing anymore, then it's not your version of the truth I have to represent. I'm focused on making the best damn documentary I can. Otherwise, I've got nothing. And my career has slipped down the sewer."

"So, you're going to do whatever it takes, then. Even if it means you hurt the people you're supposedly trying to help."

"I'll be at the gallery show, if that's what you mean."

"And if you don't get the footage you want? If you get turned away by a hulking bodyguard I hire to be on watch for you?"

Daley purses his lips. "There's more than one way to strip an air-plane of its materials."

Without waiting for my reply, he steps past me to open the door. I follow him, crossing to the walkway outside, where the door shuts behind me. The dead bolt turns.

A handful of hours remain until my show tomorrow, each of which I need for one reason or another. I descend the outdoor staircase to the ground level and my car. Uncertainty zips in my head, my torso, tightening my stomach.

Daley is convinced I've done something wrong—Geri Vega certainly is. And as much as I'd like to stay and argue the opposite, I slide into the driver's seat of my car.

The entrance to the 8 freeway is unregulated this time of day. I fly past the darkened stoplight. Once I am enveloped by the roar of high-speed traffic, I inhale a breath that feels like it might fracture a rib. Then I release a scream.

28

FIONA

Interview Transcript

Fiona Seng: Are you recording? Should I look—? Where should I look?

Daley Kelly: Yup, you're just going to talk to me. Right here. Yeah, don't even look at the camera. I mean, unless you want to address the audience. Then, go for it.

FS: Got it. Okay.

DK: Okay, ready?

FS: Yes.

DK: Let's start by you stating your name and what your profession is.

FS: My name is Fiona Lang Fa Seng. And I'm an artist.

DK: What art do you create? Tell us about it.

FS: I mean, I could talk about it for hours. [Laughs] I make modern sculpture using materials I find out-doors. Oftentimes—well, most often—I find myself influenced by my . . . adolescence.

DK: Tell us about that. The origins of your art.

FS: [Inhales] Well, it's . . . uh . . .

DK: Whenever you're ready.

FS: I've done this a lot, so— [Laughs] Yeah, okay. When I was thirteen, my parents decided we should do a family trip to Calgary. Four days in British Columbia. They had never been, and growing up in San Diego, we—my sister, Violet, and I—had never spent a ton of time in the snow. I mean, we had gone up to Mount High and even Big Bear, but it just wasn't a regular oc-currence. This was going to be an exotic experience, my parents promised.

DK: And what else was exotic about it? About your mode of getting there?

FS: Yes. [Makes a noise] Of course. That was one of the most interesting parts, and the one that really captivat-ed investigators later—the airplane. My dad had just obtained his pilot's license for small, private aircraft, and he wanted to fly us himself.

DK: Did that make anyone nervous? Your mother?

FS: Yeah, we were too young to know how . . . unusual it was, in hindsight. But my mom, Janet. Yeah, she was nervous. I think she trusted my dad, implicitly—they were extremely tight, never had a fight in their life together. But I remember on the day we took off, she kept fiddling with her prayer beads.

DK: Prayer beads?

FS: Her rosary. She kind of rolled them around in her hand that day, like the action was calming to her. She also could have simply been stressed out with preparing to take a vacation and packing three suitcases. My dad packed his own, at least.

DK: I'm kind of jumping ahead here, but do you think your dad intended for . . . any of this . . . to happen? There's been speculation in the past that your dad may have wanted to leave your mom.

FS: My parents argued from time to time, but they loved each other. They would do anything for each other, and they valued each other as equals.

DK: Okay.

FS: Anyway, my dad was a good pilot. We figured out later that what happened next wasn't his fault.

DK: What happened next?

FS: We were almost to Canada, and flying over Washington State. Everything was fine. Normal for a four-seater plane. A bit of turbulence occasionally that felt like a kiddie ride at a carnival. If we looked down, then we knew we weren't on any kind of controlled amusement attraction. It's kind of wild to recall it.

DK: In what way?

FS: Similar to a roller coaster, in a Cessna airplane, you start climbing upward, and you're watching the ground and kind of processing how high up you're going—but in a ride, then you reach the summit and you drop down on a track with all the other scream-ing passengers. In the Cessna, it felt and looked just like a roller coaster in that you're practically outdoors. Without the massive hull of a major airline aircraft that's ferrying hundreds of people in a pressurized fake-indoor setting. You have about a foot—let's say, two feet—of aluminum, insulation, wiring, and other stuff I'm sure, that separates you from the literal clouds that you're passing through.

DK: What did you see up there? How high up were you?

FS: I think we were at ten thousand feet. So, not nearly as high up as commercial planes.

DK: And what did you see up there when you looked down?

FS: [Laughs] I tried not to. At first, I watched the ground become smaller and blurrier until the earth became squares of brown and green. Then I could no longer tell where we were, what state we were flying over, or how long we had been in the air. It all seemed to blend together up there. At one point, though, after I fell asleep and then woke up, I glanced out below—saw the brown-and-green patchwork quilt, between holes in the clouds—and nearly lost it. I was so panicked for a moment that all that was keeping us aloft was an engine I could wrap my arms around, in a passenger plane that my dad borrowed from a friend.

DK: And what happened then?

FS: Then is why I've thrown myself into my art. To kind of continue to process what happened.

DK: Which is?

FS: The gas cap came undone, leaking all of our fuel to the sky. Then we began to drop.

DK: Talk about that. About the drop, after the engine cut out.

FS: It's . . . everything you think it might be. Everything you imagine in your nightmares. It's the sudden drop that never resumes the climb. The drop just continues as a free fall, with your heart always dragging behind the rest of your body, slightly higher in your throat than it would normally rest in your chest.

DK: Mmm.

FS: You know? Maybe that's too poetic. But it felt that way.

DK: Then what happened? After you landed.

FS: Well, I blacked out. The first night out in the wild, my parents died. Almost instantly with the crash. It was—

DK: Sorry . . . During the crash, you blacked out?

FS: During the crash and afterward.

DK: . . . For the entirety of the three months that followed?

FS: No, let me try again. I meant that I lost around a day's worth of time. I don't recall the crash, my parents dying in the landing, or that first night. It all happened really fast, relatively speaking. I know in hindsight that I was moving, affecting things; Violet and I ended up eating some snacks before we ever left the airplane. But I don't remember any of that.

DK: Did your parents cry out when you crashed? Or did they die on impact?

FS: I don't know.

DK: Did you get snacks for all four of you? Or just you and Violet?

FS: I don't know—I mean, just me and Violet. It's hard to recall, since I was in a daze. The memories that I have from that time are fuzzy.

DK: Are they a blur or nonexistent?

FS: Nonexistent, I think. As much as they are when you're awake but you have no memory of doing anything.

DK: So you were . . . sleepwalking, then?

FS: I guess. I don't really know. Probably?

DK: And while you were sleepwalking, you ate, you drank, you helped your little sister out probably, and tried to care for your parents as they lay dying or injured, and then you managed to get out of the plane?

FS: Yes.

DK: But I thought your parents died on impact? You said they died during the landing?

FS: They did. I'm sorry . . . did I say something wrong? You're all looking at me kind of . . . differently. What did I say?

DK: Nothing. You did great. So you are stranded out there alone with your little sister for several months. Tell us about that.

FS: Uh, yeah. It was awful. I try not to think of the details too often. Lots of wandering, searching for help. Lots of despairing and then waking up and doing it all over again.

DK: What was your saving grace? How did you get rescued?

FS: Um. Hikers. They . . . uh, they spotted us through some crazy miracle. We made a fire—to keep warm, you know—and they saw the smoke.

DK: Fascinating. Thank you for sharing your story with us. I know that wasn't easy.

FS: No, actually. It wasn't.

29

Violet

Distinct and stoned
A path to time alone
She lures me closer with a smile
Gray cushions her frame
Two rocks' ringing blame
Tears from heaven ping the tile
I had to let go

Typing out the last line on my phone, I review the poem I wrote while stuck in traffic coming back from the registrar's office to officially withdraw from classes. The overall vibe is haunting, and it's exactly as I feel myself: haunted by what-ifs, by things left unsaid. After realizing I may have seen my mother dying, the image of stones along a moss-covered path surfaced in my mind.

In my apartment, I lay my head against the soft, squishy backrest of my couch. Stare at the bumpy design of my ceiling. A crack formed sometime over the last month, when I know it wasn't there before.

Leaving campus and saying goodbye for good to the beige buildings, I felt conflicted. Regret that it took yet another attempt at higher education to confirm it's not for me. And gratitude that this round introduced me to some interesting reads, and Professor Tran. As she mentioned in one of the first lectures I attended: creative writing in particular is so helpful to reveal details in our subconscious that we may have forgotten. "Kind of like therapy in that way," she added.

Ah, therapy. Fiona might be more open to me recording my memories if I told her it was the only therapy I would ever accept. Since I bailed on the gallery dress rehearsal last week, she hasn't called to check in. She's definitely pissed. I'm sure hearing Wes yell in my ear at the bar while I was on the phone with her didn't help.

Fiona's fear of me writing my memoirs is unfounded. Although she's harped on the dangers of it practically each time I've seen her, my sister should stop conflating my memoirs—and controlling our narrative in the public space—with full transparency. My writing will be anything but. It's more about the journey for me, rather than some desire to share my thoughts in stream of consciousness.

I check my phone. No new messages, although Wes said he would be here ten minutes ago. Irritation arm wrestles with worry as I wonder if he got lost or if he's stuck in traffic. Or maybe he decided he didn't want to see me again after our last interaction, when I snapped at him for biting my lip.

The haiku I scribbled on a sticky note during breakfast returns:

> Never more than here
> Always wading in past tense
> Sure of catharsis

My phone pings where it sits on my coffee table by my feet. A notification that VeryGeri posted a new video. "Another one? Doesn't this woman have a job?"

After our visit to Phuong-the-prince-of-paper and the psychic, I watched all Geri Vega's posted and shared content on social media.

Searched for the lies she's told and the half-truths she's touched upon. Fiona is the artist, but I think after my hours of scrolling, I could sketch a lifelike portrait of Geri Vega's face.

I open my Instagram app. Seems I've been watching her posts and her favorite hashtag—#GirlSurvivors—a little too closely, as the algorithm lands her latest reel at the top of my feed.

Geri sits opposite the camera, speaking to someone just out of sight. She wears the same outfit I saw in a post a few days ago, so this must have been filmed by Daley Kelly during that time. The bottom-feeders.

She speaks earnestly, adopting the same heartbroken yet determined expression she wears to spout lies in each video on her grid. "I've tried and tried and tried now. Each effort to connect with those girls—excuse me, women—has been rebuffed. You know? I wouldn't do this if my hands weren't tied."

"'Do this'? What does that mean?" the interviewer asks, though curiously not in Daley's voice.

Geri purses her full mouth. "Get their attention. I've gone to their homes, had representatives reach out for a meeting, and done all these media placements, but Violet and Fiona have ignored every one."

At least she's admitting to stalking us, confirming the tickle on my neck that keeps me peering over my shoulder.

"And I really wouldn't say this about someone I cared for if it weren't true: Henry Seng, their father and the pilot of their plane, was not in the right headspace to be flying them all."

"In what sense?"

"Well . . ." Geri hesitates. "In the sense that he was acting increasingly out of character during the weeks before the flight. Forgetting things, confusing things. Calling me other names."

"Can you go into more detail?"

She shakes her head, bouncing her soft curls. "I can't. This is information that his daughters need to hear first."

"Why come forward after all this time? Why now?"

Geri dips her chin. "Honestly? I held out hope that Henry was still alive. That he would contact me somehow."

"But he never did," adds the interviewer.

"No. No, he didn't—"

I close out the app before another word can slip through my phone's speakers.

"Not even when you kept pestering him in the afterlife." I smile, taking joy in the little—petty—things. "The world is going to figure out very soon that you're a liar, Geri Vega. An unstable charlatan who pretends to be kind and compassionate but then steals money from clients and throws it all at the ether while searching for dead people and someone named—"

Alicia. The person the psychic confirmed Geri asked about in their sessions. And according to Fiona, a person I once hung up on while using the landline phone as a seven-year-old. Did Geri know—care for—my dad's first girlfriend, Alicia? Did my dad have two girlfriends the summer before our flight? Although I visited the psychic over a week ago, I still haven't worked out what Geri's familiarity with Alicia might mean.

A knock sounds at my door. I cross to it, then find Wes, appearing unbothered and unhurried in my peephole.

"Hey, you found it," I say, stepping back to allow him to enter.

"Now I see why you're at the Quick Shop so often. It's practically your backyard."

"Why do you go there?" I ask as he pauses between my living room and kitchen. "Or is that you on the floor above me, always ranting about more applesauce and cartoons?"

He does me the courtesy of a laugh. "I have a mailbox at the UPS office about a mile from here."

Interesting. He doesn't give out his physical address to just anybody.

"So what's this research you need help with?" Wes walks with heavy footsteps to my L-shaped couch and coffee table. He slides onto the middle corner seat like he's been here hundreds of times. I smile, taking in the image of him in my personal space.

"Yeah, I need information relating to Geri Vega and a woman named Alicia."

Wes claps his hands and points at me. "So that's why we went to a psychic to tell us about your . . . new prospective psychic. I knew I was missing something." He grins.

"And what's that?"

"Alicia. She's your cousin or something, right? You reacted all"— Wes opens his eyes wide—"when our psychic mentioned the name last week."

"Not my cousin. But thanks for the zombie impression."

"No? I could have sworn otherwise." The grin lessens. "You don't really talk about your family."

"Neither do you," I reply. We've hung out twice since our visit to Pacific Beach, each time meeting for bare-bones tacos, while skirting the topic of my sister. Instead of more personal issues, we discussed school. And the flawed expectation that we all must succeed—be productive members of society. I open my laptop, then close out a window tab in my browser regarding legal terms. Click a new tab.

"That's easy. I have an older brother, who I don't talk to, and my dad, who I don't talk to."

I pause scanning images of women named Alicia on a website that offers "your heart's desire." If what you desire is kink. "Are you from San Diego?"

Wes shakes his head, and long wavy hair catches across his forehead. There's something about his scent here in my apartment—a confined space. The smell is earthy, pungent. Nothing like when I normally see him outside or in an airy bar. "Milwaukee."

"Wow. How did you get out here?"

"Hitchhiking, mostly. But once I arrived, I got an apartment and enrolled in school. It's been a strange year."

"Sounds like it."

"What about your family? Granted, Alicia isn't a cousin. Is she your mother?" Wes scrolls on his phone, so he doesn't see the flash of pain across my face. He hasn't hinted at knowing my past, but that doesn't mean he's not fully dialed in.

"No. Just someone I'd like to get in touch with."

"Did she wrong you? I saw you searched for 'defamation' earlier. If you brought libel charges against her, you could probably get a pro bono lawyer to take your case. That's what I learned in Business Law 201, at least." Wes cracks his knuckles. "Do you have anything to eat?"

"Do I have any beef jerky?" I tease. "Wait here."

He does, while I retrieve a rope of it I bought yesterday. I fix up a plate of sauces that I've been working on—my homemade Dijon mustard, a cream-based dill dip, and peanut butter mixed with turmeric—then deliver the spread to the coffee table.

Wes raises both eyebrows. "Are you a chef?"

I laugh. "So far from it."

Although with each chapter I finish writing, I feel more creative across the board. I guess I've always loved unique twists on food.

While he digs in to the options I brought, he tells me about the latest psychology course he dropped because it "wasn't serving" him. I can't help smiling while I listen—amused by this philosophizing twentysomething and also wishing I had his self-assurance.

"If something isn't benefiting you, you got to let it go. You know?" He licks his fingers.

"Yeah. That lesson is starting to take hold." I look up from my laptop to find Wes peering at me.

He slides from the couch down to the floor. Joins me where I sit at my coffee table.

"When you invited me over today, for the first time, I didn't know what to expect." He gives a soft laugh. He slides a hand across my thigh. "Not actual . . . research."

"Well, I'm full of surprises." I turn toward him, open to whatever this might be. Ever since I bumped into him at the Quick Shop, he's been in my thoughts. The tingle in my skin when I go to sleep at night and the bedsheet traces my body. His scent is arousing in a way that I've never considered the smell of anyone to be before. It's carnal. Primal in its allure. Like an animal instinct I've been ignoring all my life.

I slip a hand to his jaw, and then he kisses me. Tremors careen down my stomach, between my legs, in a vibrating thrill. His fingers trace my collarbone, grazing to my chest, and I lean forward into his touch. It's been years since I slept with anyone, and the times that I did, I knew less about them than I do now about Wes.

We stand and I lead him to my bedroom, to my full-size bed. Sheets are rumpled and halfway off the mattress, but it doesn't matter. We fall down together, passion making my hands frenzied as I unbutton his pants. Pushing them down his backside, I grab on to his hips as he climbs on top of me.

His thumbs hook into my underwear, prying them lower. I take off my top, and then his mouth finds my breasts through the tan fabric of my cheap bra. His tongue winds its way between the cups, down my belly, between my legs, and I arch my back as he explores my skin.

"I want to taste you," he grunts. "All of you."

Sharp pain tears across my inner thigh, and I rear backward like branded cattle. "Ow!" I shout. "What the fuck?"

Red marks—teeth marks—where Wes bit me are stark on my olive skin. Half moons, deeper than any adolescent love nips, brighter red, where he drew blood.

I stare at him, my chest rising and falling from fear rather than lust, nearly naked in my underwear. "What did you do? Why did you do that?"

Wes returns my stare with wide eyes of his own, horror drawing his face. "I—I'm sorry. I thought you were—I thought—"

"That I was into . . . what—whatever that was?" I sputter. "You fucking bit me," I say.

Wes stands, scanning the mattress for something. He grabs the keys that fell from his jeans. Embarrassment, shame—then anger—flutter across his face. "You're going to play that game? Pretend that we didn't both know what was going on?"

I yank my legs to my chest. Slide off the side of the mattress to stand against the wall. "I'm not into S and M, and I sure as hell didn't give you that impression."

He pulls his shirt down his chest. "Yeah? Great. Me neither."

Stalking from my room, he strides toward my front door with me behind him. He turns the handle, then whirls on me. "You know, you would do better to be more up-front with people. With yourself. Because I didn't misread anything back there. You're just a liar."

As I listen to his footsteps retreat down the hallway, to the open stairwell that leads to the ground floor, I remain fixed in my bra and underwear. Not at all sure what the hell just happened.

My heartbeat slows its panicked beat. My breathing calms. The wound on my inner thigh continues to pulse bright red in a jackrabbit rhythm.

Although shock spools through my system, something else twines along with it. Something pleasing.

A new thought comes to me, more nauseating than Wes clomping down the stairwell after seeing me nearly naked: he knows more about me than I've allowed anyone else to learn in almost twenty-five years. And he's aware Geri Vega is out for more than a pound of my flesh.

30

Henry

The Wild

White paper wrappers that protected the items of the first aid kit litter the ground in the woods just removed from our campsite. Bandages that were pristine in their packages are face down in the mud beside a roll of gauze, an eye shield, superglue that's been emptied, a pocketknife, and adhesive tape that's been ripped open and unwound. The only thing missing that I can tell at first glance is the small pair of surgical scissors.

"Fiona," I call, raising my voice. "What is this?"

She doesn't respond, though I know she's lounging around in the passenger seat. She keeps saying how hungry she is—how lethargic—even though I brought back the marmot for dinner last night. Each time I offer her what's left of the meat, and before it spoils out here without a refrigerator, she drops her jaw like she might vomit.

"Fiona?" I call again. No response.

I bend down, trying to salvage some of the tape or maybe a bandage, when something pokes my thigh.

"Daddy?"

I resume standing. Violet peers at me from behind a tree trunk that wasn't flattened in our crash landing. "Hi, little bao."

The nickname I used for her when she was a chubby baby—her round face and cheeks resembling a bread bun—strikes us both as odd. Violet tilts her head to the side. "What are you doing, Daddy?"

"Oh, I just found this stuff, out and scattered. Do you know how the first aid kit got here?"

Violet shakes her head. "Don't we need that stuff? If we get scratches or something?"

I nod, my smile tight. I'm trying not to scare her worse than we all already are. "That's right, little bao. But you know what? Your ying ying was a healer in Chinatown, and my po po was before her in China. We have everything we need from Mother Nature. Don't you worry about it."

Violet seems put off by the nickname again, but less worried. The more I talk about my mother and grandmother, the less anxious I feel too. The shame and fear that I've been feeling for months now seem lightened in a way. Is it recalling that I come from good stock? That our family has survived other perilous moments in our line? Maybe.

"Vi!" Fiona shouts, tramping up the hillside. "What are you doing back here?"

Her cheeks are flushed, making her paler than usual. Brown hair is matted to her head after the rain deluges and subsequent sweaty, muddy hikes searching for campers or help of some kind. I keep telling her to stay put, that I'll handle the reconnaissance—there's a pack of wolves, for God's sake, roaming the area—but she refuses to listen. Typical teenager.

When I was her age, if I were to be so disobedient, I wouldn't have made it to fourteen. I would have been drawn and quartered, then served up to my cousins for dinner in a rich broth noodle soup.

How did I get here? From poor kid in Chinatown, to member of the military dishonorably discharged, to mall security regional director, to failed pilot? How did each milestone of my path, surrounded in hope, end in failure?

Stress resumes coupling with anxiety in the space behind my eyes, and I can feel a headache forming. I focus on my daughter Violet's face and fight to stay present. Here. For her. For Fiona too.

"Violet, little bao. Are you hungry?"

My youngest nods. "Yes."

"We're going to get something to eat. Why don't you come with me?"

"No!" Fiona strides up the mountain. She grabs her sister's hand and yanks her down the hill by several feet. "No. You're staying with me, Violet."

"I'm going to need help, Fiona. And you're not exactly being a good teammate lately. How could you dump out the first aid kit?"

"Excuse me? You did that!" Fiona steps in front of Violet in a protective stance. "I watched you do something this morning when it was nearly still dark out. You woke me up, rummaging around in the cargo compartment, and then you came out here. You went off somewhere else after that, and I walked up and found all of this. The bandages, the gauze, the tape, the butterfly clips—all muddy. Just like you left it. When you came back you were all dirty like you rolled around on the ground."

I shake my head. She's been paranoid ever since Janet died—understandably. I don't know what she's talking about, but I admit I haven't been myself. The headaches have been worse, and the fatigue has been otherworldly.

"Fiona," I start in a soft voice. "I didn't touch the first aid kit. I was rummaging around for something that might help me dig. Look . . . I wanted to tell you both later, after we had something to eat. I went and buried your mother this morning."

Fiona gasps. She takes a half step away, down the hill. "You did that . . . without us?"

Violet's big brown eyes grow even wider. She's beginning to appear gaunt, my little bao.

"Believe me. Your mother needed to find peace. With the wolves roaming around, it wasn't an option to leave her under the tarp and stones."

"But . . . you didn't wait for us." Fiona begins to sob. She lifts a hand to her mouth, then grips her own face.

"I couldn't. Our high elevation was only going to preserve her for so long. And you didn't want to see her like that. You should remember her like she was in life."

I want to, at least. I wish someone else had been there to do the job.

The wind picks up, twisting through the trees. Branches rub together in a soft thrum of white noise. Animals chirp nearby, the birds issuing a call-and-response volley of song.

When Fiona's sobs dim to soft hiccups, I take a step toward them. "I would never deliberately harm us by damaging the first aid kit. I hope you believe me."

"Why wouldn't you sabotage the kit?" Fiona glowers. "After what you did to Mom?"

Violet peeks out from behind her sister. "What did he do?"

"I didn't do anything to your mother," I reply. My patience is wearing. "She slipped on a wet rock during a storm. She split her head open out of sheer terrible luck and uneven terrain."

The truth sounds so much more brutal aloud in front of seven-year-old Violet, but God, she's seen and heard so much worse now.

I haven't always been Dad of the Year. Staring my oldest in her beady eyes, I decide I won't let her turn Violet against me too, not when we need each other out here. When I need them.

I may have failed Fiona by not being there for her when she was little—by not being more present, when she was always asking me to play with her, or begging me to take my medication alongside her mother's pleading—but I have a shot to start over with Violet here. To be the only parent Violet will ever need. If Janet—I mean, Fiona—thinks she can change that, well. She wasn't paying attention when I single-handedly brought back a marmot, then roasted it for them to eat.

"Look, girls. I can't keep saying how sorry I am for all this mess. But it's not anyone's fault. And we need to find more food tonight."

"When are we getting rescued?" Fiona shouts. "Where is that other goddamned person you were talking to on the radio?"

"I don't know, Fiona. Don't you think if I did, I would tell you?" I shoot back. "I've been messing with the radio every day since we landed."

"Every day? All six of them? All day, all twenty-four hours, during the times that reception might be the best?"

"Yes! What do you think—that I want to stay out here? With the blankets we packed for a vacation, evidence and reminders of your mother across every suitcase, sock, and snack that we've decimated?"

"You killed her!" Fiona shrieks, her face twisting in rage. "You did this. You crashed our plane on purpose. I don't know how you did it, but I'm sure you did. You did it just so you could get us all alone out here and attack Mom. You gave us God knows what to eat, you've barely done more than take a leisurely hike each morning, you haven't made any kind of plan or even tried to get us rescued. You wanted all of this. You're a monster."

Gone are the heavy sobs that shook her shoulders moments ago. Fiona stares daggers at me, certain of her truth. My fingers curl into a fist at my side. The disrespect, the hysteria rolling off Fiona in sheets, would easily deserve a backhand. I've never hit my kids. But I've also never crash-landed with them, been stuck with them, and had to bury their mother not two hundred yards off.

I would give anything to have Geri with me now.

Biting back the fury that chokes my throat, I try and make eye contact with my youngest. "Violet. Come with me now. We don't have to listen to this."

"No, Violet." Fiona grabs her hand. "Don't go with him. He's going to . . . if he doesn't find something to eat, you'll . . . you can't go with him."

Violet wrests free. "You're scaring me, Fi. I'm going with Daddy."

"You can't! He's going to—he'll hurt you, Violet. He'll kill you too!" Fiona blurts out.

I drop my jaw, shocked. Speechless.

"You can do what you want, girls," I mutter. "I'm going to try and find dinner."

When I reach the summit of this ridge, brambles and branches snap behind me. Violet trails below, but she follows my path. My heart lifts a little.

More footsteps snapping twigs and brushing leaves. Fiona marches up the incline. "Wait, Violet. Take this."

A bird swoops low, nearly touching my head. It flies higher, to the top of a cluster of conifers that have probably seen everything there is to experience out in these parts for hundreds of years. Probably, we're not the only cursed family to meet their demise here. I wonder how many have come before us.

I slide a hand into my pocket, then yank it back. Cold-tipped pain startles me. As Violet's tiny strides hurry to catch up to where I've paused, I wrap my hand around the object. The surgical scissors from the first aid kit fit in my pocket as if they have always belonged pressed to my body. As if I placed them there myself.

I pull them out an inch from the fabric, then dull sunlight highlights my smudged fingerprints on the steel.

"Daddy? Everything okay?" Violet asks, her small voice pricking my ears like needles.

I swallow. "Yes, little bao. Everything is going to be all right."

31

FIONA

I stare into the long mirror hung on my wall. Faint creases at my temples have taken on greater depth recently, likely thanks to prep for the show tonight. I've got a lot riding on it—Darleen does. And I've internalized much of that strain into the pleats of my skin.

Despite the show beginning in less time than it takes paint to dry, clothing options cover my bed instead of my body. I am not remotely ready. My pieces are all down at Hughes Gallery, primed for the professional photos scheduled to happen in an hour, but I'm stuck at home still debating what to wear.

Yes, the artist, who went into painstaking detail getting her artwork just right, over months, can't seem to decide between off-the-rack dresses now. I sigh, then lift a hand to my neck. "Get it together, Fi."

I rub the knots in my neck that formed and set up permanent shop this year as I craned my head to ensure each twig, feather, rock, and mound of clay stuck in exactly the correct angle to achieve whatever emotion I targeted: Pain. Anxiety. Frustration. Chaos. Claustrophobia. Fear. Love. Feeling the haunted breath of regret forever gracing your skin.

My mother was only thirty-three when my parents died. As a housewife, whose duties were admittedly stressful, she never reached the point of needing the jars of night creams that line my bathroom sink.

"Fiona?" Someone knocks on the wood of my back door.

Peeking around the corner of my bedroom into the hall that leads directly to my driveway, I catch my sister's worried expression. Violet shades her view into my house.

"You're still here," she says.

"Yeah, can you tell why?" I cross to her and unlock the screen in my bra and sheer black tights.

Violet doesn't reply. She steps inside with a wince.

"What happened to you?" I ask.

She unzips her jeans, pushes them below checkered underwear, and points to a bandage on her inner thigh. Other bandages cover the pads of her index finger and thumb. "I got bit."

"Bit? That mosquito must have been part piranha."

"It wasn't a fucking mosquito. It was a guy. The guy I've been seeing . . . kind of."

"Jesus. Are you okay?"

Violet grunts. "It's fine."

"Consensual?"

"Fiona, does it look like I wanted to be bit that hard? Why would I—"

"I don't know, I was just—" I shake my head. "Wait a minute. This was the guy you ditched me for during my gallery dress rehearsal?"

Violet knew how huge that was for me, and how much I needed her support. Her opinion, her perspective.

She doesn't even bother to look contrite. "Yeah. Well, yes and no. He came with me to the psychic."

I close my eyes. Try to shrug off my sudden irritation. Violet already got handed some pretty rough karma. "Got it. Fine. I'm sorry about your . . . injury."

"Thanks."

"Anyway, I need your help. Come in here."

Violet follows me to my bedroom. She stands in the doorway, opposite a framed photo of us with our aunt at my high school graduation. She appears as morose now as she did then as a twelve-year-old. "What am I looking at?"

I hold up a black lace number that flares at the hips and hits midthigh. "This? Or—" I wave a red poly blend that buttons at the neck and hugs all the way down. A no-frills cheongsam.

Violet grunts, then nods to the red one. "Mom would have liked that one."

"What do you like?"

"The red."

"Thanks." I stand in front of the full-length mirror in the corner of my room, then shimmy the fabric over my head. Violet crosses to zip my dress up my back.

"I mean it. Thanks," I say again. "After the last year of making every little painstaking decision myself, I was absolutely stuck in here."

"Sure. Happy to help."

Finally dressed and ready, I turn back to my little sister. The morose expression remains unchanged. "So, why are you here?"

She fidgets with a bandage. "I know today is huge for you, and I don't want to mess anything up. You've worked so, so hard for all of this."

"What is it, Violet? You're making me nervous. And I'm already a ball of nerves for the show."

"It's about the Alicia woman."

"Go on."

Violet leans against the doorway. "So, someone named Alicia called the house when I was a kid, before the plane crash, right? And Geri Vega consistently talked to the psychic about Alicia while asking about Dad when he never came back from the flight. My gut says they're related somehow. But I couldn't find a link between an Alicia and either Geri or Dad. Not online at least."

I sigh. "Of course not. Because Dad had more secrets than the CIA. What does she matter?"

Violet purses her mouth. "Geri Vega is all over social media and TV, begging us to speak with her, and I think Alicia is the only leverage we have against her continuing to splash our shit across the public eye—she's never mentioned Alicia in any of her interviews. There's something more there. I feel like Vega doesn't want us to talk about her. To figure out who Alicia is."

I cross my arms. "You think maybe we could use the info? My effort to convince Daley Kelly that we're still the victims of the crash—"

"And of the circumstances that took our parents." Violet lifts her chin an inch.

"Right . . . Yes. That effort flopped. If we learn something about Alicia that could get Geri Vega to stop talking finally, maybe we get Daley back on our side."

My phone's screen lights up with a text from Darleen. Probably wondering where I am. I motion for Violet to follow me back into the front room. Marshall snores on the couch beside the door, having deigned to raise his head when Violet entered, but that's it. He must be starting to like her. "Are you remembering anything about Alicia, now that you're writing again? You remember hanging up on her when you were a kid?"

"No. I can barely remember my last apartment address." Violet stops short at the edge of the hall. "But I did recall my journal. Mom gave it to me right before we got in the plane. Do you?"

A light-blue water-stained cover. Pages of paper stuck together from mud and rain and tears. Little Violet's soft kid-hands scribbling—writing down the date, the number of wildflowers we ate, the weather. Drawing. Notes that a seven-year-old finds important. Letters to family. And, without a doubt, some indication that our parents survived the plane crash. Proof of our lies and the smoking gun that leads to the devastating secrets we have been guarding since we were rescued.

I turn and face her. Violet, the adult who has struggled through so much pain, trauma, and failed connections to lead her to scarred fingertips and a human bite mark on her inner thigh. "Do I remember the journal you're describing?"

A smile tugs up the corners of her mouth, the first I've seen on her in weeks. "Yeah."

"No, I don't. I'm sorry. Not at all."

———

Music emanates from the long windows of the Hughes Gallery. Violet and I arrive with ten minutes to spare before the opening, as people are beginning to line up outside. A man raises his phone as we approach the door and pass the rail-thin security guard who will be checking names against a list of invited guests and doing crowd control. Part of me wants to glare at the man lifting his smartphone, probably grabbing a pic for his socials, but I can't. I'm too nervous.

"Here we go," Violet says, all smiles. She must be pretty upset about the guy she was seeing—her assailant—given this sudden shift in attitude. I knew she would be supportive tonight but didn't expect the drive over together, the reassuring arm touch, or the open expression she wears.

"There she is!" Darleen squeals. She strides from the back of the gallery to embrace me. "We've already made three sales. *Convenience Store Wrappers*, *Airplane Map*, and *Notes from the Wild* were all sold at auction about an hour ago."

"Holy crap," I breathe into her hair. Pulling back, I search her face. "That's good. Really good. A great way to start off the actual show, right?"

I know it is, but I need my art dealer to confirm it. To blow new air beneath my little artist's wings and make my hopes for tonight take flight.

Darleen nods, a determined line pursing her lips. "Oh, yes. We're off to a good start. And I got text messages that Benny Zimmer's team and *Art Lover's Magazine* are joining shortly. They're all just finishing dinner at Top of the Market, and then they'll be right here. You okay, Fiona?"

I exhale a breath. "Yes. Yeah, I'm fine."

"Anxious?"

"Excited." I scan the room, the pieces that I created from my—yes, blood—sweat, and tears, extracting them from the core of my soul. My experiences in the past that no one and nothing can take from me, and which are my gifts to the world. No one has to go out and check anyone's asinine social media account or a stupid hashtag for an interpretation of the events. They can come straight to the source and buy one.

People begin to file into the gallery. Violet returns from touring the room. I noticed she stopped at each piece, circling the ones that were elevated on columns and otherwise standing in quiet reflection before those backed against a wall.

"What do you think?" I ask, holding a champagne flute that Darleen gave me.

Violet nods, appreciatively. "They're good. They're all good, Fiona. You did it. I think you really pulled this off."

I stop watching people and their reactions to face Violet. Search her expression for veiled hurt or criticism as only sisters can manage simultaneously. "Do you mean that? What happened to the last indifferent several weeks?"

Violet has barely expressed more than passing interest in my art. Even when she came to my house for the interview, and when I actively solicited her opinion and help on the mountain piece—that darn thing I began first and finished last—Violet was never more than placating and guarded. I understand why she may have been reserving her true feelings about anything I was creating. There's so much wrapped up in my art that concerns her.

She sips her own coupe of seltzer water bubbles. "Not indifferent. Just . . . busy."

I want to retort, *Busy? Didn't you find new free time after quitting school again?* She texted me that surprise tidbit the day after she ditched me, and I didn't have the bandwidth to reply. Not with the show looming so soon at that point.

Now, I touch her elbow. If she wants to present a united front for my potential buyers and art critics, I'm all for it. She hasn't spoken to me about her memoirs in several days, and I'm hoping maybe she's dropped the idea.

"Well, regardless, I'm glad you're here."

Quincy speaks to a man wearing thick yellow-rimmed glasses. I don't recognize him, but when I catch Quincy's eye, he lifts a hand, waving enthusiastically.

"I think you're being summoned." Violet turns toward the hallway that leads to the kitchen of the restaurant next door. "And small plates are coming out. Bye."

She winks, then scurries toward the dumplings being served on cocktail napkins and cream-colored dishware.

The evening is a blur. Though only scheduled for three hours, I'm lost to the comings and goings of Quincy, Darleen, and random art acquaintances that I last met in New York, Venice, or Palm Desert. Briefly, I feel at the center of a vortex where myriad phases of my life come together in the same place at the same time, leaving me dizzy with champagne and rattled joy. This must be what having a wedding feels like.

Conversations hush as noise erupts by the front door. The security guard—Wallace—loudly tells someone to get lost. The line along the glass window and the sidewalk hasn't emptied once over the last two hours, and now cell phones emerge to film the scene.

"What is going on?" I ask, reaching Darleen's side.

She holds up a finger, speaking into her phone. "Yes, I have two other interested parties looking at *Feathers for Dinner*. No, that's not good enough. Yes, both already offered above that. Well, if you're not interested in owning a piece of history, that's on you."

Darleen mutes the call. "Fiona, honey, I'm this close to closing on *Feathers*. Whatever is going on at the front, Wallace and Quincy will take care of it. Enjoy yourself. I'll be right back."

Violet catches my eye across the room, where she stands with an empty amuse-bouche plate in hand. She shakes her head, just barely. Enough for me to understand, though not enough for anyone else to detect the silent conversation between us. Something is wrong.

Lights flash along the sidewalk. Bright white spheres that disappear in a blink. Camera flashes. A microphone on a handheld stick, smaller than a boom mic, emerges above the crowd.

"Oh no," I whisper. Daley Kelly argues with Wallace at the front entrance, loudly but not so loud that he overwhelms the music still spinning from the DJ's booth in the back corner of the gallery. He's got at least five people with him. Quincy stops his conversation with someone in the front window to stare wide eyed at me.

"What is he doing?" he mouths across the room.

I shake my head, then pause. Daley brought more crew members than he said he would, and Wallace is enforcing the agreement; we said he could have four people with him to operate cameras, lighting, and a mic, and told the security guard in advance to expect that number. Daley is in breach of contract with five people. And I won't give him the satisfaction of ruining my night.

Fueled by champagne and indignation, I stalk toward the entrance. Daley snaps toward me, pushes his way past Wallace and the doorway.

"Sir! You can't—"

"There she is," Daley says. "Fiona, tell this guy we agreed—"

Every eye in the room lands on my face. "You need to leave," I say.

Bodies outside jostle from the line or turn to stare directly through the window, eager for a better view. Someone marches forward.

"Fiona," Daley interrupts. "We only need a few minutes of your night."

"Who is we?"

In my peripheral vision, Violet crosses to me, then abruptly stops. "Oh, shit," she says.

Geri Vega fills the doorway, despite barely cresting five feet five inches in heels. She shimmers in a white satin blouse and black leather pants. Her makeup hugs every contour, smooths each wrinkle, and amplifies the loud mouth that breaks into a smile. "Fiona. Violet. I'm so glad we could finally meet face-to-face."

She strides forward, her arms open, then pauses not three feet away from me. I stand gaping at this woman, whom I've only seen smearing my family on public platforms, completely confused. Daley whips out a handheld camera in the ensuing shock. Someone else, a woman who acted as key grip during my in-home interview, jockeys with a miniature boom mic above the crowd. Onlookers pulse at the doorway, along the wall of the gallery—some still clutching now-cold plates of dumplings.

"You weren't on the guest list," I reply, dumbly. Benny Zimmer and an art critic I recognize from my last trip to New York push in behind Daley's key grip.

"What's going on?" Benny asks me directly, though we've never spoken before. "Where is Darleen?"

Where the fuck is Darleen? I cast a glance around the gallery, to the wall where three of my pieces are spaced exactly four feet apart, but she must still be in the back room, haggling with buyers. Given the drama staring me in the face, I'm surprised word hasn't already traveled to the mid-Atlantic.

"Please leave," I say again to Geri Vega. "This is not the time or the place."

"She's right. This isn't a free-for-all." Quincy surges forward from the corner. "I'm the owner, and you people need to go."

Geri Vega pouts, not insincerely. Almost as if she genuinely expected the party would shift to honor us both. "I'm only here to right a wrong."

"On camera? For ratings, and attention for your fabricated stories?" Violet glares, but she hasn't moved to my side yet. I hope she doesn't. The last thing I want from this debacle is Daley getting the still shot featuring the three of us that he so desires.

Tension soaks the room while Geri deliberates her response. "I . . . I guess I wasn't clear in my purpose in doing all those interviews. I've been trying to tell you girls—women—"

"Tell us, Geri! We're on your side!" someone shouts from the doorway. Some jerk who lined up for my show, apparently hoping this meeting would happen. More voices take up the call: "Tell us, Geri!"

Quincy shouts to Wallace, "Enough of that. Knock that off! Shut the door!"

More groans and angry replies rise from those still waiting to get inside. "No way! You can't do that—I've been out here!"

Daley grins, recording every humiliating second. "Fiona, is there anything you have to say to Geri?"

"What could I possibly say to the woman who's interrupted my very first dedicated gallery show? A woman who has sworn publicly to love my father, yet she attacks his oldest daughter's life's work? I don't have any words for that kind of person."

Clapping begins to catch among the guests inside the room, but Geri Vega lifts a hand. The applause quiets.

"I allowed my silence to carry on too long. Really, an incredible amount of time. Out of respect for the dead and as a licensed psychologist who took an oath of confidentiality." She pauses, as if drawing strength from the room's growing anticipation. "But now, seeing as how Fiona Seng is able to boast this much support for her work—the art that she's made on the broken bodies of her parents and the trauma of her little sister—"

"No, no, no. Do not include me there—" Violet growls.

"It's got to be said. Fiona Seng should be thrown in jail, not lauded for her clearly exploited memories. Fiona Seng tampered with the gas cap that ultimately led to her parents' deaths out in the wilderness. Her father, Henry, told me during one of our sessions that he caught her manipulating it somehow."

"You were his psychologist? That's how he knew you?" My stomach twists.

"No way Dad was in therapy," Violet murmurs.

"We met at a college alumni association dinner." Geri Vega nods away, undeterred. "Then I started treating him as a patient, for a year before the plane crash. We became romantic—against my professional judgment—two months prior to the trip. When I first reached out to you, Violet, via social media, and you, Fiona—"

"I never check social media," I say.

"Well, when I first reached out, I meant to share my memories of your dad. To confess our relationship to you in private and then evaluate for myself whether Fiona could have done what Henry suspected. But the longer you ignored me, then began lying to Daley here"—she motions to the slimy turncoat, who continues to film on his handheld camera—"the more I felt called to honor Henry and his experiences. The world—everyone who donated to you over the years, and the police—should have all the information. They should come to their own conclusions about you."

The crowd stills. All eyes weigh like bricks on my face. "And you're saying that my father told you I was lurking around the airplane, then damaged it as a thirteen-year-old—while it was owned by his friend and stored on his friend's property?"

Car doors slam. Two police officers in blue uniforms approach the gallery's entrance. Geri Vega knits her eyebrows together. "Children younger than you were have committed worse crimes."

The police officer and his partner who questioned me two weeks ago step toward me. Detectives Molesley and Hummel. Daley angles his camera, probably to ensure the cops are clearly shown at my elbows.

Heat flushes my skin as I endure this nightmare of a show. My peers in the art world, fans, Violet, Quincy—even Darleen, who has returned to stand in awe at the back of the room by the kitchen hallway—all watch with greedy eyes, lapping up the horror.

I meet the selfish insincerity of this woman, Geri Vega, head-on. "I didn't tamper with the gas cap of the plane. And everything that I did out in the wild, I would do all over again."

32

Violet

The Wild

Dear Fi Fi – I miss you. You ar here with me but I cant tok to you. Not nemore. It has bin very hard. Mommy left. Daddy is all I have left. And I cant tell him.
Mommy showd me sumthing that was only for me. A secret.
I want to tell yu so much.
But I'm afrad of wut you mite do.
And the wuman is back again. Shes scaring me more then last time.

4 yellow flowers ate
1 blackbird song
Daddy barryd Mommy
1 marmut ate

33

FIONA

The police cleared everyone out of the gallery. The DJ was asked to stop playing his music, and the catering staff was dismissed. Geri Vega tried to hang back, probably to provide Daley with even more footage of my career dreams melting into the sidewalk sewer drain. Then an officer shooed her home, just like the rest of the gallery guests. My guests.

A young man with slicked-back hair, Officer Pineda, jots down notes on a pad of paper. He strikes the balance of making eye contact with me, probably gauging if I'm lying when I say Geri's accusations are unfounded, while keeping a record of phrases I used to describe her behavior: "harassment," "unhinged," "inappropriate," "devastating" that she would choose tonight to crash my life.

The police officers I met with earlier, who accepted both Violet's and my renewed statements a few weeks back, even joined the fun. Apparently, someone—likely Daley—called the police to report two homicides that occurred decades ago, whose perpetrator could be found at Hughes Gallery this very night. Anything to get the additional drama of police uniforms on-site while Geri confronted me. Detective Hummel questions Quincy in his office back in the hallway that connects the gallery to the block's bars and restaurants. Detective Molesley peers at me, while Violet speaks to him at the front.

"Can I go home now?" I ask Officer Pineda. I've given them every detail I can.

He waves to Molesley. "We're all done here."

"Been done for quite some time actually." Fatigue winds through my muscles, probably amplified by the champagne from earlier. This was supposed to be a new chapter—the best yet, after a long series of false starts.

Molesley approaches us. "Ms. Seng, I'm not sure you get how serious these accusations are against you. If what Ms. Vega says is true, that you did tamper with the gas cap of your family's aircraft, there could be criminal charges ahead."

"Charges? For what?"

Molesley lifts both eyebrows. "That'll depend on how much water these statements hold. What we find as we're reviewing the file. Since the case was never closed, I might even call up my old friend Captain Vo and get his take on it, from today's lens."

"How can you even investigate anything like—like what Vega's saying? It was twenty-five years ago," I add. Panic ratchets my throat, and I work to keep my features impassive. Calm. As innocent as an angel painted in acrylic.

Molesley puffs up his cheeks. "If you didn't have anything to do with the accident, then there's nothing to worry about. You can go now. Good night."

I cast about for the words to convince Molesley that further review of our case isn't worth it—that the police won't find anything compelling if they dig into Vega's theories and resume the active investigation of our parents' deaths. Then Molesley catches his reflection in the glass of a mounted shadow box on the wall. He pats down the thinning hair above his forehead, turning his head from side to side until it's to his liking. The corners of his mouth lift in an appraising smile.

How much attention is Molesley getting at work, thanks to this spate of media interest in us? Does he really think there's some mystery to be solved at the heart of our ordeal, or does he enjoy the spotlight as much as I suspect Geri Vega does?

Anger—disgust—tightens my jaw as I cross to Violet where she waits by the front. We walk to my car across the street. We are each silent, passing the two remaining police officers standing on the sidewalk. Darleen left a long time ago.

From Darleen's perspective, the night was a success. We sold three out of the dozen pieces that were on display, two of them via phone call to New York and London—of all places. My star is rising, according to Darleen—but that was before Geri Vega, with her baseless accusations, showed. The other nine pieces will need to be picked up and moved tomorrow. If I were a more depressive person, I might suggest Quincy chuck them in the trash.

Earlier, Violet said she would Uber home when she was ready and that I shouldn't worry about her during my big night. While Officer Pineda asked me questions, then Detective Hummel followed up before handing me back to Pineda, I was relieved to spy Violet's short dark hair waiting in the corner. She could have grabbed a rideshare home, but she didn't.

We get into my car. I start the engine. As I pull forward, then make a right-hand turn toward the freeway ramp, my throat locks. Sobs work their way up my jaw, choking my mouth. I've never worked so hard or so long on something in my life, and it was ruined.

Violet clutches my hand on my leg. She doesn't say anything, because there's nothing that can make this better.

"I'm going down, Violet," I manage, when the sobs peter off. "Geri Vega isn't going to quit with her lies. And she's starting to convince the public. The police."

My sister stares straight ahead, probably to ensure I don't hit the divider as I merge onto the 8 freeway. "Fuck the public. And we'll get the police to see reason."

"How? We've tried finding ways to discredit her, and aside from learning she owes someone a lot of cash, we've come up empty. Filming the documentary was our plan to get our version out there to more people, to remind everyone that if we don't say it, it didn't happen. Now Daley is planning to use our interviews against us, and he seems to think Geri Vega is truth personified. Or ratings personified, once the film is finished and distributed. How are we supposed to compete with that?"

My heartbeat is in my throat again. New tears blur my vision as the lights from SDSU appear ahead.

Violet is quiet. She clears her throat. "The only way we have left."

"Which is?" I glance at my sister as lamps above the freeway cast her in a yellow filter.

"We find my journal. I *know* there's something in there that can help you, even if you don't remember it. We go back to Washington and dig it up, wherever it is. And we do it before the police get overexcited or any more obsessives start supporting Geri's theories."

My exit ramp appears. I slow down in the rightmost lane, ensuring I hit my blinker like the rule follower I am—like I've always been. "But what will the journal prove? Violet, you were seven. What could you possibly have written that would help now?"

"An account of our lives out there. Proof that our parents didn't die on the first night—the result of the plane crash that you supposedly caused."

"Contradicting what we've been saying for decades? That would only cast more suspicion on us."

"It's the truth. Isn't it?"

At the bottom of the ramp, I catch Violet staring at me from my peripheral vision. The stoplight's red haze is a stark command to sit under my sister's scrutiny.

"Isn't it?" she asks again.

"Violet, we've been over this. You don't want to revisit any part of that experience. Let alone go up to Washington. Take it as a gift that you don't remember so much of it."

She shakes her head. Black hair falls over her shoulder like a mourning shroud. "That's crap. And anyway, since beginning to write again, I can recall certain images and memories of Mom. Those are the gift."

The light turns green and I pull through the intersection. When I don't respond, Violet huffs. "Well, I'm not letting you go to jail for some half-formed thought of some fame seeker. You didn't kill anybody. And I'm going to prove it the only way we can now—with or without you."

I won't go to jail. There's no way. The police, despite all their grandstanding or any public bloodlust, can't make murder charges stick against thirteen-year-old me for possibly contributing to the crash. My sister won't take any chances, though. Not after finally reconnecting with me. And that's a problem if her protective instincts drive her up to Washington. Plus, if Violet's goal is to find the journal and use it to prove my innocence, like it's some unerring factual record—

I take a sharp breath. "Violet. You didn't recall the journal until a couple of weeks ago, right?"

"Right."

"You never mentioned it to Daley?"

Violet stares straight ahead at my driveway. I pull in, then park, touching my car's bumper to the fence that separates my yard from my neighbor's property. "Vi?"

"I . . . I don't know. Ever since he approached me—no, this business with Geri Vega all over TV—I've been thinking about the crash and the Alone Time more. Remembering stuff. It's hard to know if I'm recalling a detail for the first time or the twentieth because it all seems to blend together, once I have it. I don't know if I remembered the journal before or after I did the interview."

Daley's determined expression as he was kicking me out of his office in North Park enters my head. *There's more than one way to strip an airplane of its materials.*

Daley didn't get the footage that he wanted at the gallery show tonight. Which means now he'll do whatever it takes to salvage his career and this documentary. Especially if he thinks there is a relic of a Papyrus store decomposing in the Pacific Northwest, just waiting for someone enterprising and clever enough to track it down.

I cut the engine. "Violet, I'm not letting you do this alone. I'll come with you. We'll get your journal together."

"Really?" Violet lifts her eyebrows. Then she winces beneath the dome light, rubbing her thumb and index finger together. "Perfect. We leave tomorrow."

———

Quincy agreed to store my art pieces in the gallery until I could come get them in . . . a few days? Although another gallery owner might have said they didn't have room, I think the pity he felt for me worked in my favor. Darleen seemed of the same mind when I told her I needed time to reflect on all that's happened. She didn't question it, which told me last night was as bad as I thought it was.

Although Violet initiated the itinerary, I tried to anticipate what we would need, traipsing into the wild almost twenty-five years to the day. My weather app said it wouldn't be nearly as rainy or as cold as I remember it was then. Still, I packed two ponchos for us each, a week's worth of hand-held food in a hiking backpack I've never worn, water bottles, charcoal for filtration, flares, two cordless and charged cell phone batteries, and a locked case that contains my unloaded handgun—ammunition stored separately. Basically, the entire contents of my oh-shit emergency kit that I always keep fully stocked. When I asked Violet if she had a similar bag, she mentioned a hoard of Twinkies. I dropped the subject after that.

Last-minute flights and a rental car were equivalent to a monthly mortgage payment. But it also felt good to process the transaction—to feel like we might get a head start on Daley.

On our way to the airport, a police car passed us with its siren off. Both Violet and I watched it continue in the opposite direction from the rearview mirrors. The officers I spoke with at the gallery didn't say anything about restricting me from leaving the state. Still, I kept an eye on my speed the entire route to long-term parking.

Inside the airport terminal I scanned gates, restaurants, and bar seats, searching for dark hair and black-rimmed glasses. Anyone with oversize luggage that might accommodate a boom mic or camera equipment was subject to a double take from me. If Daley Kelly is as desperate as I believe he is, he won't waste time on a coastal road trip. When I told Violet my suspicion, she agreed that he'd be on the first flight out to our publicized crash site.

Once Violet and I were walking the Jetway to the commercial airplane's open hatch, I started to hyperventilate—for reasons distinct from any rat race with Daley. I haven't been on a flight with my sister since we flew home from Washington without our parents. Violet, for her part, was sweet and as supportive as she could be without experiencing this part of PTSD for herself. Failing to fully recall the last traumatic midair event due to a young age at the time has its perks.

But I found my seat on the aisle, as close to the main entrance of the plane as possible. Violet got settled. Then the pilot announced we were off.

The flight was easy. A few bumps, passing over Oregon, then into Washington in November. But nothing like what I was imagining during the ascent to thirty thousand feet. Three hours smeared across my mind in a blur, like finger paint across canvas.

As we disembarked, I tucked a cocktail napkin into my backpack. Proof that I confronted this part of my fears.

While I was torturing myself, firing all my brain synapses as I expended enough mental energy to solve quantum physics, Violet was even quieter than usual. I asked her at the rental car counter if everything was okay, but she gave some mundane answer, not nearly appropriate for our destination.

Violet was nervous. The closer we got to the national park that consumed our parents and stole our innocence, the less verbal she grew. Almost as if Violet were regressing to that seven-year-old who wrote half-formed phrases in a journal she left there when the rescue crews finally found us three months later. The heavy snow and competing state catastrophes that sucked up public resources were to blame for the delay, the governor's office later apologized to us—to our aunt. They searched for us, but in an entirely different part of the state, while Mounties canvassed the region surrounding Calgary that we meant to land in.

Trees along the freeway nearly crowded out the sky, then the two-lane road through the backwoods of forest; some might call them "beautiful." For me, as I drove at an incline, always climbing in elevation, the landscape felt ominous, increasingly threatening with every foot the sun dropped in the sky. By the time we arrived at the log cabin motel advertised as "rustic and romantic" on its website, I was shaking head to toe.

Behind a knotted wooden counter, a young man with a thick beard smiled hello. "Welcome to the Lost Pines Hotel. Have you been to the Olympic National Park before?"

Violet saved me from losing my mind over this stranger's well-meaning greeting. She slapped down her ID, and the man's gaze immediately tracked to the bandages on her fingers that were soaked through with red.

"Yes, unfortunately," she replied. "Hopefully this visit will be our last."

34

VIOLET

The Wild

Daddy died in the crash and animals carried him away. Daddy died in the crash and ~~Fi Fi~~ animals carried him away. Daddy died in the crash and animals carried him away. Daddy died in the crash and animals carried him away. Daddy died in the crash and animals carried him away. Daddy died in the crash and animals carried him away. Daddy died in the crash and ~~Fi Fi~~ animals carried him away. Daddy died in the crash and animals carried him away. Daddy died in the crash and animals carried him away. Daddy died in the crash and animals carried him away. Daddy died in the crash and ~~Fi Fi~~ animals carried him away. Daddy died in the crash and animals carried him away.

35

Henry

The Wild

Fiona whispered something into Violet's ear, halfway down the hill, too far for me to eavesdrop. From where I waited, Fiona towered over her little sister.

She's always been stronger than she looks. When Fiona was nine, she broke through two wooden boards in her karate class that not even the teenagers could break. Last year after she watched some movie with Janet, Fiona challenged me to an arm wrestle and I nearly lost. What could she do with that much strength out here, buoyed by as much stress and fear as we all are stewing in? Mothers have been known to possess supernatural energy to protect their kids. Would Fiona experience that kind of strength—that kind of frenzy—to protect her little sister?

After Janet was found dead, then abused by animals, I buried her. I wept for a solid hour out there by myself, not caring if the whole pack of wolves came upon me. She held our family together and was often the only thing standing between me and the mental hospital. I'll never forget the way she held me after both of my tours. And yet, it wasn't enough.

Geri's stalwart advice and therapy were balms to the wounds that never healed. When she became more than my psychologist, when she and I became lovers, I knew there was a line that had been crossed. But I was used to striding fully across those, norms and regulations be damned. Being with Geri, confiding in her as we lay across hotel pillows and later in her pristine Del Mar bedroom, itself free of kid toys and someone always asking for a snack, I only felt peace. Geri calmed me—my fears of never being whole again. And for that reason, I have no regrets about her. Even though it led to such a rift between me and Janet, and subsequently, me and Fiona.

Fiona glared at me while she whispered in Violet's ear. She passed something—a flat rock—to Violet, slipped it in her pocket. I would never have characterized my oldest child as dangerous. But, then again, I haven't been paying much attention to anyone but myself during the last year, while she's grown to my height in that time alone. Fiona's fits of rage became commonplace over the summer, and I think she blamed Janet for allowing our family to fall apart, for the tension that permeated even the most mundane mornings over toast and jook.

Before I found Fiona crouched beside Janet's body, then Violet shell-shocked nearby, it had been around thirty minutes since I last saw my daughters. The rain had begun to subside after Janet took off, and I slipped away while the girls were still huddled together under the tarp. I was so frustrated with the whole situation, I pocketed my knife, then left without telling the kids. I needed space. After wandering into the area of trees that grows most densely toward the mountain's base, I think I sat down for a while. Twenty minutes or so. I finally snapped out of my daze, and found a layer of rainwater had gathered in the crease of my shoes. When I happened upon Fiona at her mother's side, she was muttering to herself.

I wondered to myself then, as the girls and I trampled through the woods in the near darkness, back to the campsite, newly rendered a family of three. Did Fiona inherit whatever it is that runs in my family? The purported ability to commune with the spirit world—to communicate with the other side, the way my grandmother did in China as the healer of her village. Was Fiona talking to someone? Or was she arguing with herself, riddled with horror about . . . something else?

"Violet, we need to go. Sun's setting." I lift my hand to shield my eyes from the rays slicing through the horizon of trees. "Let's go, little bao."

"I'll be okay," she says to Fiona, who remains on the hillside.

Okay. As if Violet could be in danger with me, her father, right beside her. I huff. "Let's go. Now."

"Vi, be careful. What he did to Mom, he could do to us. Don't forget that."

I scoff—sick to death of Fiona's paranoia and ready to shout about it—when Violet grunts, reaching the plateau where I stand. I scan the slope to tell Fiona to dry out the bandages that she, probably, destroyed herself, and then I stop short. Fiona has already begun the descent without a backward glance. Fine.

I throw Violet a smile. "Let's go find dinner."

We climb up and underneath a stretch of forest that lines the valley-facing side of the mountain. Patches of fading sunlight warm my neck, my face, and I wonder how insulated the snow parkas are that the girls wear. I have no idea, personally. Janet bought them.

Birds trill to one another while Violet and I stalk between tree trunks without speaking. Although I didn't tell her to be quiet, Violet just senses these things. Always has, since she was a baby. When to ask aloud, when to be silent. When to babble, when to observe. She's an old soul. She's more mature and better able to handle adversity than any one of us.

Sunrays slant between branches, landing on her round, rosy cheeks in the cold weather. With fatigue, hunger, and what I suspect is the beginning of dehydration despite all the rainwater we keep harvesting—if I look at Violet from the corner of my vision, she resembles Janet. Maybe my mother.

We walk for a half hour, cutting high, then low again along this ridge. Animal tracks washed away in the last rainstorm this morning, forcing me to rely on sight and audible indicators that a meaty meal might be near. Feces lie in a neat pile beside a pair of boulders, hard little pellets. Nothing to get excited about.

"Daddy? I'm hungry."

"I know, little bao. I am too. We'll keep going another few minutes, then—"

A branch breaks ahead. I hold my palm up—signal to Violet to stay still. From my pocket, I withdraw the knife that's come in handy more times than I ever thought it would.

Something stains the hilt where the blade meets the handle. I angle the knife into the sun, between the shadows. Dried blood remains, unwiped from the last time the blade was used. But when was that? I used it to cut into the dinner from two nights ago. And I always make sure to clean my tools—whatever I'm using.

A twig snaps. A low growl rolls across the bushes elevated on the next ridge. Gray fur is visible not fifty feet off as an animal crouches.

I stare straight ahead. "Violet, honey. Don't move."

She stops short. "Daddy?" she whispers.

Another growl. Closer this time. There's more than one of them. Trees jostle as if one of the animals is descending from the branches. Is that possible? Or is that the wind picking up?

The earth tilts. I flail, then find a small hand in mine. Violet stands fast while I steady myself.

"Are you okay?" she asks.

Shadows move ahead beneath long, leafy trees that are different from the conifers so common to this place. The branches dip to the ground as if melting into weeping willows. One branch begins to crawl along the dirt, picking its way across the roots and rocks embedded into its path, heading straight toward us. Another growl rumbles, louder this time.

This isn't happening. "Do you see that?"

"What?"

"That. The branch—the—the leaves."

Violet shakes her head. "Daddy, I see lots of trees. Can we go back to the plane now? Fiona is probably worried."

I focus on the deep brown color of her eyes. The shine to her matted hair flat against her scalp. Concern pinches thin eyebrows—that look like mine—and the slight bridge of her nose is wrinkled.

"Daddy?" she says again.

"But did you hear that?"

Violet withdraws from me, just a bit. "I . . . Hear what?"

Swinging my gaze along the path, I search for that possessed tree branch that was quivering toward us. Listen intently for the sound of predators hiding in the bushes ahead.

Nothing. Everything appears as it did three minutes ago. "I'm sorry, honey. I must be more tired than I thought. I've only ever felt this way once before, when—"

Another twig snaps. Rocks kick down a hillside nearly covered in foliage, tumbling to our route below. "Did you—?"

Violet shrinks backward, her eyes wide. She nods.

"Listen very carefully, little bao," I whisper. I turn my shoulders an inch so I can see her in my peripheral vision, but otherwise I maintain my stance. Present strength. Aggression. Violence.

"On my count . . ."

"What?"

"One . . ."

"Daddy, wait."

"Two . . ."

"Daddy, I don't know what you want. What is out there? Are you sure something is out there?"

"Three."

Violet stands still. "Daddy, what do you want me to do?"

The earth shifts again, but I will myself to remain grounded. Dig deep within my core to pull the only word from my chest that matters. "Run."

36

Violet

At the edge of the parking lot, a weather-worn map beneath plexiglass presents a massive field of play. Literally. In the bottom left corner, a key shows icons for interesting landmarks. The official buildings across the nearly million acres of Olympic National Park are also noted. All two of them, located at opposite ends.

"We never stood a chance." I turn to Fiona, to make sure she's seeing what I'm seeing, but she's already walking toward the wooden cross that marks the new trailhead.

Since we were rescued, certain changes have been made to the park. Instead of having to hike for hours into the forest, a new road allows us to drive seven miles closer to the crash site. We'll only have the remaining six miles to hike to reach our destination.

"Let's go," she calls. The giant backpack Fiona wears with everything we could possibly need out here—everything we didn't have last time—bobs like it's nodding along to a club mix. She's off at a brisk pace, but I pause to soak in the view of our rental SUV. We'll be back to it before long. Certainly before we need to bust out the camping equipment that Fiona insisted she bring.

In November, the parking lot is nearly empty. Only a handful of vehicles—hikers more intrepid than I would be under normal circumstances—are parked beside ours. A dirty red wagon sits all the way in the back, as if the driver abandoned it during their own *Into the Wild* trek. None of them look as clean or shiny as our rental SUV. If Daley did fly up here, we beat him to the starting line.

The first mile is easy. Well-worn paths within the forest are only slightly muddy from a recent rainstorm. Still, as a native San Diegan, I slip twice down a slick decline. I manage to remain upright each time but earn a hard look from Fiona in the process.

"You done playing back there?"

I raise both eyebrows. "Wasn't it my idea to return here?"

She doesn't reply. Instead, she hitches up her pack and continues on, it seems at a faster pace.

Stark white-tipped mountains are evident above the tops of trees while we navigate overgrown roots. Mount Olympus, looking Grecian and regal. Our plane landed somewhere east of the snow caps, in an area that we later learned was akin to rainforest. Chirping birdsong, the noise of tall grass rustling, and the rhythm of tiny rodents scurrying beside us, hidden from sight, take me back. A strange sort of peace hugs my shoulders, although I know I should be terrified.

When I returned to my apartment two nights ago, after telling Fiona my plan, I wondered if it were even possible to find my lost journal. I recall writing in it—or rather, I recall the light-blue color and the earthy, sweet scent of its leather exterior. And I recall stashing it when those hikers found us, after wandering beside the river that was so swollen for the winter, I watched a grown moose drown in it. At that point, without a working pen for months, I drew in it with berry juice, and wrote brief words with charred twigs from our campfires.

The journal was dirty and worn, and I had multiple hiding places for it. Whenever the wolves came to sniff around our campsite, Fiona and I would tuck what food we had in the single plastic trash bag that hadn't been destroyed, then hightail it to a tree we both were able to climb. I never minded the frenzy that took over when the animals came searching for scraps. It felt like a game to me. Something to break up the monotony of survival. But Fiona would break out into hives, sweating whenever she had to climb a trunk, insisting that ants and other bugs were drawn to her "sweet blood."

Miles two to four pass over the hour that follows. The Quinault Rain Forest is thick, lush, and green at this time of year. Raindrops pattern my jacket in uneven streaks, remnants of the last storm that drip from the branches overhead. My muscles ache, reminding me that junk food as a favorite vice is not a great choice. Fiona is booking it, despite the ten pounds on her back, and I'm relieved when she pauses beside Lake Quinault on an embankment. We only saw this expansive body of water on our way out, when a rescue crew drove us past in a Land Rover.

"You okay?" Fiona asks. She pauses sipping from one of the giant water bottles she brought.

I set my own down. "Yeah. You?"

Fiona stares across the sparkling surface of the lake during mid-morning. The other end of it is invisible to my eyes, as it turns around a bend of green. This part of the park, the portion we didn't experience and have no negative association with, is beautiful.

Once I was old enough to access the internet and felt ready to learn more about the time warp I call Olympic National Forest, I did some digging. I learned that white explorers in the late 1800s desired to reach the Pacific Ocean through the forest and the mountain pass of Mount Olympus, after growing tired of the roundabout trail south that was both costly and dangerous. It took them six months to make it through, along with a team of "wilderness experts" who curated supplies and rations. Learning that, I felt impressed two girls such as us survived during three.

"We need to keep going." Fiona takes off down the path, sweat lining her underarms in the long-sleeve wicking T-shirt she just happened to have in her closet. She pulls a wide-brimmed hat—that she ripped the tags from when we stepped out of the car—low over her eyes. I adjust my own hat, grateful she brought one for me too. As she pauses to tighten the long laces of her hiking boots, I'm struck by how prepared she was for this scenario, despite the last-minute notice.

The miles and hours that follow are harder than I expect them to be. My running shoes—that honestly haven't clocked above a mile in too long—are holding up fine, and so are the loose-fitting pants, long-sleeve shirt, and jacket I chose. It's my body that's protesting louder than my heavy breathing.

"Do you need more water?" Fiona asks as the river rapids loom into view.

The current tumbles, rolls, bucks downstream. "I need a new set of quads. Are we planning to cross that?"

Fiona shakes her head. "We didn't do it then; we're not doing it now. I mapped out a better route that goes around it."

We break for lunch beside the riverbank. Cloud cover that's been constant since we exited the car parts for the sun to make an appearance. A slice of light sparkles along the water like something out of a museum tableau.

The weather is forecast to bring rain showers in the afternoon, which is why we pushed so hard during the morning. Once I swallow my last bit of sandwich and a protein bar that Fiona offers me, we get to our feet.

Leafy trees lay ahead, a rainforest of dense foliage from the ground up. I scan the meadow behind me, the sight of the river, bearing in mind that the parking lot lies several hours south. The hike so far, while difficult, has been a first-time experience for me. None of my ghosts haunt the lush greenery we pass or the patches of wildflowers that stubbornly remain despite the colder temperatures. Farther on, the dark, enclosed world of my nightmares stands stoically waiting for us to reenter. To try our luck again at getting out in one piece.

Fiona exhales. "Ready?"

I rub my index finger and thumb together. Though both are bandaged, the pain that comes with the motion is comforting. Stabilizing. "Let's go."

A worn path of wooden logs installed here makes the incline manageable. We work our way through the thick tunnel of trees, leftover morning dew soaking the shoulders of my jacket, leaving sloppy, wet kisses on my neck beneath my ponytail.

Once we reach the plateau, the path narrows. Trunks are more closely grown together. As if nature or the park curators didn't want anyone climbing past this point. Fiona and I take to pushing off from the trees for leverage.

I grunt, my foot slipping on a ledge of slick leaves. "Was it this bad before?"

Fiona leans into the incline, using her height. "No. I think these were planted here. There used to be a legit trail. Not big, of course. But, like, from the animals in the area."

Even at the shallow landings between slopes, the area is encased. Air here is thick, dense without the circulation of the meadow below. A half mile passes at the slight degree gradient, but for my sedentary muscles, it feels like a marathon.

When we emerge from the thick dome of trees, I breathe deep. I turn toward the valley, to survey our progress for the day so far. Fiona pauses as well, the agreement to take a minute to rest unspoken.

"Violet." Fiona's voice is tense. "Violet, is that—?"

I whirl at the phrase no one wants to hear in the middle of nowhere. "What? Where?"

"Relax. It's not—it's just that the hill ahead, where the plane crashed. It's not there."

"What is that supposed to mean? Mountains don't just move."

We've still got a ways to climb, but I scan the green horizon. Above the tree line, the rock face—the cliff's edge where my family all stood and admired the natural wonders, before they became our prison guards—has disappeared.

"Are we in the right spot?" I ask.

Fiona narrows her eyes. She consults the app on her phone that provides latitude and longitude. Lifts it higher, then angles it down. "I don't know. This was working fine back in the parking lot. We should be able to view the ridge from anywhere up here."

Another hour passes as we choose our footing carefully along the dips and hills of the soggy earth. Our route leads us up a sharper incline as we approach our campsite, dark-green—almost black—trees acting as a shroud the farther we go.

When at last we reach the cliff's edge, it's clear that the mountain remains where we left it. Obviously. It's the rainforest that has grown up and around it, to heights I wouldn't have thought possible. Vines twine among the highest branches, connecting the living creatures above and beneath us, entangling each limb in a network of photosynthesis.

The sun has begun its descent in the sky, but a few final rays bounce between tree trunks and swaths of branches—across something metal. Aluminum.

I take a sharp breath. The carcass of our passenger plane.

"What is that still doing here?" I whisper. Every cell of my body activates, vibrating in such close proximity. We're still another hundred feet away, at the edge of the ridge, but far closer than I ever envisioned when I suggested this trip. I thought that death trap was hauled away ages ago.

Fiona purses her mouth. "Too expensive to airlift out. I thought you knew."

Gazing around us, with only dull sunlight dappling the ground, I feel my stomach churn. So many moments that my family lived were swallowed whole by this instant camouflage. Even the plane, an industrial eyesore among the natural growth, is hidden from the valley below.

Fiona turns to me. "Where should we start looking? Do you remember your last hiding place?"

I flinch. "Fiona."

"We should probably orient ourselves. There's a ton of new plants here. Then we can fan out for the journal."

"No . . . Fiona. Do you see that?" Lifting a shaking hand, I point below, to the pinprick of light blinking in the forest, along the path we just took. It's a few miles away. Maybe more, given the optical illusion of so many treetops smushed together.

"Is that the river?"

"No, that's farther." I look up at the sky. Cloud cover thickened while we were under the branches.

The pinprick blinks again. Then again. It bounces. As if someone is using a flashlight to watch for exposed tree roots and rocks jutting from the uneven terrain.

"Violet, that's . . . what is that?"

The sharp light extinguishes. Its absence casts a black shadow across the expanse.

Nausea roils my stomach as I meet Fiona's tense stare. "Someone is out there."

37

Henry

The Wild

We sprint through the forest, away from the path, the rocks, the view that lulled us into false security. I leap over a fallen tree trunk, then yank Violet over it with me. Stand and scurry along its base to a different tree, thicker and wilder in its twisted limbs. We launch ourselves up the bent branches, using the eyes as footholds, until we are ten feet from the ground.

We pause. Violet peers up at me, fear making her little heart beat like a rabbit's against my arm. I hold my breath, listening, anticipating the sound of dozens of paws tramping down the earth behind us, sniffing us out faster than we can climb to a higher vantage point of safety.

Leaves rustle. A twig snaps. Silence stretches on for minutes. Then a new growl rumbles across the sky—thunder.

"Daddy, I'm scared," Violet whispers.

"I know, little bao. Just sit tight."

"No, not about the animals. It's . . . well . . ."

"Yes?"

Violet looks up from hiding against my elbow. "The woman. She's come back."

"What woman?"

"Don't you remember? I told you yesterday. When you were cutting down more wood for the fire."

I don't remember—either cutting down more wood or chatting with Violet about some imaginary friend. I did notice the stockpile under the plane's belly appeared larger this morning. But meeting Violet's anxious gaze, I go along with it. We have bigger problems to worry over. "She's not real, little bao. Whatever happened."

"Daddy, I'm scared," Violet says again. "I think she's trying to hurt us."

I sigh. Withdraw my arm from around her. "You're just tired. Hungry. I promise, no one is trying to hurt you."

Except for maybe the pack of wolves that I swore was only feet away. "When you were three years old, you also used to talk to a blue puff ball named Viper who had only one leg."

"This is different," she whimpers.

"What are you doing up there?" Fiona glares at us from the ground, her arms crossed. "I thought you were finding dinner."

I scan the area, the path we just ran like startled chickens. "We were. I was. But we heard something. Didn't you, Violet?"

Violet looks up at me, then her sister below, her eyes still glassy. "Daddy, can we eat something now?"

I sigh, searching for a meal between patchwork leaves. "I'm working on it."

We pick our way back to the ground with caution, although we only managed to get a few feet up. I've climbed higher and run from worse, but that was a decade ago—and without the dead weight of a child. I probably shouldn't have brought Violet along. The more time I spend out here, the less I feel society's normal rules apply.

"It's getting darker," Fiona says, her voice dripping in criticism. "What's the plan?"

"The plan," I begin, my tone sharp, "was for me and Violet to find food. Since you disobeyed me by leaving camp, you can help. Go searching for droppings of some kind. That direction." I point toward the wolves. Or where I thought the wolves were. The fact that none has come loping toward us, its hungry tongue lolling from its mouth, says I might have imagined the pack.

I rub my temples, willing myself to stay here. With the girls. In reality.

"Fine." Fiona huffs. "Good thing I'm brave. God forbid you two were left to your own devices."

I shoot Violet a look that she doesn't return. Violet stares after her sister. "Can I go with her?"

"No, best that you and me stick together." I traipse into the brush, then point out blue berries, vibrant and lush despite the time of year and the cold. "Don't eat these. These are a quick way to a harsh death."

Violet shudders, her little shoulders up to her ears. "No berries."

"You guys!" Fiona shouts around the rocky mountainside.

We move quickly to join her and find Fiona crouching near where Violet and I started running. "This looks fresh."

Smells it too. A small bush nearly covers a steaming pile of feces.

"I knew the wolves were out there," I say more to myself than my disbelieving girls.

Fiona rolls her eyes. "Seriously? I haven't heard any howling this whole time. This could be from anything. A marmot."

"Not a pile this size—"

"Daddy," Violet interrupts. She tugs on my jacket sleeve. Drops her voice to a whisper. "Daddy."

"What is it, little bao?"

Fiona scoffs. Probably jealous at the nickname. "Whatever left this, it's still close."

She creeps into the thick of the forest, away from the path formed by animals and hikers during better weather. Her feet should crunch among leaves and rocks, but she moves like a ghost, making little to no sound.

"Fiona, I don't think that's a good idea." Was it another marmot that scared us into sprinting up a tree? Or another animal, a predator tracking the marmot—tracking us?

Away from the stark sunshine that washes the cliff's face during the morning, this part of the mountain is steeped in branches, leaves that blanket the ground, and damp darkness.

Fiona continues farther in, hunched over like a witch seeking out children to eat. She even clasps her hands closer to her chest, like she's hiding something. A bomb? A grenade, more likely.

I shake my head. Press my temples between two moist hands. "Stop it."

"Are you okay?" Violet asks me.

Fiona pauses in a shadowy clearing covered in moss that I've never visited before. "Check this out."

She stands several feet from a carcass, freshly slaughtered, blood still oozing from lateral wounds. A Roosevelt elk. Spanning at least six feet across, a beast like this could only be taken down by a team.

I turn in a circle, scanning the surrounding shadows. Was I right all along, then? Was there some threat on the path, coming for Violet and me? A banana slug, bright yellow, pulses on the branch beside me, and I reel backward.

"Fiona. We need to leave. There must be a pack nearby. Or a bear. Or mountain lion. If not a pack, something large enough to tackle this animal and walk away."

My oldest whips out the pocketknife from the emergency kit that was so recently covered in mud. "I'm not leaving without something to eat."

She stabs the meat, sending a ripple across the animal's hide. Tugs the knife until it begins to serrate its way down the chest. She stops short. Tugs again but makes no headway.

"Shit . . ." she starts. "I need help. The meat, it's too . . ." Fiona bursts into tears. "I just can't do it."

A twig snaps somewhere close. Violet whirls, searching for the noise this time. I didn't imagine this one. "Fiona, we need to go. We're too small a group to defend this kill."

Fresh tears trail through the dirt streaks on her cheeks. "I'm not going back down with nothing to eat."

With new vigor and both hands, she rips—claws—at the elk until she's able to get a hunk of flesh in her hands. Chills undulate along my bones in some primal reaction, watching the blood drip from her long fingers, squelching in her grip.

A new growl resounds in the forest. This elk's killer.

"We're leaving. Fiona, come on." I grab Violet, swinging my gaze left and right, sweeping the forest floor for rocks to trip us up. "Fiona!"

Stumbling footsteps follow us. At the edge of the forest, before the path that lines the rocky face of this portion of the mountain, light stretches beneath the leaves. A zone of safety encroaching on nature's underworld.

Fiona falls weak kneed onto the earth with a noise that sounds like the air is knocked out of her. The ground is drier here. Less forgiving to land upon. She clutches the bloody carcass, now covered in pebbles and leaves.

"We need to get that over a fire, immediately," I say.

Violet takes two steps backward. "Daddy, I'm so hu . . ." She falls against a rock, toppling over.

"Vi!" Fiona rushes forward, but the sight of her macabre hands stops her from helping.

I grab Violet by the arms, lift her from under her shoulders. Lucky she didn't hit her head against the stone. "You okay?"

"I don't know," she replies in a little voice. Her skin is pale, her pupils large. Bones small to begin with are much too pronounced.

I reach in my pocket, the inside pouch, for the plastic baggie of meat that I saved from the other night. Violet needs it more than I do. "Here, little bao. Have some."

Placing a strip in her mouth, I watch as my youngest chews, then swallows. Saliva pools in the corner of her mouth. "Tastes funny," she says.

"What did you give her?" Fiona asks from over my shoulder, alarmed. "Did you—?"

She rips the bag from my hand, then holds it to the draining sunlight. Moonlight has begun to reign in the sky. "You have more? You can't give this to her, Dad!"

"Fiona, your sister is hungry, and I've told you, it's not—"

Her features twist. She huffs, working herself into a frenzy, like a mirage I once had in the desert of a woman—an artist—come to kill me.

"If we get out of here alive, she'll never forgive you for this. I'll never forgive you. You're a monster! A fucking maniac!" Fiona flies at me, and I jump away from where Violet crouches by the forest floor.

"Fiona! Calm down!"

She swings the pocketknife at my belly, missing me by inches. I flail backward, grab on to a bush to right myself. "What are you screaming about?"

"Don't act like you don't know, and don't make me say it in front of her!" Fiona snarls, but doesn't look directly at Violet. Violet watches us with wide baby-deer eyes.

"Fiona," I start, my voice low and slow like a lion tamer's. "I don't know what you mean. The meat was marmot. How many times—"

"There are no fucking marmots up here. I haven't seen any," Fiona whispers, her expression wild. "All I know is that you killed Mom and then you brought us *dinner*!"

She screams, swiping at me again with the knife, and I stumble, nearly fall to the next ledge twenty feet below.

"What do you think I did? What did Alicia do?" I shout, desperation—realization—taking hold.

Fiona pauses. "What did you say?"

"Shh." Violet lifts a finger. She points toward the forest's interior. Her mouth opens, parts. A shiver trips down my back as I process the single unspoken word.

Wolf.

38

Violet

Interview Transcript

Violet Seng: Is this—am I good? Just tell me when to go. I think we have an hour until another class starts here.

Daley Kelly: Just a sec; the boom is—okay, I think we got it. Great. [Claps hands] Let's start from the top. Tell us your name and what you do.

VS: My name is Violet Seng. I'm a writer.

DK: When did you first realize you wanted to be a writer?

VS: Ah, well. I was probably ten years old or so. I mean, I wrote before then, but too much of the act was associated with trauma.

DK: In what way?

VS: [Exhales] Well, when I was seven years old, I was given a blue leather journal right before my family and I boarded a plane for a family vacation in Canada. I immediately started scribbling in it and drawing pictures. At that age, I was doing very basic writing, but I had already asked my mom for one—a notebook or something to write "my dreams"—and I did pretty well with it. Like, I remember writing a full entry the day that we boarded the plane . . . I totally forgot about that until just now.

DK: What did it say?

VS: I wrote, "Today we go to Canada. I am excited. Mommy said I could go snowshoeing with Fiona this time." Or something like that. Very short and sweet. [Laughs] But in hindsight, it was . . . special. The clear desire to write something great.

DK: And when did that change? When did that desire leave you?

VS: After the plane crashed. My dad was flying it with my mom in the copilot seat, and I remember the perfect weather that day. No gray clouds below us as we flew, just sunshine above and to the left. I fell asleep for a little while. The whir of the plane's engine, the loud— so loud—whooshing of the air around us—not at all like a commercial flight—

DK: Which you've since flown?

VS: Right. We had to take a commercial flight on a larger airplane on the return journey home, you know, after everything. Not at all like that. No, the air whooshing and the engine, and the . . . the kind of comforting pressure of the giant headphones around my ears all made me very tired. Lots of excitement for a kid at that age.

DK: Right.

VS: So, while Fiona and I were stranded, I wrote in that journal almost every day. I mean, wrote very small sentences or doodled, almost every day. Then after everything that happened, I didn't pick up a pen again until I was ten years old. At that point, my writing got a *lot* better. But I still didn't start pursuing writing until much, much later. More recently.

DK: And what happened exactly? What was the trauma that occurred that made writing so difficult for three years?

VS: Death. Total mayhem out in the wilderness. Family members. Strangers.

DK: Tell us about the crash.

VS: [Exhales] I really don't . . . I don't remember it. Or rather, I remember coming to and the plane being on the ground with all of us—my mom, my dad, my

Elle Marr

sister—I mean. We were all there. But my mom and dad, they died on impact. Fiona and I walked away from the plane, but my parents . . . they were beyond saving.

DK: How did you know that, as a kid?

VS: The blood, mostly. Like I said, I don't remember the plane crash—

DK: Like, you blacked out?

VS: Maybe. I just don't remember it. It was a long time ago, and I'm sure I have some kind of cerebral protection in place to defend against the memory.

DK: Mmm.

VS: Yeah, so, they were obviously deceased when we landed. Broken glass and blood everywhere. The first night was the hardest without them.

DK: Did you know how to survive in the wild? Build a fire?

VS: [Shakes head] Nope. Not as a seven-year-old. But Fiona was so much older than me, by six years. She at least had absorbed the lessons our mom and dad shared during camping trips in the past, and stuff our dad had told us about his time in the marines. Plus there was an emergency kit with a spark igniter in the cargo compartment. Fiona knew how to build and maintain a fire.

DK: That's very lucky. A thirteen-year-old isn't usually known for survival skills.

VS: Yeah, that's true. We got extremely lucky.

DK: In the past, I'd read that you and your sister were able to use the plane as a kind of home base—a shelter during the park's many rainstorms while you were there.

VS: Right. It was intact.

DK: But you said just now that the plane had broken glass upon an impact that was severe enough to cause your parents' deaths.

VS: Well, yeah. Not all the windows were blown out, and my parents—my dad went through a hole in the windshield, while the rest of the glass didn't shatter. And my mom, she must have knocked her head pretty bad against the plane's metal frame or something. She just never woke up. I don't know what happened. But the rest of the plane was okay. It was the fuel leak that did us in, not anything mechanical.

DK: Got it. Tell us about the period that followed the crash. How did you two survive three months in the winter of Washington State?

VS: We did what anyone would do. We scavenged. Tried to remember what berries were okay to eat and which weren't.

DK: How did you avoid the predators in the area? There are some pretty effective hunters out there. Bears. Wolves. Coyotes.

VS: Yeah, we were definitely on edge with all of those in proximity. I remember being obsessed with marmots too. But I don't think I ever saw one.

DK: Marmots? Like, the big rodent?

VS: Yeah. They're bigger out in the Olympic Forest, around the size of a bear cub. But I only know that from the internet.

DK: Gotcha.

VS: Anyway, there were some nasty mosquitoes and other bugs too. Honestly, after everything, I'm surprised some kind of disease or infection from a skinned knee didn't get both me and Fiona. There are so many ways I should have died. Probably deserved to in some way.

DK: As a seven-year-old?

VS: I know it sounds innocent. A child. A seven-year-old. But once our plane crashed, our ages, our respective understandings, strengths, and weakness—all of that fell away. Any idealism or moral compass that two kids could have had was gone in the name of living to the next day. It wasn't about who had been paying the most attention to the birdcall lesson at summer camp that year, or who was stronger even, more muscular. The question was: What are we willing to do to make it back to hot water and heat and a roof? We sure as hell didn't have parents to go home to. So we just, every day, had to choose to eat something we thought might not make us sick, walk a mile for exercise and to keep up our spirits, and drink rainwater that we thought was clean and unsullied by fecal matter. The three months passed as slowly as they sound like they did. Especially in the winter.

DK: How were you finally rescued?

VS: Some hikers spotted us. The sun had just come out that day, after like a week of overcast conditions. They said the reflecting light off the airplane—or something—caught their eye, and they called for help after that.

DK: They had a phone that worked?

VS: Yeah, and reception. They were a few miles away from us.

DK: So what did you do?

VS: We . . . uh . . . it was so cold. So we started a fire to keep warm while we waited. First responders didn't arrive until around three hours later.

DK: You must have had a lot of free time, waiting to be rescued.

VS: Yeah, we did.

DK: What did you do then?

VS: Oh, I mean, we had a deck of cards, I think. I don't really remember.

DK: Now, going on twenty-five years later, do you think—could you ever imagine yourself going back to visit the site of the crash?

VS: It . . . it would take a very . . . [Pause] No. I can't comprehend a scenario where things would be that desperate that I would voluntarily return there. It would have to be pretty bad.

DK: Even if it was at your sister's request?

VS: Fiona knows better than to do that.

DK: Is there anything new you want to share? What about your father? Henry Seng. What do you think of the claims being made about him cheating on your mother?

VS: [Sighs] Uh. Well, he was complicated. My dad had a brilliant mind that was pretty damaged during his time in war zones as a marine. Sometimes I would wake at night to his screams, and my mother hushing him back to sleep like a child. I don't know, personally, if my dad cheated. But my parents loved each other. That's all I can say from my own memories.

DK: Okay, I think we got it.

39

FIONA

"Over here!" Violet calls, waving her illuminated phone to get my attention. She points to beneath one of the plane's wheels, remarkably still intact. "I think I used to keep the journal here."

Tall grass reaches the foot ladder of the cockpit. The inside of the cab is empty, stripped of materials, just as we left it. A Clif Bar wrapper, from a curious hiker probably, lies on the metal floor of the pilot's side. "I don't see anything."

"Well, no. I mean, I don't either. But do you think we could have buried it here? I feel really certain I used to wedge it underneath the wheel."

"Violet. Why would we have buried your journal beneath the airplane, knowing it would be investigated by the FAA and anyone else who decided to hike up here? That makes no sense."

Violet drops her phone, throwing us into shadows. "Well . . . I'm trying at least. Whatever."

She stalks back to the edge of the forest and the cliff, where the light is still good. The sun disappeared past the mountains long ago, though my phone says it's only four o'clock. Since then, the shadows have stretched out, filling the negative space between trees and along well-worn trails. We have around an hour before night falls. Possibly enough time to seek out the journal.

I don't blame Violet for getting frustrated. What has grown up beside the encumbering weight of a passenger plane and without two children running in circles from boredom and fear resembles nothing of our onetime home. Thick trees have sprouted—or maybe, resumed their original spots—to block out the scattered view of the meadow, the river, and the sloping hillsides beyond that taunted us while we were stranded. The image of the crash site was so embedded in my mind, I thought I'd recognize it immediately, as soon as we approached. Naive, in hindsight.

Returning to this spot—seeing the cadaver of our aircraft—is jarring, and I try to focus on finding the journal so we can hightail it home. Back to the motel and proper warmth. As I scan the ground for places that might hide Violet's notes, I pluck a few items: a turquoise feather, an empty snail shell, an animal's tooth.

At the least, I'll have new materials for my next gallery show. If anyone cares to attend. If I'm not arrested days from now.

Daley's betrayal at the greatest event of my artistic career was a slap to the face. It cut through the happy buzz of champagne, dousing me in a reality I have long known but also ignored when convenient: people don't want to befriend me or admire my work; they want to profit from it, from my story. No one actually sympathizes with something beyond their comprehension. They ogle it.

"What about over here?" Violet shouts.

I follow her voice another twenty feet east. She stands nearly level with a tree that's grown from a larger and much older stump.

"I think this is the big mama tree. The log we used as a bench. Do you remember it?"

I nod, examining the base. The plane hit it straight on, knocking the tree down but leaving the stump. "I think you're right."

Violet smiles. "It's kind of coming back to me."

We spin around. Our plane crash-landed much closer to the cliff's edge than I remember as a teen. Fear skitters down my arms as I scan the short distance from where we stand to nothing but air.

"I'm going to look around here, where I think we used to sit," Violet announces. "Did you bring a shovel?"

I point to where my backpack sits by a shrub. "Rear pocket, the fold-up kind."

Violet retrieves it, then locks the pieces in place. She nods appreciatively at the serrated edge on one side. "Multipurpose. You thought of everything."

"There's even a pickax feature." I scan the leafy terrain. "Didn't you have another hiding spot over there along the forest edge?"

"Yeah," Violet grunts, attacking the cold ground with the shovel. "But it's all forest now."

"Past that other stump, then?"

Violet points her chin toward the mountain's summit. "Yeah. Check there."

I walk into the trees, where the more recent saplings give way to sturdier trunks. Bushes, rocks, and broken branches litter the moss-covered ground. Plants twine around each other, forming a quilt of interwoven greenery. Narrow archways hover closer to the earth, as if small animals routinely run beneath.

I scan the mosaic of materials lining the forest floor. A flat rock the size of my palm catches my eye, nearly hidden beneath a bush with pointed leaves and red berries. I've been searching for one like it for months. Dusting off the wet dirt underneath, I pocket the stone.

"Anything?" Violet calls.

"No."

A half hour passes. I search for familiar signs of our residency—any indicator that Violet hid her journal beneath an adjacent stone—but every plant, tree, and weed begins to resemble each other. I might doubt that this is the correct ridge, if it weren't for the ever-present Cessna.

Night rushes in while I venture deeper into the forest. Firs and cedars mingle together, ferns and flowers clustering underneath in the growing shadows. The mountain's side is draped in vines from this vantage point. I stare at the gray rock face visible through looming branches that frame the view. The branches snake from a trio of moss-covered pines—almost like a doorway.

Something important happened here.

My mother's voice returns to me. She begged me to help with a task. *All you have to do is keep it still while I pull.*

I walked with my mom along these trees the first night, to assist while she plucked a bird. Our dinner. Mixed emotions rise to my throat, recalling the way she made lemonade from any situation—even one as bad as ours was then.

A large tree surrounded by brittle branches low to the ground, and tall, lush grass draws me in. Did we defeather the animal here? Dirt around the grass is less compacted than I would have thought, and I'm able to sink the toe of my boot into the ground an inch.

Once the plumage was removed, Mom went to work on dressing the meat. The echo of my shrill teenage screams as blood splattered my shirt returns to mind—as if the sound has lingered, waiting for me to return all this time. This was the spot.

Leveraging a stick that I find nearby, I begin to dig. I lift wet dirt, moss, and plant roots before I hit something. I lower to my knees. Something hard and hollow is buried several more inches deep. Tossing the stick aside, I dig with my hands.

"You see something?" Violet asks. At this elevation, her voice is nearly obscured by the beginning of a mountain song—haunting wind currents that almost sound human, calling to us.

Violet and I, we took to burying items here, to feel closer to our mother after she died. We would lean against the same tree trunk that she did while preparing our dinner that first night. We toed the earth where her own shoes made indentations, which we treaded carefully around, trying to preserve them.

My fingers grasp an object more substantial than another hunk of earth. A black handle. The first aid kit.

Cold air blasts through the trunks to wind up the back of my jacket and scrape at my skin. I stare at the top of the plastic box with the snap lid. We used to store items we thought were valuable in this. Small pieces of food that we didn't want to leave out while we were asleep, too scared to give the wolves any reason to come for us.

Using the flat part of the stick, I dig around the first aid kit until I can wiggle it free. My hands are nearly frozen at this altitude and with the sun dipping behind the trees, but I grip the latch, then snap it open. Plastic cuts my skin. I gasp as red dots bloom along the scratch.

"Too bad there aren't any bandages in here," I murmur aloud.

I lift the lid, fully expecting spoiled rabbit meat to greet my nostrils. Instead, the surgical scissors are the only original items that remain and which came with the box. Beside them is a plastic bag containing a blue book.

Violet's journal. New chills careen across my back, taking in the relic from our haunted childhood.

Probably, there's mention of our parents within its pages that proves the plane crash didn't kill them—the truth, that our parents survived the first night. Despite Geri's rumblings, that I was responsible for the damage to the gas cap, which led to our parents' supposed deaths upon impact, Violet's entries will confirm Mom and Dad battled for survival alongside us, at least initially. Until they both lost.

Violet pauses searching at the Cessna's tail. "Fiona?"

I take the book from the plastic bag, then slip it into my unzipped jacket. Pocket the scissors for good measure. "Nothing here. I'll check another spot."

A metallic click resounds in the enclosure. I whirl to the edge of the path, where Violet and I arrived from the trail below. Daley Kelly points a handgun into the trees, aiming directly at my chest. My backpack lies open at his feet.

He takes a step toward me. "Drop the journal, Fiona."

"Daley." Adrenaline pulses in my limbs. My hands tremble, caught in the act. "Did you follow us? Is that my gun?"

"The journal, Fiona. Give it to me."

My mind races to catch up. To grasp this new surprise. "What?"

"What are you doing here?" Violet asks from by the plane's wing. She takes a step toward him, toward us.

"You wrote in that journal every day," Daley says. "You said so during filming for the documentary. And I'm betting my future Oscar that you wrote down the truth of what happened in it."

"We've told you the truth—and the police—over and over again," I reply, rising to my feet.

"Bullshit." Daley scoffs.

The bouncing light that Violet saw on the path. It wasn't some trick of the setting sun, or otherwise. Daley followed us all the way from San Diego, just like I thought he would.

"Put the gun down, Daley." I haven't moved my hand from my pocket. Stark fear makes it impossible with a live barrel staring at me.

Stupidly, I loaded six rounds before we left the parking lot. I was so traumatized by wild animals last time, I didn't consider what could happen if the gun were taken by someone. A person who's declared me a liar.

Daley nods, ignoring my command. "Fiona admitted that your parents made it through the first night. They survived the crash. Coupled with what Geri told me about your dad, I need to know the whole of it. The public does."

"You can't prove anything," Violet says, bristling. "Give it up, Daley. Go home."

"I can't. Not without that journal."

Involuntarily, I glance to Violet. "Daley, I made a mistake. I messed up the initial timeline. I shared with you that our parents didn't die instantly the first night, but they barely made it into the first day. Violet didn't understand the difference, and it's a matter of twelve hours. I'm sorry it was misleading. Can you put down the gun now?"

"If only it were that simple, Fiona," Daley says. "After you flubbed the timing with me, I sought out Leroy Palmer, the lone hiker of the three interviewed by police who was still alive and willing to chat for the documentary. And guess what Leroy said?"

Tension ripples across my shoulders. My hand twitches, clutching the journal through my jacket pocket so hard that my knuckles ache.

Daley nods. "He said he first noticed the sun shining off a structure in the middle of nowhere of this massive nature park. The airplane. Later on, after he waved to you and got your attention—shouted so that you could hear that help was coming and made the call to the responders—he started climbing the trail toward your campsite. He noticed then the plumes of smoke. But in your interview, Fiona, you said he noticed the plumes of smoke first. You're the only person who recalled that."

"I . . . I can't be expected to remember—"

"You started burning something after he waved to you, Fiona. What was it?"

The memory of searing heat hits my nostrils. It was the blood-soaked shirt that our dad had been wearing when he returned with dinner in a daze, then regained consciousness while eating, his eyes open the whole while.

"I told you," I manage. "Paper. Insulation. For heat."

Another lie. I considered throwing Violet's journal into the flames, but she flipped out when I suggested it. We agreed to bury it instead—to come back for it when attention had died down. As time went on, Violet seemed to remember it less and less. I thought it best to let our ghosts lie where they were.

"Once you left the gallery, I figured you'd make a run for it, Fiona," Daley continues. "Head to Mexico or Canada to avoid more scrutiny for your misdeeds. Violet, though—she said she would only ever return here under the worst circumstances. And this situation fit the bill."

Violet remains twenty feet off, disgust blazing across her features. "Fiona has only ever protected me. She was a good kid to our parents. You're so far off, you're in Hawaii."

"Fiona had anger issues. You might have been too young to know, Violet. She was written up in school several times that year, and she once attacked your mom with the rice cooker. She visited the plane herself the week before your flight."

Violet darts her eyes to mine. "Fi?"

"I was curious about the plane," I begin. "And my dad wanted to talk with the owner about a few things, so he agreed to take me with him. I wanted to know how it all worked up close. Wanted confirmation visually that we weren't going to fall out of the sky. Ironically. But I wasn't violent."

Everything Daley recounts is true. I was a rebellious, angry thirteen-year-old who learned that her dad was cheating on her mom the summer beforehand. It wasn't a happy time, and I had two meetings with the school principal during the beginning months of the eighth grade.

Daley clicks his tongue. "More lies. Too long, where family crimes are concerned, law enforcement looks the other direction. My mom left us because my entertainment executive dad was a serial abuser who charmed the local police into ignoring her complaints."

Ah. So his story isn't as cut-and-dried as his mother "walked out on him when he was a kid." She was driven to it by his dad. Speaking of omitting the truth.

"Now, I redirect attention where it's needed," he continues. "And I'm going to do that—with the journal that you're still holding on to, Fiona."

He points the gun at my knees. "Give it to me."

"Daley, I just scribbled in it. It's nothing!" Violet shouts.

"You don't know that. I think you wrote about how Fiona attacked your parents, how she finished what she started with the gas cap. Is that it, Fiona? Is that why you came up here, to cover your own ass?"

Daley creeps closer. His steps make no noise, as if he slithers, hovering above the ground by an inch. "Geri seems to think so. She was your dad's therapist, and Henry told her things he didn't share with anyone. Like during especially stressful times, he left his body. And someone else, a spirit he called Alicia, inhabited it."

Violet and I gape at him. At this unhinged attention seeker.

That's who Alicia is? A *spirit*? Geri Vega did ask her psychic about her. But Alicia called the house and spoke with Violet.

A new memory returns to me: of my dad shouting the same name. *What did Alicia do?*

"That's ridiculous—" I start.

"You believe that shit?" Violet hisses. "You're a fucking hanger-on, Daley Kelly. A rubbernecker. Peddling dumbass stories manipulated to justify your actions. Leave us alone!"

Daley points the gun at Violet. "Your parents deserve justice, even if your dad hallucinated or was into the paranormal."

"This isn't making any sense." Violet shakes her head. "You're not making sense."

"It's time, Fiona," Daley says. "To come clean. About what evidence you made Violet burn before the first responders arrived, and the ways in which you profited from your trauma at your parents' expense. You're a public disgrace, manipulating the millions of GoFundMe donors. They deserve to know."

So, he's one of those. My critics have said from the beginning that I'm exploiting my family horror to make a dime. I shake my head, feeling the journal's weight all the more, wedged in my palm. "Okay, fine.

I'll go on record about what I burned in the campfire before we were rescued. But I'm not giving you the journal."

"Good thing I have the gun."

I square my jaw. "The journal is Violet's. It belongs to her."

"That's right. I'm taking it." Violet moves toward me.

"Put the gun down, Daley," I say, ignoring my sister. "You're going to hurt someone."

"Fi? My journal." Violet's hand remains outstretched.

"Why? Because I can trust you?" He laughs in a sharp bark. "Not a chance."

"Fiona. Give it to me." Violet's voice rises. "Fiona."

I glance toward the edge, where the cedars, the big-leaf maples, and the firs all cede to the free-falling air. "No. No one needs to read this."

"What? What do you—that's my final connection to our parents. To Mom."

Violet starts toward me and I break into a sprint.

"Stop!" Daley shoots the gun, but I don't pause, don't look back. The crack echoes, announcing our location for anyone within miles. Sparkles shine in the near darkness below, the clouds not yet returned. Though the river is far too removed, way farther than I could possibly throw the bound book, I have to get it away from Violet and Daley. Chuck it as hard as I can and hope that it lands in a hidden pond, puddle of water, its pages open and flailing in the rush of wind.

"Fiona, no!" Violet shouts, and then claws are on my legs. Her nailed grasp unrelenting as she tackles me from behind. "Fiona! What is wrong with you—give me the journal!"

We wrestle on the ground, rolling in the leaves, while I try to hitch a knee up, to regain traction in the soggy earth and continue to the cliff, only feet away at this point. I stretch my arm—the journal—as far from my body as I can, then toss it with a flick of my wrist toward safety and freedom. It flies, shifting, circling across a rock, sailing forward, taking with it all the sordid details of the Alone Time and before.

"No!" Violet shrieks.

Footsteps pound the earth, and then Daley emerges upright beside us. Clapping his hands shut in an alligator grip, he snatches the journal from disappearing into the void.

Daley pants, breathing heavy and still clutching Violet's most personal thoughts. Her hopes. Her confessions.

"I had my doubts," he starts, speaking to me. "About coming up here. But those are long gone. Seeing how desperate you are to keep this secret."

I set my jaw. Tears pool in my eyes, unbidden and against every cell to my core. "It's not my secret to keep."

Silence falls around our trio. Even the trees seem to pause, no longer bending to the soft wind coursing between branches.

"Whose is it?" Violet asks in a tiny voice—a pebble of noise on the ledger of things remembered by the mountain.

"Yours."

40

Violet

The Wild

I had to let go. I had to let go.

41

ALICIA

The Wild

The girls are staring at me, wide eyed and gaunt after the last week. Night has fallen, but the whole moon leers at us from above, casting sharp light between the trees with no clouds in the sky. Something moves in the forest beside us, out of sight for now. But Henry needed me. I'm sure whatever is there won't stay hidden for long.

At least I think it's been a week that we've been stranded. I've been in and out only a few times. After the plane crashed. When Janet was mouthing off. When dinner was needed. And before then, back in the desert when Henry and those soldiers were starving and needed someone to step up and handle the sitrep.

Throughout our relationship, I've been there for him. The surgical scissors from the first aid kit are heavy in Henry's pocket—same place I put them after throwing the kit in the mud. Violet needed to trust him more than she does Fiona. The older sister has been trouble, making Henry's life more difficult, since the day I met her several months ago, when she was launching kitchenware at her mother. If Henry is to survive out here, she's got to be handled next.

I run a hand along my frame—Henry's frame—and take inventory. He hasn't been eating much, though he feels wiry, his pulse pounding beneath his skin. He's ready for whatever caused him to call out to me—physically or emotionally, however it happens.

"Girls," I begin in my own voice. Lighter than Henry's, but it's never seemed to bother them before. "What is going on?"

They glance at each other, confused. I wish there were an easier way to get my bearings. Several months ago, when Henry was needing me more and more due to the stress of having an extramarital affair, I found myself speaking and acting through him more frequently. Chatting with his girlfriend. Doing laundry. I even resumed consciousness a few times, mid–phone call with his wife, introducing myself before I could figure out what was happening.

"Daddy?" Violet whispers.

Fiona doesn't take her eyes from me. "We were tracking an animal. While wolves were tracking us."

"Oh." I look down at his hands, now rough, calloused, and blistered. Something pokes Henry's backside. Reaching behind, I retrieve a bowie knife from where Henry tucked it against his belt.

Bending at the knee and crouching low, I motion to the girls. "We should return to camp."

Fiona shakes her head. She casts a harried glance between the trees. "It's too late for that."

"Fiona—" I use my Henry voice, deeper and more authoritative than my natural timbre. "Move, now." I scan the path, but I don't recognize where we are. "I'll follow you."

"What? What is wrong with you?" Fiona hisses. "You want me to march down there by myself—get eaten so you can sneak back with your favorite child later on?"

I hesitate. Searching for the right response. I never had any children of my own. "Girls, please—"

"You don't know where we are, do you?" Fiona asks, her brow pinched. "You always know our location. You use the stars to tell me what direction we're standing in, and you can guess our elevation based on the atmospheric pressure. You've lost it. You're nothing but a whacked-out monster who'd sacrifice his family just to go to Canada on vacation!"

Something black pounces from the trees, a blur of fur and snapping teeth as it lands on Fiona. She screams, falling to the ground, as another mass leaps toward Violet, grabbing the girl by her foot and dragging her five feet to the forest's edge.

"Violet!" I scream. I barrel into the fray, punching, kicking, landing a blow to an animal's head. It yelps, then bites down on my fist. I rear back, feeling the flesh tear from Henry's knuckles, then shove the beast off. Primal sounds bellow from my throat, and the wolves skitter away back to the darkness of low-hanging conifers.

Fiona pants, coughing on the ground. A scratch lines her jaw, and her shirt is ripped beneath her jacket. Violet whimpers beside her, clutching her foot. The sneaker she wears, dirty and discolored, appears intact.

"Move, girls," I say, getting to my feet. The surgical scissors shift, stabbing my thigh, and I pull them from my pocket. "They're still watching us—"

Sixty pounds of muscle knocks me sideways, rolling toward the ridge's edge. The wolf turns to Fiona, and she reels backward, knocking her head on something hard behind. It spins back to me, and I grapple with the mass of fur, twist away from the wolf's snapping teeth. I push it from me in a surge of adrenaline, then feel the ground disappear. Claws snag on my coat, dragging me with it over the side as it topples, turns over, free-falling to the treetops below. Flailing, I grab an exposed root that instantly gives, dropping me another foot.

Air snakes between my ankles. Soggy socks are like rings of ice along my skin—Henry's skin—and a surge of regret for him swells within me. I'll continue on after this. But I don't know about him.

Movement overhead catches my eye. Violet peers over the edge. A little hand reaches for me. "Daddy," she says.

"Violet."

Small fingers twist toward me. A brave offer of help. If I take it, I'll pull her down with me. No doubt about that. She weighs a maximum of fifty pounds, whereas Henry weighs closer to two hundred.

"I'm okay, Daddy. Grab me." Violet holds on to something behind her. Another tree root?

"Really," she says. Earnest terror makes this child appear older than her seven years. Did she inherit her father's ability to channel spirits when necessary? Who is speaking to me now?

I grasp her palm. "Pull me up, little one."

She pauses. "No. That's not right."

"What?"

She doesn't move. The earnest terror shifts. It becomes confusion. Concern. "You saved me from the wolf, didn't you? That was you back there?"

"Violet?" A gust of wind spirals up my jacket, through the shirt Henry wears. "Violet, pull, darling."

Her grip lessens. "Darling?"

"Little one, I need your help. Now."

"Little . . . ? But that's not right. I'm not 'little one.' I'm . . ."

"Violet, Christ! Help me. Where is your sister? Fiona!" I shout. Moaning is the only response I get. She must be disoriented from the attack.

Violet shakes her head. "I'm not 'little one.' Who am I? Little . . . ?"

Blast. This is a test. I'm failing the test. Henry has a pet name for her, and I have no clue what it is. Sweat courses down Henry's body despite the sharp chill at this altitude, with only an arm gripping a tree root and supporting his weight.

"Little . . ." I kick the side of the mountain. Pain pinwheels from Henry's toes to his knee.

"You're the woman that comes. You killed my mother, didn't you? Fiona thought it was Daddy, but it was you."

"Little . . . sweetie."

Innocent brown eyes widen. Then her small features turn to stone. "You killed Mommy. And you're coming for us next."

42

Violet

Fiona and Daley stare at me from the edge of the cliff. My skin vibrates with déjà vu as I process Fiona's implication that the journal protects my secrets, not hers. Covered by the plastic bag all this time, the original color blue remains crisp in Daley's grip.

"What does that mean, Fiona?" I ask, willing my voice to steady. "What secret of mine are you keeping?"

She struggles to her elbows. "Don't, Violet."

"No, I want to know. What do you think I did?" I get to my feet. Brush the leaves and twigs from my pants. "Tell me."

Daley darts his gaze from my face to Fiona's. He retreats several yards to safety, then opens the plastic bag.

"What is he going to read in there, Fiona?" I continue. "Is that the real reason you came with me? To keep something hidden from me?"

Fiona was not interested in this trip. She preferred to wallow and wait for the police to come for her, but I pushed the idea—wanting to protect her for once, the way she tried so long to do for me. Now that we're here, and we find that Daley "Stalker" Kelly has followed us, she whips out a new theory that I've done something wrong. Convenient.

My finger and thumb press together, and I twist my digits so their respective scabs catch, then tear open. The pain is immediate and sharp, a relief. An expression of the anxiety burbling in my chest, threatening to explode up my throat.

"I'm here because I wanted to help—" she starts.

"—yourself, I know." New pain sparks from my fingers—and something else. Determination? Resignation? I don't understand why Fiona would betray me like this. Although she's always hinted at some terrible action on my part. Looks like her lifelong goal to keep me in the dark is going south. Pain surges in my chest, in a different way. The revelation that Fiona still wants to shield me from an awful truth carries a bittersweetness to it. A stab to my heart that both rejuvenates and atrophies the long-ignored muscle.

Waves of emotion swirl within me, threatening to overwhelm as tears fill my eyes. I rarely cry. The rising moon, the crisp air, the sense that all I'm looking at was here, in some way, when both of my parents were still alive, leaves me feeling bereft. Yet empowered.

Daley flips a page, reading. "This is . . . this changes everything. Your parents didn't die the first night, like you've been spouting for years. The police are going to want to see this. Everyone will."

"Why is that?" Fiona asks.

He hesitates. "I think you know. If what's written here is true— turns out, I've been concerned with the wrong sister."

"What are you saying?" she snaps. "What do you think you know about Violet?"

"I didn't see a confession. But where there's smoke, there's campfire." He resumes pointing the gun at Fiona—and me. "Now that I have what I need, I'll be leaving. Fiona, I'd highly suggest you come with me. You don't want to be out here alone with Violet again."

Snippets of poetry mingle in my mind. Being in the exact setting of my stories, my memoirs, the lines I crafted while bored out of my mind in a lecture hall, seems to amplify the scenes from my memory. The clearing used to be wider, much wider, after the Cessna leveled so many of the preexisting trees. The ones that survived were smaller, shorter. My mother hunted for edible mushrooms and flowers in the thick forest beside the crash site.

Her constant calm and aura of love return to me now. Even while she lay dying.

"This way." I start walking, through what used to be the campsite. Fiona and Daley lift their heads.

"Where are you going?" Fiona asks.

I don't reply. Before long, my feet find a worn path that was well established decades ago. I follow it like an old friend.

> Distinct and stoned
> A path to time alone
> She lures me closer with a smile

Leafy branches droop low, nearly touching the ground. I hunch over to pass underneath. Footsteps follow me, tramping through the brush. Daley seems content to keep Fiona's gun held high while he scans my journal.

"This is some Stephen King shit," he murmurs aloud.

> Gray cushions her frame
> Two rocks' ringing blame
> Tears from heaven ping the tile
> I had to let go

A path slopes upward to my left. I turn over my shoulder to Fiona. "Does that lead up to the ridge?"

Fiona nods. "That's where he died."

Grasses have grown over the stones haphazardly scattered by nature and animals over time. I take note of the gray, shiny surfaces peeking through the green.

The trees begin to thin, ceding the way to a meadow. It's smaller than I remember. Bulky rocks line the edge of the flat terrain, slick and wet after a recent rainstorm.

"Be careful," I say to Fiona. "This is where . . ."

Fiona nods. "I'll be careful."

Two flat stones form arbitrarily placed steps above the soggy ground. Professor Tran's voice and the dull echo of the lecture hall return to mind. *Creative writing in particular is so helpful to reveal details in our subconscious that we may have forgotten.*

Daley looks up from the journal. He scans the lush grass at the edge of the mountain. "What is this place?"

Fiona moves past me, farther in. She pauses beside a boulder in the field, nearly halfway submerged in the earth.

Here, in this mournful setting, images and sounds flood my brain. Raindrops. My own cries. My father and sister happening upon me nearby. My mother, before she died, rubbing her fingers together as she would her rosary, in the same motion I have done for decades.

My gesture. I got it from watching her. Without conscious thought, I do it now. The pain is immediate without bandages, and comforting.

"Well, I've read enough," Daley says, slapping the bound book closed. "I'll leave the police to decode everything, but your parents seem to have died separately according to this." He lifts the journal. "And a few entries show your dad may have been to blame for your mom's death. Plus, the last entry is more than bizarre."

"What does it say?" I ask.

A smile tilts his mouth, dripping in disbelief. "You don't remember what you wrote? I think you will once the police ask you about it. Once the world learns all about it in my documentary. Everyone who ever sent you a dime or wasted more than a second thought on you two is going to be livid."

He whips out a cell phone, juggles it with the gun still in hand. "Damn."

"No service?" I ask, already knowing the answer. My own has been spotty since we climbed up to the landing, and I doubt here in the meadow is any better.

Daley peers across the wet grass. A long pause follows, as if he's considering his options. Both survivors of a plane crash, notoriously private, are under his control in the very place that made them famous—that might make him a famous and successful filmmaker. "Maybe up there on the hillside the reception will be better. Let's go."

I catch Fiona's eye. Daley wants to use my journal to further bolster his documentary—something that strikes me as pretty criminal. Abhorrent. It would be so much easier to exploit our trauma if neither Fiona nor I were around to call him out. Could he want to get us into an enclosed space to attack—versus having to chase us down in the wide, open meadow?

My mother's bones lie somewhere close by. I never knew where my father buried her, or if she was buried at all, but she's close. My skin tingles with the certainty.

Fiona peers from the ground, where she sits against the boulder. "Daley, don't do anything stupid. We can give you more interviews. We can support the premiere of your film."

She stands, visibly shaking. Tears pool in her eyes, as if she too senses this could go badly. She takes a step toward him. "Daley, please."

"Don't come any closer. I just need better reception—relax." He keeps the gun raised as high as his cell phone. Not at all reassuring. "Start walking."

"Daley," she says again.

"Walk." His voice is terse. When I looked into his background, after he first pitched me the idea of interviews, I didn't find anything unnerving. No history of violence. But things have changed since the last month: He's got a loudmouth fame seeker for his documentary, gracing every daytime outlet there is; so many more eyes on him after the police hinted at resuming their investigation of the plane crash; and then, his very public interruption of Fiona's gallery show, the optics of which made him seem aggressive, maybe a little unstable. Daley's got to tie these loose ends together. Right now, he needs to curate a story that benefits his film. A pair of unruly former tabloid celebrities like Fiona and me, who will assuredly contradict him, can't be good for business. Not anymore.

Fiona throws me a sneer. "This is all your fault, Violet. It was your idea to do the documentary—the interviews. We managed to avoid the public eye for so long, and you kicked us down this rabbit hole."

"Me?" My stomach twists, fearing she's right. "I didn't suggest anything until Geri Vega started doing live streams everywhere."

"Oh no?" Fiona starts walking. Her fists hang at her sides. "Because I pushed us to meet with Daley, right?"

"You might have," I say, following her. "God knows you're more of an attention whore with your *art* than I would have thought."

Angry words that I've thought to myself during my darkest moments when I felt abandoned by her trip over my lips into the open. Fiona half turns, now in the middle of the meadow.

"Oh, nice, Violet. Very original. Attack the thing that differentiates us. I'm able to be successful in my creativity, and you continue to take up space on your couch."

I wince. "I've been writing since forever. You know that. Just because I only recently committed to it, doesn't mean—"

"My art makes money, Violet. Yours has only ever led to trouble. Look at it now, your journal."

We both swing our gazes behind, to Daley, who steps wide of a fallen tree branch in the tall grass. The journal remains tucked under his arm.

"And your memoirs, my God. You'd think a more rational, healthy person would realize her *passion* is a curse to be hidden, not shared."

Heat flushes my cheeks despite the clammy air. Thunder rumbles above. Is Fiona baiting me? "I would be healthier if you hadn't left me, completely cut me off. You just stopped talking to me, let me think I was all alone in the world—again."

"You're being dramatic."

"Yeah? If the great and capable Fiona Seng says so, maybe I'll become an actor. Whatever you think, sis. Just tell me all the answers that you have in that self-important brain." Fresh tears prick my eyes as I plod forward. Baiting or no, Fiona's words sting. The rocky face of the hill is close.

Fiona stops again. "You want the answers?"

"Keep moving," Daley says. "Enough talking."

"No, Violet wants to know all that I know." Fiona whirls, her eyes wild. "She wants the secrets, and you do too, don't you, Daley? Don't your future viewers? Your executive producers?"

"Fiona." Emotion swells my throat, choking my words.

"Do you want to tell him, or should I?" She bounds closer to me at an angle, swinging wide in her route. Kitty corner to Daley and his gun.

"Tell him what?" I cry.

She levels me with her gaze. Doing what she always does best. Doing what is necessary. "You killed Dad. You let him fall to his death instead of helping him up. All because he didn't call you the pet name he had for you."

My mouth falls open. Chills ripple across my shoulders, my body responding to her words faster than my mind can process. "You're lying. He slipped and fell from the ridge. That's what you told me happened."

Daley stands still. Frozen in knee-high grass.

"Because I didn't want you to carry that burden. Because you were just a kid." Fiona glares at me. "But I heard you. He couldn't remember that he called you 'little bao' because he was dangling from a cliff, fighting for his life. And you let him fall. Pushed him from the edge."

Wetness splashes my skin—rain and salty tears. Lightning streaks behind the clouds, illuminating the hate that twists my sister's face—and in my mind, flickering to life the scene she describes.

Pull me up, little one.

My father's shocked expression as he fell twenty feet.

The sound of branches breaking on his way down.

Sharp pain that struck my backside as I landed hard on my tailbone.

I shiver as understanding washes over me in a cold deluge—a wave that snakes down my throat. Throttling the ideas I took with me about the Alone Time into adulthood.

Daley's batshit revelation about my dad and Fiona's venomous accusation crash together. Our dad had a nickname for me when I was a baby, but he had no recollection of it when faced with his own death, and that terrified me. Not because I was a petty child who wanted the crown of favoritism in that moment—because he wasn't himself. He was someone else.

Alicia. The spirit who used to come and go, who scared the living shit out of me when she would inhabit my dad. Geri Vega was telling the truth.

Memories I stamped out ages ago surface like snippets of film: the ramrod posture Alicia would adopt that contrasted my dad's normal hunch at the shoulders. The loping gait she used while walking along the ridge and the angry way she tossed the contents of our first aid kit into the mud. The appraising way she looked at me, as if sensing I knew something was off about my dad.

My own little voice whispers clear as birdsong in my memory: *You killed Mommy. And you're coming for us next.*

My lips tremble as I meet Fiona's searching gaze. The truth billows, surges behind my teeth. "Yes. I did."

Fiona lunges, but she darts past me. Daley fires the gun at my sister—misses. He screams as she reaches him—stabs him with a silver-tipped weapon. The surgical scissors that we stashed in the first aid kit?

They struggle, Daley's yelps rising above the crash of thunder. Fiona rears back and connects the scissors with Daley's chest, again and again. Her own screams add to the primal chaos until Daley lifts a hand and she stabs through flesh. He howls an animal cry, gripping his palm and the scissors as he tears them free.

Fiona stumbles backward, struggling to stay upright on the uneven ground. Daley attacks, catching her long ponytail in his fist. He yanks—exposes her fragile neck to the moon. Steel blades flash across the stars as he raises them high, the gun lost to the tall grass.

"No!" I scream.

Fiona whimpers, grunts—gripping Daley's shirt—as her other hand searches her pocket.

Daley stares her dead in the eye, inches from her face. "You're just as violent as your sister. Both the girl-survivors have been parading as the victims all these years, abusing their parents' memories and deaths, just to get a leg up over the rest of us."

"Daley, please—"

"Don't." Daley shakes his head an inch. "When I flew up here, I thought I was coming to talk to you both. Find out what you were hiding. But now, I know that was a pipe dream. We can't all leave here together. Geri was right about you all along."

I scan the grass, willing myself to see clearly in the near darkness. The gun. The gun. Where is it?

"We can—"

"Shhh." Daley tuts. Cloud cover shifts overhead, and then his blank expression glows in the starlight. "I'll ensure the narrative is finally made accurate."

The scissors drop, searing the air toward my sister's flesh.

Then another object rises, faster, arcing toward Daley's head. Fiona slams a flat rock the size of my hand across his skull.

Daley doesn't make a sound as he stumbles. He looks up in time for Fiona to hit him again, and again across his face, the scissors lost. Arms flailing, clawing at my sister as she strikes him like she's working a piece of flint.

He crawls away, whimpering, while Fiona watches. Stumbling back across the meadow, Daley trips, then falls in a heap in the grass.

My sister straightens, her back to me. Grass is knee high in this meadow, the blades reaching for her. My eyes must be playing tricks on me because the tall grass seems to climb her body, to her thighs, before another image snaps forward from the past.

My mother reached for me. She was dying, blood bubbling from her skull, and nearly unconscious where she lay on her back in the meadow, just removed from the forest. But she saw me and stretched a hand forward.

I crept to her, too scared to disobey. Her eyes stared above toward the gray sky, unaware of my silent tears. Her lips parted. She said, *Your father . . . Be careful, my girl.*

Then hands grabbed me, pulling me backward.

"Violet?" Fiona calls. "I'll be right back, okay? I'm going to get my bag."

A tremor starts at my shoulders, then twists down my spine. My knees buckle, forcing me to the damp ground. Rain begins to fall in earnest.

"What is it?" Fiona asks, startled.

A single white flower in this patch of grass is nearly crushed by my knees. I meet Fiona's pinched gaze. "Mom warned me about Dad."

43

FIONA

When the helicopter landed in the meadow, it was louder than I would have guessed. Last time around, when Violet and I were found by errant hikers out to break some world record of days living among coyotes, the weather was too turbulent to send in a helicopter for us, and the ground was too saturated. We had to be evacuated by first responders and a park ranger in a jeep, then driven across the terrain, along the river, to reach the parking lot and a whole team of paramedics. This time, they all come to us.

Once I made sure Violet was okay and it was clear Daley wasn't getting up, I found the discarded gun hidden in a tall patch of grass. I sprinted to where I'd left my backpack at the crash site. Grabbed the rope I had brought and the first aid kit and returned to tie up Daley and treat his wounds as best I could, despite the rain. Stanch the blood. Violet remained where I left her, pressed up against the rock face. After my revelation that she killed our dad, and her own realization about our parents, I didn't blame her.

Violet thinks our father killed our mother. He followed Mom after she left the campsite to seek out dinner—I could overhear their conversation while they shouted—and I remember wondering if it was safe for us to be left alone, just us kids. When he walked off, he seemed different. A stiff posture that contrasted his normal hunch.

If this Alicia person—spirit—took over then, the way that Geri Vega suggested to Daley, I wonder if it sensed my mother was at odds with our father. If Alicia mistook a fight between spouses as something greater: a threat against Henry that needed . . . neutralizing.

Violet nods where a police officer interviews her by the forest's edge. We moved toward the shelter of the trees after I climbed the rocky hillside and found my phone's reception worked just fine from that altitude. Daley was right about that.

Before paramedics got him settled into the helicopter to deliver him to the closest hospital, I searched his pockets. I'm not ashamed to say it. I needed to know if he was recording us. What I found left my stomach knotted worse than when he forced us at gunpoint to march across the grass: he had taken pictures of the final page of Violet's journal. Of her last entry, written in berry juice. His phone was set on facial recognition to unlock its screen, so I quickly went through and deleted everything as the rain petered off. No one should have access to Violet's thoughts at that point—not even me.

Violet clutches her elbows as she approaches where I stand. The police officer I spoke with earlier said they would give us a ride back to the parking lot in the park ranger's jeep. That we would need to drive to the station after that to give an official statement. Despite Daley's wounds, he was going to live. Anxiety floored me then, as I imagined all our secrets finally coming to light—everything that Daley uncovered and swore he would feature in his documentary. But then, I always knew this day might come.

If only I truly were a violent person, I would have known better where to stab.

Violet coughs. She tugs the jacket she wears tighter across her frame so that the panels overlap. "Hey."

"Hey."

She looks around us, confirming no one is in earshot. Not right now. "I've been thinking. Everything that happened to us out here is finally starting to make sense. Like, I'm recalling more and more, now that the most important moments have come back to me."

I tuck my hands into my jacket pockets. They're empty, of course. "That's good. Right?"

Violet only nods.

"But I still have some questions, myself," I add. "What do you think about . . . about speaking with Geri Vega? About Alicia. About all of that summer."

As our dad's mistress, therapist, or confidante—whatever Geri was to him—she has more insight into his headspace. Alicia's headspace, apparently—although that's going to take some time to digest. I'm still not sure I believe a spirit took over our dad's body. But there was absolutely a different, separate personality in the proverbial cockpit at times.

Despite Geri accusing me of orchestrating harm to my parents, Daley will confirm the opposite is true—that my parents both lived through the crash. Or he will if he is as dedicated to the truth as he was going on about. I know, after the last twenty-four hours, I'm ready to learn more. I need to know the whole of it.

"Off camera, though," I say.

"Yeah." Violet rubs her fingertips together, wincing. "I'm in for that."

44

VIOLET

Six months later

Bodies spill from the doorway of the Hughes Gallery, people dying to see Fiona's creations up close. Gone is the DJ who was bumping music the first time around. No catering staff hovers beside art lovers now. A freestanding table of alcohol, including some champagne, occupies a corner of the gallery, but the vibe is otherwise completely different. Less formal, less pressure. More emphasis on the art, the inspiration behind it, and the woman who escaped the wilderness—not once but twice.

Sure, a news crew parked on the sidewalk outside, hoping for a chance to speak with the artist of the hour. Thanks to Detective Hummel, who volunteered to provide security for the do-over event, the crew didn't linger for long. The slight interruption barely seemed to register for Fiona, however. This evening was billed as the gallery show she should have had before Geri Vega and Daley Kelly crashed the last one, and Fiona has enjoyed a near-constant circle of fans and art critics. She's a wanted commodity tonight.

Everyone who was invited came. Fiona actually suggested I invite the guy I was dating before everything went south six months ago— Wes. I shook my head. I have no desire to get rough between the sheets again. Even if there was something magnetic about him—about the feeling of his teeth on my skin. Truthfully, I often thought about contacting him, once we returned to San Diego. He came into my life at a time when, as the psychic said, I was experiencing some difficulty. His quirky presence was a fun—exciting—contrast to the moody clouds that seemed to follow me everywhere. He gave me permission to stop measuring myself, my progress, by others' expectations.

Instead of reconnecting, I deleted his number from my phone and stopped going to the Quick Shop down the street. Part of me was sad about cutting ties. But the change to my culinary routine is forcing me to actually learn to cook, the traditional way on a stovetop and with fresh ingredients. Eventually, I hope to work up to my mom's delicious steamed fish recipes. And, well, anything beyond unwrapping a Twinkie and dipping it in homemade honey glaze will be a step up.

Since Daley Kelly's hospitalization, and his subsequent slap on the wrist for harassing us and then threatening us with intent to harm, things have resumed an almost normal cadence. Although our lawyers said they could push for attempted murder charges against Daley, Fiona and I would have had to testify against him—to go on record about the circumstances that led us back to the crash site. And that wasn't happening.

These days I'm writing in a lot of coffee shops—a novel. I decided completing and publishing my memoirs is something I don't need to pursue at the moment. Not given Fiona's revelations while we were each desperate for a way to distract Daley from firing the gun. Her effort to dissuade me from putting any memory to paper was Fiona trying to protect me against recalling how I allowed our dad to fall to his death—against creating a paper trail of evidence that would contradict the official story we gave the authorities. Fiona didn't realize then that I knew, as a child, Alicia's secret: Alicia killed our mother, and she was coming for Fiona next—and after that, if I became a liability, me.

Fiona recounted that I was disturbingly calm on the ridge after our dad died. I tried explaining that "the woman" had taken over, but Fiona didn't understand. She made me swear not to speak of my "evil imaginary friend," or otherwise, again. So we didn't. Fiona has since apologized for denying me the chance to talk things out together—to process what I did in order to survive and protect us. Missing out on that closure ultimately led me to bury as many details of the experience as possible until Geri Vega began reaching out. These days, it's pretty weird to feel grateful to Geri.

"Vi." Fiona waves me over to where she stands with Detective Molesley. It's the first time she's been unattended by art people since doors opened. For the last two hours, her art dealer has been taking calls in a back office and running out with updates every now and then, while Fiona has been surrounded by people whose names I don't know.

Detective Molesley tips an imaginary cap to me. "Fun evening, isn't it?"

"Definitely. Though it's strange to be here after the last time."

Fiona nods, scanning the room of her guests. Detective Molesley twists his mouth to the side. "Mr. Kelly knows not to join. His lawyer would kill him."

As soon as Daley exited the hospital, our legal team issued a cease and desist notice. There was no way we'd allow him to use—or misuse—our interviews after he threatened us with a gun. Signed contract or no. I'll never know whether he would have shot us, but I know he wanted my journal more than anything in that meadow. And he'd already bent the gamut of morals and ethics, following us up north to Washington State after abusing our trust, and pumping Geri Vega for information in the name of his documentary after she contacted him, searching for us. This many months later, I'm still processing how brave Fiona was—for doing the unthinkable and attacking someone before he could attack us.

"How's Ms. Vega?" Detective Molesley asks. A couple laughing by the front door draws his attention. He turns back to Fiona. "Any word from her?"

"Not recently. Although she did invite me to be a guest on her new podcast."

"She got one of those?"

Fiona nods. "Yeah, she did. She discusses trauma from a psychology angle, I guess. She's doing pretty well."

"Good for her," he says.

"Yeah, it is."

I keep quiet. I haven't spoken to Geri since our face-to-face months ago, even though she and Fiona have maintained a nice buddy-buddy correspondence. Since then, Geri says our new interaction with her set her off on a path of righting old wrongs. She even got in touch with Phuong Nguyen, the paper prince, to repay him what she owed after a business gamble left her broke and humiliated.

Geri said she did love our dad, and that she was alternately afraid of him. Twice, she spoke with "Alicia" during their affair, including the conversation where Alicia accused Fiona of tampering with the gas cap. Since Fiona continues to deny ever touching it, Geri remains in the dark on Alicia's—unreliable—intentions. It was Daley who twisted the information into a more sensational storyline—*Father recalled daughter damaging fuel reservoir that took his life*—befitting a blockbuster documentary.

Geri said Dad's whole demeanor physically and emotionally changed while Alicia was present. Alicia would do household chores, helping out with what was needed to give Henry a break, and thoroughly creeped Geri out. Alicia explained that during those times, Henry was "resting."

"Well, I'm sorry to party crash here, Fiona," Molesley says. "I've been swamped with work and didn't have a chance to step away from Downtown until now—neither of you should visit Fourth Avenue, by the way."

"Why? What's there?" Fiona asks.

"Just trust me on that. Anyway, I wanted to give you both a brief update—"

"Fiona, sweetie, we need you." Darleen appears from the back office, red hair askew. She plucks Fiona by the elbow.

"Sorry, I'll be right ba—" My sister disappears around a partition that separates the part of the gallery on display from the resident artwork.

I lift both eyebrows to Detective Molesley. "Multitasking gives Fiona life these days."

He chuckles. "Well, it's probably better that I tell you first. I have an update on your dad."

I pause. "What would that even be?"

"Can we head outside for a moment? I don't want to spring this on you here." Molesley steps closer to me as a woman passes behind him.

I sip my cranberry seltzer. "Just, out with it."

Molesley sighs. He scans the room. "Your dad. He was found. Alive. He's been living up in British Columbia."

The clatter of cups and alcohol and conversations dulls to a hum. I struggle to speak. "Wh—what?"

Molesley nods. "Normally I would have called you into the station or visited you at your home for this, Violet. I'm sorry to be ambushing you here, but there's a press conference tomorrow. And, obviously, you and Fiona should know in advance."

"How did you find him? I don't understand." I shake my head. Although I now recall the moment he fell from the cliff, sharp pain mingles with happiness when I think of him. Positive memories that have begun to return. The buttery waffles he made on Saturdays. The scent of motor oil when he finished maintenance on the family car. The times when I was still small enough to snuggle into his arms while he called me "little bao," remaining ignorant of how much he was battling.

The room sways. My hand flies to my mouth, stifling a sob I wasn't expecting.

Molesley casts an eye at his partner, Detective Hummel, who stands at the front door. "We don't quite know how he survived, honestly. After Mr. Kelly told Seattle investigators that Fiona accused you of having something to do with your dad's death, we went back up there. I went, myself. We checked out that ridge where he would have fallen. Nowadays, there's a pretty thick bed of moss about twenty feet below. Back then, who knows what was there to cushion his fall? My guess is, he landed somewhere forgiving, then woke up disoriented. If he had a history of dissociative identity disorder like Geri Vega says—or split personality disorder, whatever the docs call it these days—I'm thinking he wandered as his other personality. And that led him north, to your original destination. Canada. Apparently, he mentioned a hotel in passing to Geri Vega before you all took off—she didn't realize the significance at the time—and he was found five miles away from it, working as a dishwasher."

In the first interview I saw with Geri, she was going on about a handwritten letter she'd received from my dad. It came in the mail the day before our plane took off and said for her to meet my dad "you-know-where." He really had hoped for them to reconnect in Canada. The balls on that guy.

That guy, who is actually alive.

I reel, trying to process Detective Molesley's updates. Steady myself on a cocktail table beneath a tableau.

Does this mean our dad left us in the wild knowingly? Or was that Alicia's decision?

"Did he . . . Why didn't he contact us? Not once, all this time?" My question comes out like a whine. A seven-year-old's.

Molesley purses his lips. "He said that he wanted to, but each time he tried, he decided against it."

Sweat dots my palms, and I clutch the stout glass of my cranberry spritzer. "Like . . . he thought we were better off without him?"

"Well, considering your mother's death remains unsolved, I wonder if it was something more. Guilt. Or maybe this Alicia person was stopping him."

"I'm sorry, I'm having a hard time . . ."

"Sure, sure. I understand. It's a lot." Molesley nods. "Whatever happened, he survived the park to make his way across the border.

He took up living under the alias Harry Song. We started asking our counterparts there, and apparently he was arrested for theft around fifteen years ago, living on the streets. At one point, he identified himself as Henry Seng while he was in custody, and the police made note of the name in their systems. They thought he was just slurring his words, especially when he mentioned something about needing to take his medication. I can show you a picture of him, if you want—" Detective Molesley reaches into his jeans pocket, but I shake my head.

"I don't—I'm not ready."

Detective Molesley nods. "After the announcement tomorrow, we'll be questioning him in Canada about your mom's death. Depending on his answers, he could be extradited back to the United States. But that's a few months away."

I work to keep all the details straight that Detective Molesley is laying at my feet now. The extradition, Harry Song, Alicia's survival instincts.

After Daley spilled the beans, and in combo with Geri Vega's revelations about our dad, the police knew all about Alicia. Yet Geri decided against talking about her in Daley's documentary—which left him with only his word against ours. For Daley's next grab for relevance, he insisted that our dad killed our mom, but the police also refused to validate that claim without further evidence.

He was pretty pissed. Without confirmation from either of the actual witnesses, Daley's assertions became moot.

Ultimately, none of that matters. My dad is alive—has been all this time. I didn't kill him.

We could be a family again. Hope swells my chest, thinking again of waffles on Saturdays and the sound of him tinkering in the garage.

Then someone drops a champagne glass that shatters across the gray tile floor. For a moment the room stills. Jazz music that Fiona selected for tonight amplifies the collective shock. Upbeat bass notes contrast the silence. Then catering staff rushes in with a broom, breaking the spell.

Conversations resume as a pit settles in my stomach. There's no coming back from the Alone Time. Not for me, at least. The little girl I was who yearned for her father's protection and comfort is buried somewhere in the Washington wilderness alongside her mother.

Detective Molesley leans closer to me. "I'm sorry."

A punch of grief for all that Fiona and I lost hovers above my shoulders like a water balloon ready to burst. I tear my gaze from the tile floor. "Thank you. Thanks for telling me. I'll share with Fiona later. After all this."

"Good idea." He turns to leave. "Hey, you still haven't seen that journal, have you? Mr. Kelly swears he was loaded onto the helicopter without it. He thinks it's still out in Olympic National. We haven't been able to recover it."

"No. Not since that day."

With a tight smile goodbye, Detective Molesley makes his way to the front. He waves to Fiona, who emerges from the back room, beaming.

"We did it!" Fiona says as she returns to my side. "We sold all of them. Between the last time and tonight's edition, all my pieces sold, and for solid prices. I can't believe it! I'm so happy."

I take her hand. She lifts both eyebrows, as if surprised by the touch, but doesn't pull away. "I'm really thrilled for you. You deserve all the success, Fi."

The night winds down with more well-wishers and admirers approaching Fiona to discuss her work. A few guests realize who I am and try to draw me into conversation, but I ignore them all. Tonight is not about me or our family's tragedy. It's about Fiona's triumph.

And celebrating when light finally cracks through the darkness.

45

Violet

Once the room empties, Quincy and Darleen begin clearing cups and napkins from the front. They step outside to sweep the sidewalk.

From under the drinks table, Fiona retrieves a wrapped gift. Red polka-dot paper covers a rectangular object. "For you, Violet."

"What? Why am I getting a gift? This is your night," I protest.

Fiona only smiles. "Open it."

I tear the paper, not bothering to keep it intact. I've never had the patience for that. Freshly cleaned blue leather appears, a color I would recognize anywhere.

"My journal," I whisper. "You kept it? How?"

"I stashed it before the authorities came, deep in a cave below the hill where Daley was leading us." She pauses. "Anyway, it's yours. You should have it."

I lift the cover. My childish scrawl in pen gives way quickly to nature's ink—dirt, berry juice, crushed leaves, and rainwater.

"What does that say?" Fiona asks over my shoulder.

"I think we set a booby trap for the wolves this day."

"I remember that." Fiona smiles. "Although I guess there were almost no wolves in Washington then. And almost no marmots. So I have no clue what Dad was hunting all that time."

I flip to the back. To the last entry that Daley said was so compelling. Tiny kid scrawl is barely legible. "What does that say?"

"Ah, I think . . . I miss Dad?" Fiona leans closer, still reading upside down.

"No, there's something else after."

I miss Dad's marmut. It was so yum.

The taste of iron floods my tongue. The coarse feeling of the charred branch in my hand. Saliva that pooled in my mouth, and the sight of glistening meat backlit by the flames of a cursed campfire. The offbeat taste of protein that caused me to gag yet reach for more.

I meet Fiona's stricken gaze. Search for a reply to soften the horror that grinds my stomach. "I . . . I don't . . ."

Fiona steps backward. She's afraid of me.

More recent memories jostle to mind. The look in Wes's eyes when he bit my thigh, the strange cologne he wore that was a mixture of salty and ferrous.

Wes has eaten human flesh. And he must have sensed we had the unusual affinity in common.

Did the psychic in Pacific Beach sense that too? Her words slide forward from my memory until I can almost smell the incense: *Twin flames collide in life because there is something to be learned from the relationship. Oftentimes the fire dies out. But there is always, always an explosion.* The connection we shared was more than some casual flirtation. And now I know why.

Detective Molesley's exhausted voice carried above the din of the gallery guests. *I've been swamped with work and didn't have a chance to step away from Downtown until now—neither of you should visit Fourth Avenue, by the way.* Wes has been busy since last fall.

Fiona clears her throat. "You know, it's very possible, I—um—I ran into marmots a few times. I think they were more represented than wildlife biologists think."

Stomach acid gathers at the back of my mouth. She's lying. But her effort to reassure me is more kindness than I deserve.

I swallow. "Thanks, Fi. I'm ready to get home now."

She nods. "Yeah. Probably a good idea."

The mountain sculpture remains in the center of the room. Sold but not yet carried off. A spotlight overhead bathes the piece in a yellow glow, highlighting the title that Fiona chose for her centerpiece: *Freedom*. I thought that was a little strange considering our time on the real version was more akin to a prison, but I didn't critique her decision. There are professional art snobs for that.

In every respect, this smaller version mimics the plateau we landed on, panicked and crying for months, down to the two wooden logs we used as benches. Typical Fiona to double down on the details. A large rock farther to the right, past where twigs and leaves symbolize the forest, catches my eye.

"Is this . . . ?" I step closer to Fiona, although Quincy and Darleen are still outside and can't hear my whispers. "Is this supposed to be where Mom died?"

"Where we found her, yeah."

"But why aren't there two stones? A path?" The large rock marks the beginning of the meadow that Fiona only hinted at with flat, dried leaves. The same place Daley attacked us six months ago, and where our father killed our mother. But I'm certain there were two flat stones preceding the big rock. I even wrote about it in my poetry: *Two rocks' ringing blame. Tears from heaven ping the tile.*

"Any depiction of that spot is incomplete without the flat stones," I add.

I must be tired to be nitpicking my sister's masterpiece. Probably, I'm still in shock at having read my last journal entry and learning our dad is alive. And yet, something about this omission bothers me. Fiona is obsessive about getting components just right for her art—for everything in her life.

Unless the scene is set exactly as she intended.

"Fiona?"

My sister clasps her hands together. A small smile curves part of her mouth, as if she's impressed by my question. "You got me. There wasn't enough space to accommodate the flat stones as well as the big rock. Call it creative license."

Ignoring the fact that Fiona dictates whether there's enough space to add something, I still don't understand. "Why did you choose to call this piece *Freedom?*"

Fiona cocks her head to the side. "It's a mountain. Most people would agree it suggests open air, wide spaces void of any encumbering buildings. General freedom from societal burdens."

The jazz playlist that's been running all night comes to an end. Silence blankets the gallery, amplifying Darleen and Quincy's conversation on the sidewalk outside. The evening was a financial success.

Fiona ushers me toward the door. "Well, I'm beat. Let's touch base in the next day or two. I have a ton of messages to reply to."

I plant my feet along the wall, then open the journal. I must have written about the stones. I must have recorded our mother's location of death in some way.

Instead of flipping all the way through, I pause on a page bearing repeating phrases. *Daddy died in the crash and animals carried him away.*

Daley called my journal "some Stephen King shit" when he attempted to steal it from me. He must have read this and thought I was losing my mind back then.

"Violet, pay attention. You were leaving? And I'm going home," Fiona says. She narrows her gaze, flaky mascara lining the tops of her cheeks after smiling in conversation all night. "I'm tired."

Her reprimand transports me to the moment of writing. Of crafting my letters carefully, under Fiona's coercive eye. *Violet, pay attention. Now try again. Daddy died in the crash and animals carried him away. Not "Fi Fi carried him away."*

I remembered this—have never forgotten this. We refined our story for months, in case we were ever rescued. "Mommy and Daddy died in the crash" because it was so much simpler than the truth: Our father, or my "evil imaginary friend," as Fiona termed Alicia, killed our mother, then suggested we enjoy a protein-packed dinner. Before I ultimately let him fall to what I thought was his death.

The second rambling entry makes sense at face value: "I had to let go," over and over again in my familiar hand.

My dad fell because there was no way I could anchor him. I had to let go.

My dad fell because he was housing a person who meant to hurt my sister and me the next time we least expected it. I had to let go.

The anguish that occupied my days and nights would have consumed my young heart and mind, if not for Fiona's constant presence. I had to let go of all that we lost while stranded in the wild.

"Violet?" Fiona calls, though she's only a few feet off. The hair of my neck stands on end at her singsong voice. "You're thinking pretty hard about something. What is it?"

Violet, pay attention.

"You were standing over me. While I was writing this." I show Fiona the repetitive phrases. During the eleven weeks we spent alone, just the two of us in the wild while we waited for help, Fiona drilled into me these two ideas: "Daddy died in the crash and animals carried him away," and "I had to let go."

The first sentence has been part of my conscious and unconscious thoughts since we left the ridge. It's only in recent years—in recent sobriety—that I've been able to separate the truth versus the fiction we told everyone. And along the way, I've gotten so good at letting go of relationships, goals, ideas of myself, that I think that second phrase downloaded just fine.

Fiona eyes the page of scribbles, her mouth in a thin line. "You know you had to, right? There was no way a seven-year-old girl could help a grown man climb back up over the edge."

Detective Molesley's revelation. Fiona still doesn't know our dad is alive.

"You had to let him drop, Violet. I hope you're not still second-guessing that, now that you remembered. And I'll take your secret to the grave."

I pause, examining my sister's earnest expression. The pinch between her eyebrows. "Yeah. Only . . . I don't remember allowing him to drop. Or his face as he did, or Alicia's shock, or whatever. I remember seeing him up close . . . and then you pulling me away."

Speaking the words feels like a fever dream. Like coming down from a high and still orienting myself to what plane I landed on, not quite recognizing reality. But is this that? Could these images I'm recalling now be what really happened? Or am I confusing things again?

"I caught you," Fiona says. "As you fell backward from the shift when you released him."

No, that's not it. Sharp hands dug into my shoulder blades, forcing my small body to retreat. When I first recalled that feeling, outside of the humanities building on campus surrounded by onlookers and the school nurse, I thought it happened beside my mother as she lay dying.

"I don't think you did," I reply. "I think you grabbed me, moved me deliberately out of the way."

Shock twists through my frame, tingling my fingertips. My mouth is dry—so dry—and all I want in the whole world is the cooking sherry Auntie Taylor kept stocked in her pantry.

Adrenaline pulses along my limbs in the empty gallery as images coalesce in my mind. Fiona's adolescent frame hunched over the edge of the ridge. Her whisper integrating itself so firmly in my head that I thought the words were my own: *You killed Mommy. And you're coming for us next.*

Fiona's insistence that she was protecting me, back in the clearing with Daley, was all a ploy. She wasn't guarding my secrets in the journal. They were her own.

"You let him go, Fiona," I reply, barely grasping the words. "Then you told me over and over again that I did it, told me how Dad was going to hurt us—me because I was the smallest. Over eleven weeks, you had me write down a confession, just in case you needed me to own his death too. Like some fucking Manchurian candidate. You killed our dad."

Certainty settles in my gut as Fiona's eyes widen. She casts a glance to the still-empty front door where her friends break down chairs and decorations outside. "Violet, that's insane. Of course I didn't. And I'll never tell anyone about you, but you have to—"

"Only he's not dead," I interrupt. "He's alive."

She stills. "What?"

I nod. Draw strength from her faltering confidence. "Somewhere in Canada. And the police are about to question him in depth about why he never announced he made it out. You know why I think he didn't come looking for us?"

Fiona doesn't reply. The petty part of me wants to withhold my theories from her awhile longer, to let her squirm. Instead, I stand taller, finally understanding my role in the wild. I did unthinkable things—yes. But my deepest suspicions about myself—that I was capable of hurting my family—turned out to be a lie planted by my sister.

I watch as Fiona's concern graduates to full-blown alarm. Indignation mingles with terror like homemade balsamic vinaigrette.

"I think it's because he didn't know how to confront the truth," I explain, meting out my words, "that his oldest wanted him dead."

Metal screeches from somewhere nearby. Shouts and horns follow, but I maintain my concentration on my sister's stoic face. Darleen and Quincy cry out, and then footsteps pound the sidewalk away from the gallery.

Our mother's weakening voice returns. *Your father . . . Be careful, my girl.* Suddenly, the words shift from the phrase that I've turned over and over in my head for the last six months since I finally remembered it—to something else.

Mom wasn't talking about our dad. "Your . . . Fiona," she murmured then. "Be careful, my girl."

I suck in a sharp breath. Take a step away from my sister. "Oh my God."

"What?" Fiona glances down at my journal as I clutch it tighter to my chest.

"It wasn't Dad or Alicia who attacked Mom. You followed her while Dad was chopping wood. While I was napping to wait out the rain. It was you."

"Violet. You're not making any sense. Dad is alive? Now I'm a murderer, twice over?" Fiona balks, but her anguish sounds forced.

"This is why I have such a hard time remembering things from out there," I continue, talking more to myself. "Not because I was some young kid. You drilled these other images and ideas into my head while we were alone for *eleven weeks*. It's a wonder I came out knowing my own name. It's the reason I didn't recall that Mom warned me against you until now, because I was so convinced Dad had been out to get us."

"Violet, please—"

"Who are you?" I ask, raising my voice for the first time since the big rock of the mountain sculpture caught my eye.

Fiona stares me down. She's always been tall for her age, then for a woman, and I never felt like it was anything but an asset in my life. Now, her height feels like a weapon.

"Who am I?" She steps toward me. "I'm the oldest child born to two people who did not handle their shit well. For many years, I raised myself—while our mother chose depression on the couch. While our father was in and out of my life and refused to take medication to control his own grab bag of unstable conditions. Neither of our parents ever gave a damn about me, or our family, until you were born. The golden child. Violet Esther."

Piles of cutlery, including a corkscrew, remain on a cocktail table draped in a white cloth. Too far away in the center of the room.

Fiona smirks, a mirthless act. "We always talk about those weeks in the wild, just the two of us, as our period of isolation. But you know what? As a child, I had nothing and no one. Often I wore the same clothing and soiled diapers for days. The first six years of my life were the real Alone Time."

I struggle to catch a full inhale. A light bulb flickers overhead—mimicking the hitch in the narrative I've built my world on.

"Did you actually tamper with the gas cap then?"

"No." She scoffs. "Why would I, when I depended on that gas cap too? It was pure—call it whatever you want—happenstance, coincidence, luck, that we crash-landed. And opportunities arose. I never—"

"Luck?"

"I never planned on anything bad happening to anyone. Mom slipped." Fiona pauses. She purses her lips. "I did follow her while you were napping, but she slipped on the flat rocks since it was raining and hit her head on that big rock. I was arguing with her again, angry that she didn't stand up to Dad that summer when she knew he was cheating on her. That she allowed us to be swept up in their drama by agreeing to this vacation meant to rekindle their fractured marriage. When Mom reached out for help in finding her balance, I pushed her away."

A mental snapshot enters my head of my mother, lying face up on the grass, the boulder just behind her. *Your . . . Fiona. Be careful, my girl.*

"And Dad?"

Fiona nods. "I really did think he was going to turn on us. He had been growing more and more unhinged, serving up *barbecue*, dumping out the first aid kit just to get you to distrust me. He—or he and Alicia—was targeting me."

"You. But not me. You didn't do anything for us."

Fiona sneers. "Don't kid yourself. If I were gone, you would have been next."

Disgust rolls through my core at the easy way Fiona justifies attacking our parents. "All of this because you had a shitty early childhood. You were there for Mom's death, you meant to kill Dad, and then you brainwashed me for decades after the fact. All to . . . what? Earn money for your art, after all, huh?"

The critics' favorite song and dance, that Fiona exploits her family tragedy to get buyers, presents a better melody now. I can almost hear it. I could dance to it.

Fiona scans the room rather than look at me.

"It's so obvious," I continue in a low tone. "Even your title screams it. Freedom—from the people you thought did you so wrong."

Footsteps arrive on the sidewalk. Darleen and Quincy laugh about something—a joke one of the drivers said.

Fiona folds her arms across the black, sparkly dress she rented for the evening. A special ensemble for the guest of honor. The evening's venerated artist.

"No one will believe you, Violet. It's all in your head. And you have the proof in your hands." She points to the journal. "If you ever tell anyone what happened—if Dad does—it will be your psychologically suspect word against mine. And the photocopies I made of those pages before I gift wrapped them."

I stare at the freshly cleaned blue journal. Although the material is over two decades old, the cover is soft, preserved as it was beneath plastic. Fiona gave me this here, in a public place, rather than risk me having these epiphanies alone.

She's not deranged—Fiona. Just cold. Calculated when it comes to protecting herself.

"Look, Vi. I won't condescend to you, pretend that I did everything for us," Fiona adds. "But I did what I thought was best—to protect myself and, yes, you. I knew, as a thirteen-year-old, that if it ever got out that I was involved in our parents' deaths, I would be called a murderer, regardless of the context. You, as a seven-year-old, would not. You would be forgiven." Her gaze drifts to the lights of the front window. "Forever and always the golden child.

"So I created the insurance that I needed, just in case we were rescued," she resumes. "Just in case the truth came out about Mom and Dad surviving the plane crash."

"You . . . Wow." I huff. "You thought of all of that, as a teenager, no less."

Fiona purses her lips. "Despite everything, Violet, this next chapter doesn't have to be a repeat of the last six years, totally estranged from one another. I never wanted to use any of the groundwork that I laid. I love you. But you—and Daley—forced my hand by insisting we go up to Washington. It's only you and me that know the whole story now."

I turn the journal over. The back cover is as soft and free of dirt as the front. Fiona took her time cleaning this.

Resentment bubbles beneath my quiet admiration. She primped and prissed up my journal to court my silence all over again. It even smells nice. Like coconuts.

"But I don't get a choice in the matter, do I?" I shake my head. "With all the leverage you coerced from me when I was seven, the next chapter will be whatever you decide."

"Violet, you don't have to believe me." She pauses. "But I hope you do."

Darleen appears in the front doorway, an open bottle of wine in hand. "Quincy and I popped open the last of the pinot. You two feel like a glass at the park across the street?"

Fiona breaks into a big fake grin, exchanging manipulation for celebration with eerie facility. "Well, I think that's up to Violet. What do you say, Vi?"

I take in Darleen's excitement. Her unknowing impulse to fete my new prison sentence. She doesn't realize I don't drink alcohol, that I haven't in over a year.

"Or maybe you prefer the chard instead?" Darleen adds. "Red or white, Violet?"

Nausea roils my stomach at the deluge of information that was confirmed tonight. I'm so afraid I might throw up on the spot that all I can do is meet Fiona's eye contact.

She smiles again, a more subdued version of the megawatt performance from seconds ago. Bile gathers in the back of my throat as Fiona gladly resumes her role as my caretaker.

"Violet will have a cranberry spritzer. Won't you, Vi?"

Without waiting for my reply, she strides forward, following Darleen into the semidarkness of the park across the street. For a moment, I imagine her figure is my mother walking away, approaching two other individuals already seated on a bench in front of a dim lamppost at the pond's edge.

I stare until my vision loses focus.

My sister was deceptive across years, hiding her secrets deep inside my own. But I forgive her. The truth is, when I knocked on Fiona's back door months ago and she answered, I forgave her for everything then, and everything that was to come. Because the thought of returning to the endless, hollow relationships that I've always endured—all built on lies—makes my fingertips flinch toward their scars. Now Fiona has ensured she is the only person in the world who can understand who I am. And in a way—a strange way—it's . . . comforting . . . to finally get that confirmation. I'm not alone.

The park smears against the streetlights. Then the outlines of two women and a man take shape, seated and waiting for me to join them. The three figures with their backs to me could be my family—my mom, my dad, and my older sister, Fiona, who has a plan for everything.

Fiona crossed the street to join Darleen and Quincy, I know. But the parts of my brain and my heart that have each yearned to recall scenes like this from my childhood are exhausted. For this short moment, I allow the fantasy to win out—just for a few seconds, now that I can, after so many years confusing reality and the fiction that Fiona created. While I may not be fully in control of this next chapter, I'm finally up to speed on the backstory.

In my head, at least, my family and I can be together again, just as we were in the Before Time.

I step onto the sidewalk.

ACKNOWLEDGMENTS

Each time I have the privilege of writing this part of the book, I'm humbled by the support of people in my life.

Firstly, thank you to the entire team at Thomas & Mercer. In particular, my incredible editor Megha Parekh, who knows how to coax the best ideas from me. To Ellie Schaffer, who worked on a previous book of mine but made the process of writing *The Alone Time* easier with her helpful, concurrent communication, thank you. Heartfelt thanks to Sarah Shaw and the entire copyediting and proofreading teams, as well as Gracie Doyle.

So much gratitude goes to my eagle-eyed editor Charlotte Herscher. Your patience and insight are enviable, and I am lucky to work on another book with you.

To my agent, Jill Marr, and the team at Sandra Dijkstra Literary Agency, thank you. Jill, your support and encouragement mean the world to me. I'm thrilled to say we did it again.

Trisha Arnold deserves all the thanks for providing her generous time and energy while explaining tarot to me. You are a treasure of random information, my Gemini friend.

To a thriller author whose books I love—thank you, Heather Chavez, for reading an early version of this book. Your feedback was so needed and appreciated.

To my sweet, dynamic, and enthusiastic family, whom I am always thinking of—except for when I get that glazed-over "brainstorming face" at dinner: I love you. Thank you for your patience with me when I disappear to write.

To my husband, who is always willing to read: mille mercis.

To the readers who dive into the acknowledgments, after three hundred plus pages—thank you for joining me on another twisted, twisty journey. I hope you enjoyed reading this story as much as I did writing it.

Lemonade makers: keep making the most out of life's speed bumps.

Finally, thanks must definitively go to my dad, who landed the plane.

About the Author

Photo © 2019 Jana Foo Photography

Elle Marr is the #1 Amazon Charts bestselling author of *The Family Bones*, *Strangers We Know*, *Lies We Bury*, and *The Missing Sister*. Originally from Sacramento, Elle graduated from UC San Diego before moving to France, where she earned a master's degree from the Sorbonne University in Paris. She now lives and writes in Oregon with her family. For more information, visit www.ellemarr.com.